Thomas Faughnan

Stirring incidents in the life of a British soldier

An autobiography

Thomas Faughnan

Stirring incidents in the life of a British soldier
An autobiography

ISBN/EAN: 9783742836793

Manufactured in Europe, USA, Canada, Australia, Japa

Cover: Foto ©Raphael Reischuk / pixelio.de

Manufactured and distributed by brebook publishing software
(www.brebook.com)

Thomas Faughnan

Stirring incidents in the life of a British soldier

Thomas Faughnan

Stirring incidents in the life of a British soldier

Yours faithfully,

Thomas Faughnan.

STIRRING INCIDENTS

IN THE LIFE OF

A BRITISH SOLDIER.

An Autobiography.

BY

THOMAS FAUGHNAN,

Late Colour-Sergeant 2nd Battalion, 6th Royal Regiment.

"Faithful unto Death."

TORONTO:

HUNTER, ROSE AND COMPANY.

1879.

TO HIS EXCELLENCY

The Right Honourable The Marquis of Lorne,

K. T., G. C. M. G.,

GOVERNOR-GENERAL OF THE DOMINION OF CANADA,

THIS STORY

Of a British Soldier's Life,

IS, BY SPECIAL PERMISSION, RESPECTFULLY DEDICATED,

BY HIS HUMBLE AND OBEDIENT SERVANT,

THOMAS FAUGHNAN.

PREFACE.

IN laying the history of my life and travels before the public, I deem it right to state that I am past the middle age; this I feel compelled to mention, because it is my opinion that no man should write a history of himself until he has set foot upon the border land where the past and the future begin to blend. When the past has receded so far that he can behold it as in a picture, and his share in it as the history of a soldier who has fought for his Queen and country, and had many narrow escapes of death. But, thank God, I have been spared thus far to confess my faults, and my good deeds look miserably poor in my own eyes, indeed I would no more claim a reward for them than expect a captain's commission.

The countries and incidents described in this work will be found, I trust, interesting to all classes of persons. The history of a soldier's life and travels is always an entertaining and instructive one. Many books on the lives of officers have been written by learned men, containing much information, and highly useful to the scholar, but they do not interest the mass of common readers. Others again pass so rapidly from place to place, and are so general in their description, the reader gets but very imperfect ideas from reading them. These extremes the writer has endeavoured to avoid. It has been my object to select the most important events of my life and to describe them in a plain and familiar style. I have not indulged in learned dissertations, my common, old-fashioned Irish school education being too limited to give that classical finish to the work which a learned writer would have done. Indeed, it has not been my intention to write a book for the learned or critical, but to give to the public a volume written in a homely style, by a non-commissioned officer, to instruct and interest the family and the common reader, as well as my comrades. If, while dilating on the exploits of my comrades in arms, I have omitted to pay proper respect to gallant foes, it is because I know that history will supply the deficiency. Time will gild with glory a Trojan defence, fitly closed by a successful retreat across a burning bridge, under a heavy fire. But come along, dear reader, and try whether in my first chapter I cannot be a boy again, in such a way that my reader will gladly linger a little in the meadows of childhood, ere we pass to riper years and stirring battle-fields.

CONTENTS.

CHAPTER I.

PAGE

Education—My Schoolmaster—School House—My Father, Mother, Sisters—Our House 17

CHAPTER II.

River Shannon—Derry Carne—Our Farm—My Sister gets Married—Cave—Still House—Still and Worm—Process—Interior—Revenue Police—Irish Wake—Funeral 24

CHAPTER III.

Advanced School—State of the Country—Emigration—Cause of Poverty—Irish Landlords—Potato Crop—Dishonest Agents—Election—Politics—My Sister Emigrates—I Enlist 29

CHAPTER IV.

Swearing in—March to Dublin—Beggars' Bush Barrack—Rations—The City—Embarkation—The Ship—The Voyage—Liverpool—Train to London—Billets—Canterbury—Join the 17th Regiment .. 34

CHAPTER V.

Medical Examination—Receive my Kit—Drill, Manual and Platoon Exercise—Dismissed Drill—Visit the City—Description—Route—The March 43

CHAPTER VI.

Arrival at Dover—First Guard—The Dead House—Ghost—The Heights—Shaft—Fortifications—Marching out—Chartists Riots—Train to London—Departure—Osbourne House—Main Dock—Route to Chatham—Siege—Sham Fight 50

CHAPTER VII.

Route to Canterbury—The March—Arrival—Chatham—Dock-yard—Furlough to London—That Great City—Join my Company—Sheerness—The Dock-yard—Get Married—Route to Weedon—Route to Ireland 59

CHAPTER VIII.

PAGE

Liverpool—Embark for Dublin—The Voyage—Arrival--March—The Train—The March to Castlebar--Arrival—Election—Route to Galway 70

CHAPTER IX.

The March—Galway—Captain Bourchier—Detachment—Regetta—Row with the Police—Route to Galway—Major Bourchier exchanges—Captain Croker—Claddagh—Attend a Camp Meeting—The City of Galway—Theatre—Route to Dublin 81

CHAPTER X.

The March—Rail to Dublin—Arrival—Garrison Duty—Castle Guard—The Old Man's Hospital—Divine Service--Tent-Pitching—Death of the "Iron Duke"—The Funeral—The Queen Visits Dublin—Buildings and Institutions—The Route 92

CHAPTER XI.

Arrival at Templemore—The Route to Cork—Embarkation for Gibraltar—Queenstown—The Voyage—Storm at Sea—Gibraltar 106

CHAPTER XII.

The Landing—Barrack—Garrison Duty— Old North Front—Smuggling—Market—Queen's Birth-Day—The Dinner—Speeches—The Route—The March—Embarkation for the Crimea—The Parting—The Voyage—Arrival at Malta 121

CHAPTER XIII.

Maltese—Departure—A Captain Commits Suicide—The Funeral—Small-Pox—Return—Resumed the Voyage—Grecian Arches—Dardanelles—Gallipoli—Turkish Sentries—Constantinople—Turkish Ladies—The Bosphorus—Voyage across the Euxine—Arrival . 134

CHAPTER XIV.

Disembarkation—First Bivouac—The March—Arrival—Sebastopol—The Trenches—First Man Wounded—Return to Camp—An Alarm—Lord Raglan—Sortie—Foraging—The Old Bridge—Col. Cole—The Siege.. 146

CHAPTER XV.

PAGE

March to Balaklava—Return—Men go Bare-footed—Snow five feet deep—Long Boots—Hard Frost—Cavalry Division—Burial Ground—Solitary Procession—Men Frozen—I build a Hut—Green Coffee—Wintry Appearance—Dead Horses—63rd Regiment—Carrying Provisions—French Sick—Terrible Climate 157

CHAPTER XVI.

Trenches—Canal of Mud—Russian New Year—Heavy Fire—On Sentry—The Sortie—Old Brown Bess—Sortie—Arrival in Camp—New style of Candle—Flint and Steel—Making Coffee—Heavy Snow—No Fire—Warm Clothing—Shot and Shell 167

CHAPTER XVII.

The Railway—Lord Raglan—Cossacks—The Navvies—Russian Deserters—The Railway 178

CHAPTER XVIII.

St. Patrick's Day—Rifle Pits—Fourth Division—French Loss—The Siege—General Attack—Flag of Truce—Burying the Dead—Wooden Huts—Turkish Troops—Divine Service 189

CHAPTER XIX.

Bombardment—Tents blown down—Siege—Lieut. Williams—Wounded—Sailors—Go to Hospital—Description—Sardinians—Discharged from Hospital—Attack on Quarries—Flag of Truce—Burying the Dead 199

CHAPTER XX.

Bombardment—The Assault—Great Redan—Wounded—The Battle—Balaklava—Hospital—Miss Nightingale—Nurses—Promoted—Discharged from Hospital—Death of Lord Raglan 210

CHAPTER XXI.

Captain Colthurst—Siege—Bombardment—Assault—Redan—The Battle—8th September—The Evacuation—Russians—British in Sebastopol 224

CHAPTER XXII.

Expedition to Kinburn—The Voyage—Odessa—Landing—Cutting Trenches—Bombardment—The White Flag—Capitulation—The

PAGE

Prisoners — *Reconnaissance* — The March — Village — Bivouac—March—A Village—Pigs and Geese—Departure—The Fleet—Return—Sir W. Codrington—Russian Spy 237

CHAPTER XXIII.

Armistice—Cessation of Hostilities—Exchange of Coins—Heir to French Imperial Throne—Treaty of Peace—Invitations—Grand Review—Removal of the Army—Embarkation—The Voyage—Ship on Fire—Arrival at Malta—Join the Reserve Battalion—Proceed to Alexandria—The Voyage—Arrival—Visit Places of Renown—Visit Cairo—The Nile—Arrival—The City—Bazaars 249

CHAPTER XXIV.

The Pyramids—Crossing the Nile—Island of Rhoda—Ark of Bulrushes—Visit Cheops—Heliopolis—Palace of the Shoobra—Palm Groves—The Citadel—Joseph's Well—Dervishes Return 262

CHAPTER XXV.

The Hospital—Mohammedan Sabbath—Departure- The Voyage—Malta—Departure—Voyage for England—Portsmouth—Voyage to Dubin—Arrival at Limerick—The 6th Royal Regiment—Promoted—Aldershot—Route for Gibraltar—The Voyage .. 277

CHAPTER XXVI.

Arrival—Spanish Bull-fights—Lieut. Jackson—Change Quarters—The Rock—Monkeys—Caves—Gardens—War in Algiers—Corfu—Voyage—Arrival—Santa Maria—Desertion—The March—Greeks .. 291

CHAPTER XXVII.

Sir Henry Storks—Albania—Visit Nicropolis—The Brigand Chief—Turkish Baths—Coffee-Houses—Turkish Ladies' Costume—Sergeants' Ball—The Route—Corfu—Route—West Indies—The Voyage—The Burning Mountain—Gibraltar—Madiera—Teneriffe—Santa Cruz—Cape De Verde Islands—Trinidad—Jamaica 303

CHAPTER XXVIII.

Jamaica—The Exhibition—Market—Rebellion—The Commission—Col. Hobbs—The Voyage—The Route—The Voyage—Route—Voyage—Queen's Birth day—Edinburgh—Calton Hill—Tolbooth—Queen Mary's Room—Dunoon—Discharged—Dalkeith—Glasgow—Embark for Canada—The Voyage—Arrival—Montreal—Kingston—Picton—The Dunkin Bill—Marquis of Lorne 317

TESTIMONIALS TO THE WRITER.

EDINBURGH CASTLE, *April 29th, 1868.*

I have great pleasure in stating that I have known Sergeant Thomas Faughnan for about nine years, and during most of that period he was Pay and Colour-Sergt. of my Company. He also was Sergt-Major of a Detachment of which I had command, and I cannot say too much in his favour, either as a soldier or a trustworthy person.

He always gave me the greatest satisfaction, in the position he was placed ; both by his high sense of discipline, as well as his entire knowledge of drill, and he leaves the Regiment with the respect of every one.

(Signed) JOHN E. TEWART,

[TRUE COPY.] *Captain 2nd Batt. 6th Royal Regiment.*

Sergeant Faughnan was discharged from the 2nd Battalion 6th Foot, in Edinburgh, May, 1868, after twenty-one years' service, with an excellent character. I have pleasure in stating that I consider him a most honest, trustworthy, respectable man ; for many years he held positions of much responsibility.

(Signed) JOHN ELKINGTON,

Colonel Commd'g 2nd Batt. 6th Royal Regiment.

ALDERSHOT CAMP, *July 10th, 1868.*

[TRUE COPY.]

ALDERSHOT CAMP, *July 12th, 1868.*

I have known SergeantFaughnan for the last five years, in the 2nd Batt. 6th Regiment, and can say that he has behaved himself very well in every way as a soldier. He was an honest, willing and sober man, he was also Mess Sergeant for several years, and gave every satisfaction, and deserves to get on in the world, and I much wish he may do so.

(Signed) SPENCER FIELD,

[TRUE COPY.] *Captain, 2nd Batt. 6th Royal Regiment.*

TESTIMONIALS TO THE WRITER.

I have known Sergeant Thomas Faughnan, late Sergeant in the 2nd Battalion, 6th Regiment, for about ten years, during which time he served as Pay and Colour-Sergeant to a Company with great satisfaction to the Captains; also as Sergeant-Major to a Detachment, in which position, by his steady conduct and fair knowledge of drill, he commanded the respect of his superiors. He has since served as Mess and Wine Sergeant to the Battalion, and has been sober and attentive to those duties. I can recommend him as a generally useful Non-Commissioned Officer.

(Signed) HENRY KITCHENER,

Lieut. and Adjt. 2nd Battalion 6th Foot.

EDINBURGH CASTLE, *25, 4, '68.*

[TRUE COPY.]

I have known Sergeant Faughnan—now taking his discharge from the 6th Regiment, with a pension, after twenty-one years' service—since the year 1860, and have served with him in Gibraltar, the Ionian Islands, and the West Indies. Up to 1865 he was a Colour-Sergeant of the Regiment, and as such was very much respected. About the middle of that year he became Sergeant of the Officers' Mess, in which position he remained up to the departure of the Regiment from Edinburgh, on the 22nd May, 1868. He was for about two years caterer of the said Mess, and in addition had charge of all wines, ale, &c. Thousands of pounds must have passed through his hands, for every portion of which he has had to account, and his remaining up to the last moment in the Mess is a proof of his having done so most satisfactorily. I, myself, have a very high opinion of Sergeant Faughnan for his straightforwardness, honesty, sobriety, ability, and steady good conduct. I am sure his loss will be much felt in the 6th Regiment.

(Signed) L. B. HOLE,

[TRUE COPY.] *Captain, 2nd Batt., 6th Royal Regiment.*

I have known Sergeant T. Faughnan for the last seven years, and have always found him honest, sober, quiet and obliging. He is a good accountant, and was employed in charge of the Mess 2nd Batt. 6th Regiment for some time, and gave every satisfaction. He was also a Colour-Sergeant and had charge and payment of a Company for some time, and resigned his colours to go to the Mess.

(Signed) W. G. ANNESLEY,

Captain 2nd Batt. 6th Royal Regiment.

ALDERSHOT CAMP, *8th June, 1868.*

[TRUE COPY.]

STIRRING INCIDENTS

IN THE LIFE OF

A BRITISH SOLDIER.

CHAPTER I.

EDUCATION—MY SCHOOLMASTER—SCHOOL HOUSE—MY FATHER, MOTHER, SISTERS—OUR HOUSE.

I HAVE for some time been trying to think how far back my memory could go; but, as far as I can judge, the earliest definite recollection I have is the discovery of how I played the truant, in stopping on the way side playing pitch and toss, instead of going to school; and how I cut all the buttons off my jacket and trowsers for the purpose of gambling with other boys. After losing all my buttons, I had to pin my jacket to my trowsers. In Ireland in those days, boys had to be content with gambling for buttons instead of coppers as now-a-days. I was late for school, and was rather remarkable, going in with my trowsers and jacket fastened together with pins. I remember well the master called me over to him. Oh! I will never forget his spiteful countenance, and how he shewed his ivories. My heart beat fast. I thought I was very wicked, and fright made my heart jump to my mouth. I had to stand my trial. Master: "Well, boy, what kept you late for school?" Before I had time to answer, "How came the buttons off your clothes, tell me straightforward at once, who cut them off, and what became of them? Hold up your head and speak out." "I—I—I—cut them off, sir, to play with the boys, and they won my buttons." "O, ho! you have been gambling, have you? I will teach you to cut the buttons off your clothes to gamble. Go, stand in that corner until I am through with the class."

"Pat Cannon, take this knife, go out and cut a strong birch, this one I have is nearly worn out. I want a strong one for this youth."

While I was standing in the corner, one of the boys, or as we used to call them, "gossoons," stole over to me and gave me a big shawl-pin, saying: "Stick this in the boy's neck who takes you on his back." I took the pin as I was told, and nerved myself up for the occasion.

"Dan McLaughlin, take Thomas Faughnan on your back."

I was brought up in due form. "Take off your jacket; get on Dan McLaughlin's back."

No sooner had I got on his back, and before the master had time to administer the first stroke of the birch, than I sunk the big pin into the boy's neck. He shouted at the top of his voice, yelling as if he had been stabbed with a knife, and fell over the other boys, causing great commotion. In the uproar and confusion I made my escape out of the school, jacket in hand. The master stood in a state of amazement. It took him quite a while to restore order among the boys. I waited outside until the school came out, then went home with my comrades as if nothing had happened, and did not go to school again for three days. The master reported my absence. My father questioned me concerning my absence from school. I then told him the whole affair, and, as I was afraid of getting another flogging, he accompanied me to the school next day.

It will be necessary here, to describe the master and the school. The master had only one leg and that was his right; he had lost his left when young, by some means which I never heard of; he walked with a long crutch under his left arm, and a short one in his right hand. He trotted very fast, considering that he went on crutches. He was in truth a terror to dogs or animals which dared to cross his path on his way to and from the school, and could most wonderfully use the right hand crutch with great skill and alacrity, in his own defence.

The school was held in the chapel, which was a most peculiar edifice of ancient architectural design. Its shape was that of a triangle, each side of which formed a long hall, one for boys, the other for girls; there was a gallery at the extreme end of the girls' hall which the choir occupied during divine service.

The structure was one story in height, and had a very high, slanting, thatched roof, with narrow gables. The edge of the gables rose, not in a slope, but in a succession of notches, like stairs. Altogether it had an extraordinary look about it, a look of the time when men had to fight in order to have peace, to kill in order to live—every man's hand against his brother. The altar stood in the acute corner of the angle, facing the men's hall, with a railing around it. Under the altar was a small hole sufficiently large enough for a boy to crawl in. One day I had done something for which the master started to punish my back with the birch. He was laying it on pretty stiffly, and had me in a tight place, when, in self defence, I pulled the crutch from under him. He fell over and I retreated into the hole under the altar. However, tracing me out, he started to dislodge me with his long crutch. For every thrust he gave me, I gave him one in return, until I found he was too strong for me, when I made one drive at him, jumped out of my hiding place, and left for home in a hurry that day. Next day I expected a flogging, but I got off much easier than I had anticipated. Afterwards —how strange—he took quite a liking to me. The number of pupils attending was over two hundred. The hall was supplied with fuel by a contribution of two turf from each scholar every morning, which he brought under his arm.

Enough of my school history—it would spin out my narrative unnecessarily. I shall only relate such occurrences as may be necessary to lead to those main events which properly constitute my eventful history. I remember my father, but not my mother. She died when I was yet a baby, and the woman I had been taught to call mother was only my stepmother. My father had married a second time, and now our family consisted of my father, stepmother, two sisters, and myself. Our house was of olden-time stone, gray and brown. It looked very gray, and yet there was a homely, comfortable appearance about it. A visitor's first step was into what would in some parts here be called "house place"—a room which served all the purposes of kitchen and dining-room. It rose to a fair height, with smoke-stained oaken beams above, and was floored with a home-made kind of cement, hard enough, and yet so worn that it required a good deal of local knowledge to avoid certain jars of the spine from sudden changes of level.

My sisters kept the furniture very clean and shining, especially the valued pewter on the dresser. The square table, with its spider-like accumulation of legs, stood under the window until meal times, when, like an animal aroused from its lair, it stretched those legs and assumed expanded, symmetrical shape, in front of the fireplace in winter, and nearer the door in summer. Its memory recalls the occasion of my stepmother, with a hand at each end of it, searching frantically for the level, poking for it with the creature's own legs before lifting the hanging leaves, and then drawing out the hitherto supernumerary legs to support them, after which would come another fresh adjustment, another hustling to and fro, that the new feet likewise might have some chance to rest. The walls of this room were always whitewashed in spring, occasioning ever a sharpened contrast with the dark brown oak ceiling. If that was ever swept I never knew. I do not remember ever seeing it done. At all events its colour remained unimpaired by hand or whitewash. On the walls hung several articles, some of them high above my head, which attracted my attention particularly. There was a fishing rod, which required the whole length between the windows to support it. There were old book-shelves, hanging between the old pewter, of which we were very proud; my father's temperance medal, which he received from Father Mathew; a picture of Dan O'Connell, the "Irish Liberator;" several other pictures, and many articles of antique and Irish origin. I need not linger over these things. Their proper place is in the picture with which I would save words and help understanding if I could.

MY NATIVE VILLAGE.

Dear Fiarana! loveliest village of the green,
Where humble happiness endeared each scene;
The never-failing brook at Drumod Mill,
The parish church on John Nutley's hill.

There in the old thatched chapel, skilled to rule,
The one-legged master taught the parish school;
A learned man was he, but stern to view—
His crutch he often used, and well the gossoons knew.

Well had the daring urchins learned to trace
His scowling countenance and his fierce grimace ;
And yet they laughed with much delight and glee
At all his tales, for many a one had he.

In all my travels round this world so fair,
Of trials and marches I have had my share ;
I still have hope my latter days to crown,
And 'midst old friends at home to lay me down,

I trust and hope to visit home again,
And sell my book to every village swain ;
Around the hearth a wondering crowd to draw,
While spinning yarns of what I heard and saw.

A man who a military life pursue,
Looks forward to the home from whence he flew ;
I still have hopes, my long eventful past,
Some day return, and stay at home at last.

T. Faughnan.

CHAPTER II.

RIVER SHANNON—DERRY CARNE—OUR FARM—MY SISTERS GET MARRIED—CAVE—STILL-HOUSE—STILL AND WORM—PROCESS—INTERIOR—REVENUE POLICE—IRISH WAKE—FUNERAL.

OUR residence was situated on a beautiful bay of the River Shannon in the County of Leitrim.

The month was July, and nothing could be more exhilarating than the breezes which played over the green fields that were now radiant with the light which was flooded down upon them from the cloudless sun. Around them, in every field, were the tokens of that pleasant labour from which the hope of an ample and abundant harvest always springs.

The bay was bounded on the east by a large wood which abounds in game of every description. Gentlemen from the surrounding counties were frequently invited by its owner, Francis Nesbitt, Esq., Derry Carne, during the shooting and fishing season. Many times I have been out with them, coming home foot-sore in the evening, after traversing the woods all day with the sportsmen. Those were happy days.

My father and the hired man, with the help of my two sisters, managed to sow and gather in the produce of the small farm. I, being the only son, was kept at school till about sixteen years old, after which I had to make myself useful around the house and farm. I was about twelve years old when my eldest sister got married. About two years afterwards my other sister took unto herself a partner, for better, for worse. After those events our family dwindled down to three, viz., my father, stepmother, and myself.

About this time I roamed about the country a good deal. In the evenings a few other boys and myself assembled in a "Potheen Still-House" to see the men who manufactured the potheen, and hear them tell stories. It was situated about two miles in a north-western direction from our residence. The country was very rugged and wild, but picturesque. Although a portion of the same landscape, nothing could be more strikingly distinct in character than the position of those hills. They formed a splendid pasture land for sheep. In approaching these hills you struck into a "Borheen," or lane which conducted you to the front of a steep precipice of rocks about fifty feet high. In the northern cover of this ravine there was an entrance to a subterraneous passage twenty feet long, which led to a large chamber or deep cave, having every convenience for a place of private distillation. Under the rocks, which met over it, wás a kind of gothic arch, and a stream of water just sufficient for the requisite purpose fell in through a fissure from above, forming such a little cascade in the cavern as human design itself could scarcely have surpassed in perfect adaptation for the objects of an illicit distiller. To this cave then, we must take the liberty of transporting our readers, in order to give them an opportunity of getting a peep at the inside of a "Potheen Still-House." In that end which constituted the termination of the cave, and fixed upon a large turf fire which burned within a circle of stones that supported it, was a tolerably sized still made of copper. The mouth of this still was enclosed by an air-tight cover, also of copper, called the head, from which a tube of the same metal projected into a large condenser that was kept always filled with cold water by an incessant stream from the cascade I have already described, which always ran into and overflowed it.

The arm of this head was made air-tight, fitting into a spiral tube of copper, called the worm, which rested in the water of the cooler; and as it consisted of several twists like a corkscrew, its effect was to condense the hot vapour which was transmitted to it from the glowing still into that description of alcohol known as potheen whiskey or "mountain dew."

At the bottom of the cooler, the worm terminated in a small cock, from which the spirits passed in a slender stream about the thickness of a pipe-stem into a vessel placed for its reception. Such was the position of the still, head, and worm, when in full operation.

Fixed about the cave, upon wooden benches, were the usual requisites for the various processes through which it was necessary to put the malt before the wort, which is the first liquid shape, was fermented, cleared and passed into the still to be singled; for our readers must know that distillation is a double process, the first produced being called singlings, and the second or last doublings—which is the perfect liquor. Sacks of malt, empty barrels, piles of turf, heaps of grain, tubs of wash, kegs of whiskey, were lying about in all directions; together with pots, pans, wooden-trenchers, and dishes for culinary use.

On entering, your nose was assaulted by such a fume of warm grains, sour barm, and strong whiskey, as required considerable fortitude to bear, without very unequivocal tokens of disgust. Seated around the fire were a party of shebeen men and three or four publicans, who came on professional business.

In order to evade the vigilance of the "Revenue Police," or, as they were called, "Still Hunters," the smoke, which passed through a hole in the roof, came up into a pasture field. On the top of this hole was fitted a wide flag, made to be shifted at will. On the top of this flag was kept a turf fire, in charge of a boy who herded sheep and goats. When the boy saw the police advancing towards the fire he would shift the flag over the hole. The police came, lit their pipes, walked off, and suspected nothing. The boy then shifted back the flag, in order to let the smoke escape. In this way they escaped detection.

Several illicit stills flourished in this part of the country, which I frequently visited during the winter evenings. When there happened to be a wake I often accompanied parties for whiskey to this still-house; it being the custom to have a supply of liquor to enliven the guests on such occasions. The boys and girls always expected a good time for fun and frolic at a wake, especially if it was an old person who gave up the ghost; therefore it was looked forward to as a kind of pleasurable occurrence to the rising generation. I became a regular frequenter on such occasions, for a radius of three or four miles. The corpse was laid out on a table, with a white curtain similar to those over a bed. On the same table, in front, were six lighted candles. At the entrance stood a table furnished with bottles of whiskey, glasses, tobacco and pipes, for those who drank and smoked to help themselves. An old woman sat at the head of the corpse, whose duty it was to start the crying on the entrance of a guest. After they got through with the crying, the host passed round whiskey, tobacco and pipes; when the conversation went on as if nothing had happened, except the loud crying, which was only the women's part, the men not joining in it.

When my stepmother's sister died, I put an onion to my eyes, in order to cause them to shed tears, which had the desired effect. Those wakes generally last two or three nights. Whiskey is passed round previous to the funeral procession starting from the house.

On returning, the processionists invariably called into a "shebeen" to have a sociable chat and a parting glass to drown their sorrows. I refrain from quoting the conversation of those peasants, as it would take up too much space, and defeat my object in laying the history of my life and travels before my readers.

CHAPTER III.

ADVANCED SCHOOL—STATE OF THE COUNTRY—EMIGRATION—CAUSE OF POVERTY — IRISH LANDLORDS — POTATO CROP — DISHONEST AGENTS —ELECTION—POLITICS—MY SISTER EMIGRATES—I ENLIST

ABOUT the time this chapter opens I had been removed from the country school (which has been already described in the first chapter), and sent to a much more advanced and better school, in the town of Drumod, County Leitrim. I continued at this school about four years, during which time I had waxed strong in mind, strength and learning. In the meantime the state of the country gradually assumed a worse and more depressing character.

Indeed, at this period of my narrative, the position of Ireland was very gloomy. Situated as the country was, emigration went forward on an extensive scale—emigration, too, of that particular description which every day enfeebles and impoverishes the country, by depriving her of all that approaches to anything like a comfortable and independent yeomanry. This indeed is a kind of depletion which no country can bear long ; and, as it is at the moment I write this, progressing at a rate beyond all precedent, it will not, I trust, be altogether uninteresting to inquire into some of the causes that have occasioned it.

Of course the principal cause of emigration is the poverty and the depressed state of the country, wages often being as low as eight-pence a-day, and it follows naturally that whatever occasions our poverty will necessarily occasion emigration. The first cause of our poverty then is "absenteeism," which, by drawing six million pounds out of the country, deprives our people of employment and means of life to that amount. The next is the general inattention of Irish landlords to the state and condition of their property and an inexcusable want of sympathy with their tenantry, which indeed is only a corollary from the former, for it can hardly be expected that those who wilfully neglect themselves will feel a warm interest in others. Political corruption, in the shape of the forty shilling franchise, was another cause, and one of the very worst, which led to the prostration of the country by poverty and moral degradation, and for this proprietors of the land were solely responsible. Nor can the use of the potato as the staple food of the labouring class, in connection with the truck or credit system and the consequent absence of money payments, in addition to the necessary ignorance of domestic and social comforts, that resulted, be left out of this wretched catalogue of our grievances. Another cause of emigration is to be found in the high and exorbitant rents at which land is held by all classes of farmers —with some exceptions, such as in the case of old leases —but especially by those who hold under middlemen, or on the principle of sub-letting generally.

By this system a vast deal of distress and petty but

most harrassing oppression is every day in active operation which the head landlord can never know, and for which he is in no other way responsible than by want of knowledge of his estates.

There are still causes, however, which too frequently drive the independent farmer out of the country. In too many cases it happens that the rapacity and dishonesty of the agent, countenanced or stimulated by the necessities and reckless extravagance of the landlord, fall like some unwholesome blight upon that enterprise and industry which would ultimately, if properly encouraged, make the country prosperous and her landed proprietors independent men. I allude to the nefarious and monstrous custom of ejecting tenants who have made improvements, or, when permitted to remain, make them pay for the improvements which they have made.

A vast proportion of this crying and oppressive evil must be laid directly to the charge of those who fill the responsible situation of landlords and agents to property in Ireland, than whom in general there does not exist a more unscrupulous, oppressive, arrogant, and dishonest class of men. Exceptions of course there are, and many, but speaking of them as a body, I unhappily assert nothing but what the conditions of property, and of those who live upon it, do at this moment and have for many years testified. I have already stated that there was a partial failure in the potato crops that season, a circumstance which ever is the forerunner of famine and sickness.

The failure, however, on that occasion, was not alone caused by a blight in the stalks, but large portions of the seed failing to grow. In addition, however, to all I have already detailed as affecting the neighbourhood, or rather the parish, of Anaduff, I have to inform my readers that the county was soon about to have a contested election. Viscount Clemens and Samuel White, Esq., were the opposing candidates. The former had been a convert to Liberalism, and the latter a sturdy Conservative, a good deal bigoted in politics, but possessing that rare and inestimable quality which constitutes an honest man.

It was a hard contested election. The electors throughout the county were driven to the town on side cars escorted by police. The excitement was fearful. However the people's candidate gained the election. There was a large amount of whiskey drunk during this election and there was plenty of fighting.

At this time my eldest sister, with her husband, emigrated to Canada. On parting with her she said she would send for me, but I did not like the idea of going to America or Canada at that time, although I heard good reports from both countries. I thought instead that I would go for a soldier. I had seen splendid, tall soldiers frequently marching past our house, when I invariably accompanied them for several miles to hear their band play. With this intention I went to the fair of Mohill, on the 8th of May, 1847. There I met a recruiting party. I went up to the sergeant and asked him if he would take me for a soldier, he answered me in the affirmative. He then told me to answer the following questions, viz: "Are you free, willing and able to serve Her Majesty Queen Victoria, her heirs and successors for a period of twenty-one years?" I answered, "I am." "Then take this shilling in the name of the Queen." I "took the shilling," and was one of Queen Victoria's soldiers, and of the 17th regiment of foot. I must say I never regretted it since.

CHAPTER IV.

SWEARING IN—MARCH TO DUBLIN—BEGGARS' BUSH BARRACKS—RATIONS—THE CITY—EMBARKATION—THE SHIP—THE VOYAGE—LIVERPOOL—TRAIN TO LONDON—BILLETS—CANTERBURY—JOIN THE 17TH REGIMENT.

THE sergeant conducted me to the rendezvous, where I passed a medical examination, and was returned fit for "Her Majesty's Service." He then ushered me into a room in which were five more brothers-in-arms.

Next morning at ten o'clock, I was taken before a magistrate and sworn-in (after which I received a half-crown), called "swearing-in-money." My sister and stepmother hearing I had enlisted came after me the following day, and tried to get me off, but the sergeant would not hear of it, and I was unwilling, as I had made up my mind to be a soldier, as I was anxious to get away from my relatives. My anxiety was soon realized, for next morning, after breakfast, we were on the road for Dublin in charge of a staff-sergeant, the distance being one hundred and fifty miles, which we accomplished in ten days. During the journey the sergeant amused us with stories of his experience in the regiment to which he belonged, marches in different countries, and several battles he had fought. It being the month of May, the roads were in good condition, the weather salubrious, and the country beautiful in the summer sun.

On our arrival in the evening we were billetted at a public house, where soon after our arrival we enjoyed a hot meal, the landlord being allowed ten-pence for the same, this being according to " Her Majesty's Regulations." After we had regaled ourselves with the landlord's hospitality, the sergeant enjoyed himself with his pipe and a glass or two of beer; he also gave us some of it to drink. I had never tasted beer previous to this, although I had often tasted " potheen whiskey." After the sergeant had finished his pipe and glass of beer, we retired to bed, slept well and dreamed of long marches. We were on the march again next morning at eight o'clock, and so every day until we reached Dublin, which we accomplished in ten days. On arriving in that city I was astonished at the appearance of the splendid high buildings, the like of which I had never seen before; they formed a striking contrast with the cabins which I had been used to look upon in Leitrim.

We entered the city from the south, marched past the Royal Barracks, along the Liffy to Carlisle Bridge, where we crossed over; thence past the Bank and Trinity College, to Beggars' Bush Barracks where we were to await orders to join the depôt of our regiment in Canterbury.

On our arrival in barracks we were told off to different companies *pro tem.* until our embarkation for Liverpool. This was my first night in barracks. I was shown a bed or cot, with three pegs over it, to hang my clothes on. We soon got acquainted with other recruits, and old soldiers, who showed us to the canteen, where there was a large company of soldiers and recruits carousing and singing. On the first post sounding, we had to answer our names in barracks at tattoo roll-call, and be in bed at last post. Fifteen minutes afterwards "out lights" was sounded, when all the lights were put out, except the orderly sergeants', who had fifteen minutes longer for theirs. "Reveillé" sounded next morning at five, when we all got up, made our beds, and were on parade at six o'clock, when we were drilled till half-past seven, were practised at setting-up drill and the goose step. It being my first drill, I was awkward; we had three such drills daily (Sundays excepted), while we were in these barracks. On being dismissed, we went to breakfast, which consisted of a pound of bread and a basin of coffee each; my appetite being good I made short work of the pound of bread. Our dinner consisted of soup, beef and potatoes; at supper we got a quarter of a pound of bread and a basin of tea. After paying for our rations, washing, and barrack damages, there were four-pence left, which I received every day at twelve o'clock, so that I could spend that much for extra food if I wanted it, some of the recruits preferred to spend it on beer.

When the daily afternoon drill was over, I generally walked into the city, to see what I could of the place. I went past some splendid shops, saw the soldiers on guard at the castle, went into the Royal, Ship-street, and Linen Hall Barracks, visited Nelson's monument, Sackville

Streets, Four Courts and Burn's saloon in the evening. After we had been a week in barracks, an order came for us to proceed to Canterbury and join our depôt there; this order was most agreeable, and we hailed it with pleasure, for we were anxious to get into our uniform. Accordingly two days afterwards, fourteen of us, with a staff sergeant in charge, were paraded on the barrack-square. After we had signed our accounts, and were told that our bounty would be paid to us on arrival at our depôt, we were told to number off from the right, and showed how to "form four deep," the command "quick march" being given, we marched off to the north wall for embarkation on board a steamer which was to sail for Liverpool at four p.m, that day. An officer accompanied us to the steamer to see us all safe on board.

Several soldiers came to see us off. I would like to tell my reader more about Dublin, but as I hope to visit it again during my soldiering, I will defer them till further experience has increased my stock of knowledge. Four o'clock p.m. was the time set for our departure; we were all well pleased when we got on board; the afternoon was beautiful so we anticipated a pleasant voyage. An ocean-ship was to me a novel place, and I had many things to learn. "What is that little flag at the main mast?" said I to a man standing near me, "That they call a Blue Peter; it indicates that the ship is to sail immediately." And what is that flag at the stern? "Why, that is the Union Jack, the pride and boast of every British seaman."

My reflections were broken by the loud, sharp cry of the ship's captain, "all on board." The last warning was given; friends hastily exchanged the farewell tokens of affection. I saw many too struggling to keep their tears back; I stood alone, no one knew me or cared particularly for me; but I was not an uninterested spectator. I dropped a few tears when I looked on my native land, which I was about to leave, and thought of the friends I had left behind me. All was in readiness, ten minutes past four o'clock p.m. the ponderous machine was put in motion; the huge paddle-wheels lazily obeyed the mandate. The Blue Peter came down and the Union Jack went up, and we moved slowly out among the shipping of the harbour. It was a clear, beautiful evening, and the water lay like an immense mirror in the sun-light; we passed the light-house which stood at the end of the harbour like a huge sentinel to guide the passage to the ocean. Onward we went; shore and city faded away and disappeared in the distance. I looked out on the wide expanse of waters; the sea and sky were all that could be seen now, except a few sea-gulls, which hovered round the ship in search of an accidental crumb that might be thrown over-board. We were fairly out at sea. The flags were taken in, and things put in readiness for rougher ocean life; for a time we moved on pleasantly. Toward sun-down a head wind sprung up producing that rocking motion of the boat, that makes sea life so much of a dread to those unaccustomed to water; at about ten o'clock our head wind changed to a side wind, and we had what the sailors call "a chopping sea;" producing a very unpleasant motion of the boat. Previous to this the recruits were in good spirits, but now silence reigned, I could see them getting pale, and one by one, go below; I felt myself approaching a crisis of some kind; but was determined to put it off as long as possible. I kept on deck in the open air, and resolutely frowned down all signs of rebellion in my stomach. From what I heard going on around me, I was aware I was not the worst sufferer; with some the agony of the contest was kept up all night long. At three o'clock a. m. we passed Holy Head; at five we were steaming up the Mersey, and were landed on Liverpool Dock at six o'clock. After a run of twelve and a half hours, here I was, standing in amazement, looking at the forests of masts, and the vast amount of shipping in the Docks. Liverpool is noted principally for its shipping accommodation, and fine docks; of these it has now over eleven miles in length, all walled in, and protected by massive gates like the locks of a canal; this renders the shipping very secure. It is a place of great mercantile importance and trade, the streets are continually in a perfect jam with heavy waggons and vehicles of almost every description. If I was astonished at the appearance of Dublin, how much more so at this great Babel of commerce. The sergeant took us to an eating-house, owned by one of his acquaintances, where he ordered breakfast, for which I believe the landlord did not make much profit; for what with sea-sickness, and fasting since three p. m. the day previous, I'll leave it to my reader to determine whether we were able to do justice to the landlord's hospitality or not?

We left the depôt at Liverpool about ten a. m. on the "Great North-western Railway" for London. I am now taking my first view of England and English scenery, also my first ride in a railway carriage. As we passed along, numerous towns and villages dotted the country, multitudes of great black smoke stacks, amid splendid steeples and church towers, side by side, rose in majesty towards the heavens.

Thus religion and industry are generally, nay always, found in close proximity; with the smoke of the furnace goes up the incense of worship; with the hum of machinery is mingled the anthem of praise. The train stopped at several stations, which were beautifully fitted up; during the journey we frequently partook of refreshments at the different stations. The train travelled very fast. After a ride of one hundred and eighty miles, in nine and a half hours, we reached London, the great metropolis of England, and the mart of the world. We were set down at Euston Station. Now my eyes, indeed, were opened wide, gazing at the magnificence of the great modern Babel of the universe. We were billetted on three different taverns, in close proximity to each other. The sergeant had to report himself at the "Horse Guards," and hand over some recruits which he had for regiments stationed at London.

He left me in charge of the billets while he was gone. We remained here five days, during which I visited a great many places. There are many wonderful things that can be seen in a brief walk through this great metropolis, if a man has his eyes open.

I should like to have had time here to take my reader to the top of some of the tall monuments; to walk with him among the wondrous fortifications of "Old London Tower," through the rooms where nobles, princes, kings, and queens have been incarcerated; to stand with him on "Tower Hill," where the scaffold and executioner's block tell their dark tales of treachery, and blood, and murder. I should like to go with my reader to Westminster Abbey, a wonderful pile, a venerable old church, and the great sepulchral home of England's honoured dead. It is worth a journey across the Atlantic to take a stroll through its cold, damp aisles and chapels; to stand amid its costly monuments and mouldering dust, where death for many long centuries has been gathering her glorious trophies; and yet her dark garlands have been recorded and embodied by human skill and art and genius. I have in a very brief space brought before my readers facts and stories; but I must defer any further description until my next visit, for I hope to see all those wonders again. The sergeant had done his duty to his satisfaction, and this being our last evening in London, he took us to the Haymarket Theatre, where we witnessed the "Colleen Bawn." After the play was over, we took the sergeant into a saloon close by, and treated him to oysters, beer, and cigars, after which we went to our billets quite jolly. Next morning, after paying the landlord and bidding him good-bye, we marched to the Waterloo Railway Station, where we took the train at ten o'clock. After a ride of about eighty miles, in two hours, we were in Canterbury, and put down at St. Dunstan Street Station, marched into barracks, and were handed over to the officer commanding the depôt of the 17th Regiment of Foot, "The Royal Tigers." We were told off to companies, and shown our quarters. More about Canterbury as my story advances. As I am now stationed here, I hope to have an opportunity of getting acquainted with this ancient cathedral city.

CHAPTER V.

MEDICAL EXAMINATION—RECEIVE MY KIT—DRILL, MANUAL AND PLATOON EXERCISE—DISMISSED DRILL—VISIT THE CITY—DESCRIPTION—ROUTE—THE MARCH.

THE following morning, reveillé sounded at five o'clock, when I turned out, made my bed, and was dressed when the drill bugle sounded at half-past.

Parade being formed at six by the sergeant major, the recruits without uniform were not required to drill that morning; drill being over and the bugle for breakfast sounding, we all sat down to a pound of bread and a basin of coffee each. We were afterwards marched to the Regimental Hospital by the orderly corporal, where we passed another medical examination, which was final, and were returned fit for service; we were next marched to the quarter master's store, and received our uniform and kit, which consisted of one each of the following articles, viz., pair boots, cloth trowsers, summer trowsers, shako, tunic, stock and clasp, shell-jacket, forage-cap, pair mits, tin blacking, pair braces, clothes-brush, canteen and cover, knapsack and straps, great coat and haversack, two shirts, two pair socks, and two towels; for the marking of which we were charged a halfpenny each. We were next taken to the tailor's shop, where we had our clothing altered and fitted; this lasted four or five days, during which time we were exempt from drill; but instead had to do the duties of orderly men by turns, that is prepare the meals for those at drill, and keep the barrack rooms clean and in proper order. After we got our clothing all right, we then turned out to drill three times a day, viz., before breakfast, club drill, ten oclock, commanding officer's parade, with setting up drill; afternoon, goose step, extension and balance motions.

At all these parades and drills we were minutely inspected by the orderly sergeant, and afterwards by the sergeant major, and if the least fault was found, ordered to parade again, which was called "a dirty parade." I took particular pains to escape the latter.

When drill commenced, we were formed into squads of six or eight men each, in line, at arms-length apart, which is termed a "squad with intervals," after drilling in single rank for a week, one squad was increased to two ranks, at open order, the rear rank covering the intervals.

The sergeant major frequently came round to each squad, and finding a deserving recruit, sent him up to a more advanced squad, in this way the most intelligent and attentive recruits were advanced; I was lucky in being one of the first sent up, and I afterwards got sent up step by step, until I reached the advanced squad, where I learned company's drill without arms; after which we were served with arms, formed into squads, taught the manual and platoon exercise, company and battalion movements, with arms.

We were then put through a course of ball practice. The distance being fifty, a hundred, hundred and fifty, and two hundred yards; the "old Brown Bess" being in use then. The first shot I fired I got a bull's eye, which was reckoned a first-class shot, and the only one I got during the practice. After we had finished the course, we were again inspected, when we acquitted ourselves to the entire satisfaction of the officer, and were accordingly dismissed from recruits' drill, and returned fit for duty as soldiers. Two days afterwards the head-quarters of the regiment arrived from Bombay, marched into barracks, band playing, colours flying, forming up on the barrack square. The men were tall and soldier-like, but very much tanned from exposure in the east. Their strength on arrival were only five hundred.

We were all delighted to meet the Head Quarters, which had been long expected. They had a long, rough voyage, of three months, having come in a sailing vessel.

After they had been inspected by the commanding officer, Colonel Pinnikuck, they were told off and shown to their different barrack rooms.

Next day regimental orders being issued, I heard my name read out "Private Thomas Faughnan posted to the Grenadier or Captain L. C. Bourehier's company." I was well pleased to hear this, it being the best company in the regiment. The whole of the recruits were also posted to the different service companies.

Being dismissed from recruits' drill, I had ample opportunities of walking out in the afternoons, and visiting some of the old places around the city; among which were the cathedral, one of the oldest ecclesiastical edifices in England.

It was consecrated by Saint Augustine, A.D. 597. Here too he baptized Ethelbert, King of Kent. Saint Martin's Church under-the-hill, said to be the oldest in England, is another time-worn structure, partly built of Roman brick and tiles. There are fourteen such old churches here, most of them built of rough flint, and very ancient.

Also the ruins of a Norman Castle, one of the largest in England, which stands near a mound known as the "Dan John;" connected with this are beautiful gardens, where the band of our 17th regiment played always on Thursday afternoon, when hundreds of the élite of the city assembled to promenade.

This is one of the pleasantest stations in England for a soldier; there is no garrison duty to perform, the only duties being the regimental guards, and they come very seldom; the men getting sixteen nights in bed between guards.

Regiments arriving from India are generally stationed here for some time, in order to recruit after foreign service and the long voyage.

The citizens are very much attached to soldiers, and treat them with the greatest kindness and respect. Our regiment were not fortunate enough to be left here much longer, for a letter of "readiness" was received by the commanding officer, directing him to hold the regiment ready to proceed to Dover at the shortest notice, which he made known to us in regimental orders that evening. After this order was read we were all on the alert, officers and men preparing for the march, packing officers' and mess baggage, whitewashing and cleaning barracks, to save barrack damages—that great curse—ready to hand over to the barrack master.

Accordingly the route came which was read as follows, viz:—

"REGIMENTAL ORDERS,
"BY LIEUT.-COLONEL PINNIKUCK,
"CANTERBURY BARRACKS, Sept. 20th, 1847.

"Agreeable to a Route received this day from Horse Guards, the Regiment will parade in heavy marching order, at eight o'clock, A.M., on Tuesday next, the 24th instant, for the purpose of proceeding to Dover, there to be stationed till further orders. The men will breakfast at 7 o'clock on that day.

"By Order,
"(Signed), Lieut. CODD,
"*Acting Adjutant* 17th *Regiment.*"

The following morning inspection of kits, at ten o'clock by the commanding officer, ordered, and afterwards medical inspection. Next day being Sunday, the regiment paraded at ten o'clock, for divine service, when we all marched to church, with the band playing; Protestants, and Roman Catholics going to their different places of worship, no other denomination being recognised in the regiment.

The barracks were inspected on Monday morning, by the quarter-master and captains of companies, the afternoon was occupied in loading the baggage waggons.

Tuesday, Sept. 24th. The regiment was on parade, ready to fall in, when the officers' and non-commissioned officers' call sounded, the latter forming in line were minutely inspected by the adjutant, accompanied by the sergeant-major, at the same time collecting the reports from the orderly sergeants, after which the companies formed on the coverers, right in front.

The rolls being called, the captains inspected their companies, that being finished, the colonel gave the commands, "eyes front, steady, fix bayonets, shoulder arms, left wheel into line, quick march, halt, dress." Then the adjutant galloped down the front collecting the reports, saluting the colonel as he reported "all correct, Colonel!" "Form fours, right, quick march;" when the whole stepped off, the band at the same time striking up, "Auld Lang Syne," marched out of barracks, down north gate, and up High Street, accompanied by such a crowd of citizens, that it is easier to imagine than describe; after marching through the principal streets, the music changed to "The Girl I left behind me," of the latter there were quite a few followed us outside the town; when the order was given "unfix bayonets, march at ease." The latter order being quickly obeyed (for we had quite a load on our backs, having the whole of our kit in our knapsacks), we were allowed to sing, chat and laugh to shorten the journey. After we had got to the half-way house we halted, piled arms, and were allowed to go into the hotel for refreshments. When we were well rested and refreshed (thanks to the landlord who had everything we needed ready), the march commenced again, and we accomplished the journey of sixteen miles in eight hours, in heavy marching order. On arrival in Dover, at four o'clock p.m., the left wing were stationed at the castle, and right with head-quarters, at the heights.

CHAPTER VI.

ARRIVAL AT DOVER—FIRST GUARD—THE DEAD HOUSE—GHOST—THE HEIGHTS — SHAFT—FORTIFICATIONS—MARCHING OUT —CHARTIST RIOTS—TRAIN TO LONDON—DEPARTURE—OSBORNE HOUSE—MAIN DOCK—ROUTE TO CHATHAM—SIEGE—SHAM FIGHT.

ON the arrival in barracks, the companies were shown their respective quarters, when we soon divested ourselves of our knapsacks and accoutrements; orderly men were told off to draw rations and prepare supper, while the remainder went to fill their beds with straw at the barracks stores; cleaning arms and accoutrements occupied the remainder of the evening. We were exempt from drill the following day, in order to get our barracks and appointments thoroughly clean after the march.

It was now getting near my turn for guard, and it being my first, I was determined to turn out in a soldier-like manner with my appointments clean and shining. Accordingly I was detailed for the western redoubt, which furnishes a sentry over the garrison hospital, that stands on the middle of a common, on the top of the Western Heights above the barracks, and a quarter of a mile from any house or habitation.

After mounting guard I was in the first relief, and my post was at the hospital; on receiving my orders from the corporal he directed my attention to the dead house, where, laid out on a table, was a body I was to keep the rats from gnawing. The corporal having posted me at eleven o'clock that night, all the ghost stories I had heard in the "potheen still house" in Leitrim, came up in my mind as flush as when they were told. While I was thinking, I heard a noise, looked round, and saw a man dressed in white standing at the door of the dead-house. I tried to challenge, but my tongue was tied. I felt paralized. I scrambled along the walk to the front of the hospital; knocking at the door, when the sergeant came out and said, "what is the matter, sentry?" "Oh!" said I, "there is a man, dressed in white, at the 'Dead House.'"

He went back for an orderly, saying something incoherent, when both went round to the dead house; and there they found everything as they had left it. The sergeant called me a fool, and threatened to report me for leaving my post; this stirred me up, and I walked up and down briskly the remainder of the two hours, which appeared the longest I ever passed in my life. I said nothing of the occurrence to the men on guard lest they might laugh at me.

Our guard being relieved, we were marched to barracks, inspected by the orderly sergeant, and dismissed. The sergeant, however, did not report me as he had threatened, whether he forgot or not I did not try to find out. The garrison consisted of two batteries royal artillery, one on the heights, and the other at the castle, a company of sappers and miners, besides our own regiment.

The troops had many guards to furnish, consequently the men got only five nights in bed between duty; besides fatigue parties were many and laborious, on account of so much uphill work; the water supplied to the garrison was brought up from a well, over three hundred feet deep, by means of a wheel, which took four men to work, they being relieved every two hours.

The heights on which the barracks stand are three hundred and eighty feet above the level of the sea. A deep perpendicular shaft containing about four hundred steps of winding-stairs, lead from town to the barracks on the heights, which tries the men's wind coming up at tattoo, and at other times when on fatigue.

The garrison is well fortified and comprises "Dover Castle," which occupies a commanding position on the chalk cliffs, about 380 feet above the level of the sea, and in the construction of which, Saxons and Normans displayed no small amount of ingenuity; the Western Heights, Fort Burgoyne, the south Front Bastion, the Drop Redoubt, the Citadel, the western outworks, and the north Centre Bastion, with Queen Anne's Pocket Piece on the Castle Heights. The harbour is well sheltered by the chalk cliffs, which end landwards, in a charming valley leading to what is known as the "Garden of Kent." During the winter, our regiment marched into the country in heavy marching order twice a week, when we generally went ten to twelve miles on each occasion, and not unfrequently encountering a snow or rain storm, returning literally covered with mud, the roads being so sloppy. These marches, with picquets, fatigues, and guards, kept us busily employed. About the end of March there was great excitement in London over the "Chartists," who were expected to break out in open revolt. The colonel got private notification that most likely the regiment would be ordered to London. We were therefore expecting an order to proceed thither to quell the riot which was daily expected. Our expectations were realized, for on the sixth of April, 1848, we got the route to proceed to London by rail, on the 9th instant, there to be stationed till further orders. When this order was given, there was great excitement in barracks preparing for the journey; we had only two days to pack and get the baggage to the station; however, many hands make light work, and we had all the baggage down at the station and everything in readiness on the evening previous to our departure. On the 9th, we were on parade at seven o'clock, a. m., in heavy marching order, the companies told off and and all reported present, when the colonel gave the command—" quarter distance column on the Grenadiers, quick march," each captain halting his respective company as it came into its place. He then addressed the men, urging them when in London to uphold the credit of their old corps, &c., after which he gave the command "to the right face," when each captain gave the command to his company, "quick march," the companies stepping off in succession, each company wheeling to the left down the shaft. On arriving at the bottom the band struck up "The British Grenadiers;" we marched to the station (accompanied by a large concourse of the townspeople), where a special train was in readiness to convey us to London. As we went on the train the band played "Auld Lang Syne," and the "Girl I Left Behind Me." One hour-and-a-half afterwards we were marching four deep, with fixed bayonets, from the Dover and Chatham Station to Millbank Prison. The streets were so crowded that we had great difficulty in reaching our destination. On arrival, we were shown into two large rooms, one for each wing, with a straw mattress on trestles for each man.

The following morning, April 10th, 1848, an order had arrived from the Duke of Wellington, Commander in Chief, to hold the troops in readiness to march to Kennington Common, where the Chartists had intended assembling in large numbers to march through London to the House of Commons, carrying a petition embodying their demands.

This was to be presented by Fergus O'Connor, one of the members for Nottingham.

The Londoners, to the number of a quarter of a million, enrolled themselves as special constables; the Chartists were not allowed to march in procession, and the whole affair passed off quietly, without bloodshed.

The troops which the Duke had posted ready, when called on, out of sight, were not required. Our regiment with several others, and a few troops of cavalry were under arms the whole day, in rear of the prison, ready to advance at the shortest notice.

While here we were not allowed to go through the city on account of the unsettled state of society; we were supplied with beer inside, the orderly sergeants of companies serving it out in our mess tins.

The troops which had been concentrated in London, from different parts of England, on this emergency, were now ordered to return; some to their former stations, others to fresh ones; our regiment was ordered to proceed to Portsmouth.

The troops had a very smart soldierly appearance, such a large number of cavalry and infantry emerging from their different quarters through the streets, bands playing, quite astonished the citizens as they marched to their destinations.

Our march was to the London and South-western Railway Station, where we took the train at ten o'clock a.m. for Portsmouth, arriving there at twelve o'clock, a distance of seventy-five miles in two hours.

We were marched to Colworth and Clarence barracks, there to be stationed till further orders.

General Orders, issued soon after our arrival, by Lord Frederick Fitzclarence, commanding the troops in garrison, the 17th Regiment was taken on the strength of the garrison, and detailed to furnish the following duties, main guard, Southsea Castle, Landport Rablin, and the main and lower dock-yard. The guards with the colours of the regiment that furnishes the main are trooped every day at ten o'clock on the Grand Esplanade (Sundays and wet days excepted): I was detailed for the main guard, which consists of one captain, one subaltern, one sergeant, two corporals, and twenty four privates; my post being on the ramparts, in rear of the guard-house, where I had a fine view of the harbour, the roadstead of Spithead, and the Isle of Wight, on the coast of which the walls of the Royal residence at Osborne House are seen sparkling among the trees; I had been well broken in to sentry duty by this time, and was not so easily frightened at my post now, as when I was watching the corpse at Dover hospital.

Numbers of nobility and gentry assemble to witness the trooping, and to see the main guard relieved. The following day, after being relieved, general field day of the troops in garrison was ordered to assemble on Southsea Common, under the command of General Fitzclarence. These reviews were once a week; my next guard was the "main dock," it is also a captain's guard of great responsibility; sentries are very strict on their posts, being furnished with "countersign," "number," and "parole," no person is allowed to pass a post without being able to give them to the sentry. There are a great many mechanics and labourers employed here; it is at present two hundred and ninety three acres in extent, one of the largest in the country; of this immense naval establishment, the most noteworthy, if not the most recent features, are the mast and rope houses, hemp stores, rigging-stores, sail-loft, and the dry docks, spacious enough to admit the largest vessels, and offering every facility for their speedy repair; of the various building-slips, one of them roofed and covered in is so large that three or four vessels can be in process of construction at the same time. When Queen Victoria and Prince Albert opened a new basin in those docks in 1848, our grenadier company formed a guard of honour to Her Majesty and the Prince. We also formed a guard of honour on the occasion of Her Majesty and Prince Albert landing at Gosport the same year, when they inspected our company and complimented Captain Bourchier on the clean, soldier-like appearance of his company. I remember Prince Albert perfectly well; he was dressed in a Field Marshal's uniform, with a broad blue silk sash over his left shoulder—he was the finest looking man I ever saw—he must have been six feet four inches in height. The dock yard also contains the residence of the superintending officers and a school of naval architecture.

This is a very lively town, the public houses are well patronised by soldiers and sailors; we liked this station very much, although the guards came often; we bathed once a week on the beach of Southsea common, which is now a fashionable watering place; a band plays here once a week in the afternoon. After we were here six months we got the route to proceed to Chatham where we arrived on the 18th October, and were stationed in Chatham barracks. If Portsmouth was a strict garrison this is much stricter—there are so many recruits here belonging to regiments in India. They are formed into what is called a provisional battalion. We were looked to as an example for the recruits. Here the dock yard duty is carried on much the same as at Portsmouth, with a little more humbugging.

We were employed here a good deal in preparing for a siege operation at Saint Mary's Barracks, above Brompton, in building a stockade, and throwing up earthworks and trenches; in the summer we had a grand sham-fight, the troops being formed into two armies, one attacking, the other defending. We were practising for this siege for over two months previously, carrying scaling ladders and moving round with them to the ditches of the fortification; it was very fatiguing work; after we were well practiced and every thing in readiness, the grand day came off on the Queen's birthday, 1849, when over ten thousand people were present, most of whom came down from London to witness this grand sham-fight. It came off splendidly, when all returned home well pleased.

CHAPTER VII.

ROUTE TO CANTERBURY—THE MARCH—ARRIVAL—CHATHAM—DOCK-YARD—FURLOUGH TO LONDON—THAT GREAT CITY—JOIN MY COMPANY — SHEERNESS — THE DOCK-YARD—GET MARRIED—ROUTE TO WEEDON—ROUTE TO IRELAND.

A FEW days afterwards, we got the route for Canterbury; on June 2nd, we marched from Chatham up High Street, with the band playing at the head of the regiment. We were accompanied by a large crowd of the townspeople outside the town, who gave us three cheers on parting; we marched ten miles that day, and were billeted in the pretty little village of Greenstreet, where the people treated us with the greatest kindness and regard.

Resuming the march at seven o'clock the following morning, and arriving in Canterbury at twelve, where we were met by several of our old acquaintances, who were pleased to see us back again, and accompanied us to the barracks. During our stay here of three months we had easy times, getting sixteen nights in bed, hardly any fatigues, but plenty of drill. On the 5th September, 1849, we marched back again to Chatham, arriving there at 5 p.m. on the 6th, after two days hard marching with a full kit weighing fifty pounds. The march tried many of our men; the weather being very sultry and the roads dusty.

The fortified lines around Chatham are the frequent scenes of military siege-operations, miniature battles and grand reviews.

In a military point of view the lines of detached forts connecting constitute a fortification of great strength, and the whole is regarded as a perfect flank defence for London in the event of an invader seeking to attack the capital from the south coast; the place is also defended by some strong forts on the Medway.

Near Chatham is Fort Pitt, a military hospital and strong fort, barracks for infantry, marines, artillery and engineers, a park of artillery and magazines; store-house and depot on a large scale. In a naval sense, it is one of the principal royal shipbuilding establishments in Great Britain, and a visit to it never fails to impress the stranger with a sense of the naval power of the country. The dock-yard is nearly two miles in length, containing several building-slips and wet docks sufficiently capacious for the largest ships, and the whole is traversed in every direction by a tramway for locomotives. There is, on an average, 3,500 shipwrights, caulkers, joiners, sawyers, mill-wrights, sail-makers, rope-makers, riggers and labourers, with 5,000 soldiers, sailors and marines, making it lively for public-houses and saloons, which are always crowded with soldiers and sailors, in the evenings.

About the middle of December, I applied to the captain of my company for a furlough; having no offence against me since joining, he had no trouble in getting it granted. I had saved most of my pay since I joined, and now had sufficient funds, with the amount allowed me from the captain in advance, to bear my expenses during my absence from the regiment; and as all my near relatives in Leitrim were either dead or emigrated to America, I had no particular place to spend my furlough, and being stationed so near London, I made up my mind to visit that great city, and avail myself of the opportunity of visiting once more at my leisure some of the principal places of note and amusement. My furlough was dated from 16th December and expired 16th January. I left the sun pier at Chatham, by a penny steamboat to Stroud Station, thence by rail to Gravesend, and boat to Blackwall; from there by rail to Fenchurch, where I took an omnibus to Cambden-Hill-Villa, Kensington, where I stayed on invitation with a friend during my sojourn in London. During my ride through the city on the outside of the omnibus, I had a splendid view of the perfect labyrinth of streets and squares, warehouses and stores, churches and palaces, which I strongly recommend all strangers in London to see. Here I am riding through the vast metropolis of England, where nearly four millions of people of all classes, grades and conditions find a home; a city that covers eighty thousand acres of ground; where is consumed fifty-five million gallons of beer and porter with three million gallons of ardent spirits, annually poured out to satisfy unnatural and voracious appetites. It takes thirty thousand tailors to make their clothes, forty thousand shoemakers to take care of their feet, and fifty thousand milliners and dress-makers to attend to the ladies' dresses; here an army of twenty-five thousand servants are daily employed, and the smoke of the coal-fires darken the country for more than twenty miles around. The splendour of the magnificent buildings and shops, carriages, cabs, omnibuses and vehicles of every description with crowds of pedestrians, impressed me with surprise beyond my powers of description. I got off at Silver Street after paying the conductor six-pence for my fare, and walked to my friend's house, where I was received in a most cordial manner. During my stay in London I visited many of the principal places of interest in the city, among which were the following, viz: St. James' Palace, an irregular cluster of buildings used for court purposes, but not as the Queen's residence; Buckingham Palace, the Queen's London residence, a large quadrangular building; Marlborough House, now the residence of the Prince of Wales; Kensington Palace and Gardens; House of Parliament, a vast structure, which has cost £3,000,000, perhaps the finest building in the world applied to national purposes; the river front is 900 feet long; Westminster Hall, a noble old structure, of which the main hall is 290 feet by 68, and 110 feet high; The Horse Guards, the official residence of the Commander-in-Chief, with an arched entrance to St. James' Park, where under the arches on each side are two noble specimens of mounted sentries. The National Gallery, devoted to a portion of the nation's pictures; in

Trafalgar Square, South Kensington Museum, the Guards Barracks, Chelsea; the General Post Office, which has a hall 80 feet by 60 and 53 high, with a vast number of offices all around it.

Of public columns and statues the chief which interested me and took my attention were the following: The Albert memorial, Hyde Park; Nelson's Column, Trafalgar Square; and York Column, Waterloo Steps. Of the public parks in the Metropolis the most important are Hyde Park, St. James' Park, the Green Park, Regent's Park, Victoria Park, Kensington Park—all belong to the nation, and are, of course out of the builders' hands; they are most valuable as "lungs" and breathing places for great London.

The Zoological Gardens, Horticultural Gardens, and Botanic Gardens are beautiful places belonging to private societies. Of places of amusement, there are three opera houses, about thirty theatres, twelve music halls and concert rooms of large dimensions (including Albert Hall), a much larger number of smaller size, and very numerous exhibition rooms of various kinds, including Madame Tussaud's exhibition of wax figures, in Baker Street; these greatly interested and amused me.

I must not forget my leave is nearly up, my furlough expires to-morrow night at tattoo. Alas, I am sorry I cannot stay longer; time seems so short, and flies so fast in this great city, but as a soldier I must never forget my duty.

After bidding my friend good-bye, and thanking him kindly for his generous hospitality, I started back to join my regiment at Chatham, by the same route I had come, arriving in barracks at tattoo, January 16th, and duly reported myself.

Whilst I had been on leave, my company (the grenadiers) were under orders for detachment at Sheerness. Accordingly we embarked at the Sun Pier, and proceeded down the Medway, by steamer, on the 8th February, arriving at our destination at two p.m., commanded by Captain L. C. Bourchier, and were stationed in the same barracks as the 72nd Highlanders, whose pipers kept playing and droning from reveillé till tattoo. This is also another of England's royal ship-building establishments; there are nearly two thousand artizans and labourers employed daily in the dockyard. The streets, public houses, and concert saloons are continually, unfortunately, crowded with sailors, soldiers, marines, and dockyard hands every evening; and not unfrequently a bar-room row takes place between the soldiers and sailors; on one occasion I saw two of our tallest and ablest grenadiers peel off their coats and clean out a whole tap-room of sailors, and that with their English fists.

On our last visit to Canterbury, what did I do but, like an Irishman, fall in love. I made the acquaintance of a Kentish beauty and promised to marry her, with the understanding that I got the commanding officer's sanction. In order to carry out this promise, after our company had been here about a month, I applied to the colonel, of course through the captain of my company, for leave to get married, which was granted, through the strong recommendation and influence of my captain; for my readers must know that it is only a very small proportion of soldiers (six to each company), and those only of the best character and highly recommended, can get leave to marry; or if they marry without leave, they have no claim to participate in any of the advantages and privileges attached to the soldier who marries with leave —such as quarters in barracks and on foreign stations, and "rations." Having received the commanding officer's permission, I was married, on the 3rd of April, 1850, at Minster, in the Isle of Sheppy, Kent. My wife then was placed on the strength of the regiment from that date. Now my happiness was complete. I was struck out of the barrack-room messing, and my wife and I became truly happy together. Instead of walking down the town with my comrades, I walked out with my wife in the evenings on the ramparts in rear of our quarters, and gazed in wonder at the massive fortifications and guns which encircled our barracks. Here we could hear the soft strains of exquisite music from the various military bands of marines, or the regiments in garrison, or, more frequently, the pipers of the 72nd Highlanders, or the sound of the evening gun re-echo over the surface of the waters from the flag-ship which rode so majestically at anchor in the distant roadstead, with the sun sinking into an ocean of fire, and the white sails of the fishing smacks glisten in the setting sun. We had been for some time fearing to be relieved from this delightful station; at length the long expected order came. The rumours which had been for some time gathering strength as to our destination were discovered to have had a better foundation than many which in general float indefinitely about our barracks, on the subject of which no one ever could discover their origin, for, you must know, soldiers are great gossipers.

Our orders were for Weedon, a small town in Northamptonshire, on the River Nene. In three days we were to embark on board a steamer for London, thence by rail. We were all rather sorry for leaving the present station, although soldiers always like fresh scenery, and always play when they leave "The Girl I Left Behind Me."

We embarked on the 18th of May, accompanied by the band, pipes, and several men of the 72nd Highlanders to the wharf; the band playing "Auld Lang Syne," as our steamer moved off from the dock, the men cheering and waving their handkerchiefs, which we responded to in a most friendly manner. We were all very happy, though we were rather closely packed together—a circumstance generally considered dangerous to good fellowship. The vessel was a small one, and being of rather ancient build did not boast all those conveniences that the new steamers possess. The voyage was a short one; the river being very smooth, the trip was pleasant, although it was somewhat inconvenient for the women and children, who were huddled up very close together. We were lucky that the weather was so fine—therefore, we had not the unpleasantness of sea sickness.

As we neared London, steamers and vessels of nearly

every size became more numerous, and the buzz of industry from the shore, with the whistling of small steamers, the splashing of wheels, and clouds of smoke, impressed us with the wondrous amount of traffic carried on through this mighty highway of commerce.

We reached Blackwall at one o'clock, and marched to Euston Station, the women and children being sent in cabs, where we took the train at three p.m, arriving in Weedon at five p.m, marched into barracks and joined head-quarters which had been there before us. About this time Colonel Styte got command of the regiment, an old Waterloo officer of great skill in military details. The Town of Weedon, which is situated in the centre of a wide and rich valley in one of the most beautiful counties in England, was declared by all our soldiers, without one dissentient voice, to be an exceedingly dull stupid place; not having much duty to perform in this quiet garrison, we were kept continually at drill; in the evenings the men had nothing to occupy their spare time except to assemble in the public houses or canteen; and on Sunday, after church to walk out of town to a certain country tavern where they unfortunately used to indulge in drink ing and carousing. In the days of which I write, those who entertained the idea of educating soldiers were laughed at as visionary enthusiasts, whose schemes, if put into practice would entirely ruin and destroy the military spirit of the army; and few there were among the com manding officers of regiments who possessed moral courage enough to combat the general opinion, even if they differed from the principle. Colonel Styte, however, the lieutenant-colonel of the 17th regiment of "Royal Tigers," was happily endowed with moral courage in equal degree with his gallantry in the field, which secured for him his present high position, and an honesty of mind and purpose he possessed that was not usual with officers of his time. He had received a wound at the Battle of Waterloo in his right arm, which entirely disabled it, and it hung down by his side quite powerless. Not being able to draw his sword, we had great sympathy for him, which he appreciated very much. He had established an evening school for the drummer boys of the regiment and for such of the non-commissioned officers and privates as chose to avail themselves of its advantages. The colonel and a few of his brother officers raised a subscription in order to provide the necessary books; and a school was established and well attended, with most excellent results; valued by many of the best disposed non-commissioned officers and men; and worked exceedingly well. Regarding the drummer boys, their attendance was compulsory. The teacher was a very gentlemanly, able man, and imparted his instructions in a very painstaking manner, which caused many of the young soldiers to attend his school willingly and try to advance themselves by his instructions.

Nothing in the regiment gave me more pleasure than attending, and the progress I made during our term served to advance my prospects of promotion in after years, which I most gratefully remember.

We were stationed in this quiet town for three months when we got orders to proceed to Castlebar, a town in the west of Ireland, and about one hundred and sixty miles from Dublin.

CHAPTER VIII.

LIVERPOOL—EMBARK FOR DUBLIN—THE VOYAGE—ARRIVAL—MARCH —THE TRAIN—THE MARCH TO CASTLEBAR—ARRIVAL—ELECTION —ROUTE TO GALWAY.

MAY 9th, 1850.—The regiment was formed on the barrack square right in front, marched to the railway station, the band playing at the head of the regiment, accompanied by a large number of the towns-people, with whom we were very popular, and who gave us three hearty cheers as the train moved from the station at 10 o'clock a.m. During the journey, the train stopped sufficiently long enough at different stations to enable us to partake of refreshments.

Arriving in Liverpool at 4.30, formed up at the station and marched through the main street down to the docks, with fixed bayonets, the band playing "British Grenadiers," where we embarked at 5.30 p.m. At six o'clock the steamer moved off slowly from the dock, the band playing "Come back to Erin," when we were cheered by the crowd from the quay.

We had a remarkably fine passage, although the boat rolled and pitched a good deal with the long swell from south-west, and we suffered but little discomfort beyond what invariably attends 900 men, 40 women and children who are imprisoned for the time being, with the fear of being drowned. Several of the women and children were sea-sick; but as for the men, their will conquered their stomach, and they were not sick, although many of them looked very pale and squeamish. Hoping to enter port in the morning, I was early on deck; we were already in sight of land; on the right the long low line of the Irish coast was visible scarcely raised above the level of the sea. Not far ahead the outline and prominent feature of the Hill of Howth stood out before us on the right with its light-house; my heart beat high with joy as my eye caught the first glimpse of the land of my birth, "my own native land."

The city, that at first looked like a white line on the coast, began apparently to lift itself upwards and assume definite form and shape, the houses and spires standing out more distinctly; on the left we saw Kingston, with the grand Wicklow Mountains in the background completing the picture. Indeed the Bay of Kingston is said to be one of the most beautiful in the world. Now we pass the lighthouse on the left which stands at the end of a long pier at the entrance of the bay, close to the Pigeon Hole where there are strong fortifications. We are moving up slowly among the shipping, arriving at the north-wall at six o'clock a.m. The order was given to disembark immediately, when huge swarms of red coats assembled on deck, buzzed and bustled about, actively preparing to disembark in good order, and fall in by companies on the quay. On the bugle sounding the whole fell in, and were inspected by the Colonel. All being correct, we marched off by fours with fixed bayonets and band playing, along the Liffy to the Western Railway station, "Broadstone," accompanied by an immense crowd of spectators. We took the train at eight o'clock for Mullingar, arriving there at ten—sixty miles in two hours—and were billeted on the taverns and public houses. Previous to being dismissed, we were formed up at quarter distance column, in front of the principal hotel, Mr. Murray's, where the Colonel stayed, when he charged the men to conduct themselves in their billets in a soldierlike manner, and never bring discredit on the corps through their misconduct among the inhabitants; non-commissioned officers were ordered especially to look after the men's interests, and call the roll at tattoo; he at the same time ordered parade with arms and accoutrements at five o'clock p.m., after which the men were marched to their different billets by their respective non-commissioned officers, where we were received with "ceade-mille-failtha" by the landlords, who had dinner ready for us in right Irish fashion, according to instructions received from the "Billet-master." After dinner we were employed in getting our appointments clean and ready for parade. At the appointed time the regiment paraded at the former place, rolls called, and companies inspected by their respective captains. During the parade the bands "discoursed sweet music" in front of the hotel. After the reports were collected, and all reported present by the Adjutant, the Colonel gave the command, "fix bayonets, shoulder arms, left wheel into line, quick march, halt, dress," the Major giving the word "steady," when the line was dressed; after which the Colonel opened the ranks and inspected the whole line (the band playing during the inspection), breaking into open column right in front, and then dismissed.

A large crowd of town and country people were looking on in amazement; one would have thought they never saw a regiment on parade before, their admiration was so great.

After going to our billets the men dressed for the evening in their shell-jackets, forage-caps, and waist-belts, cane in hand, and were soon scattered in all directions among the civilians, who soon made their acquaintance, and pledged their friendship with creature comforts in the public houses.

"Reveille" sounded at five o'clock, when we were on the alert, got breakfast at six, and were on parade at seven. After the companies were inspected, the Colonel again addressed them, telling the men the consequence and penalty of getting drunk on the line of march; after which he sent off the advance guard, and told off the rear and baggage guards. The women, with their children, that could not afford a side-car, had to ride on the baggage-waggon. After these preliminary arrangements were made, we marched off, the band playing "Patrick's Day;" the people gave three cheers on parting. After we got well out of town, we were allowed to march at ease, talk, smoke, and sing. We were quite fresh on starting, but after we had accomplished about five or six miles we began to feel the weight of a full kit, arms, accoutrements, haversack, and sixty rounds of ammunition in our pouches, with a thick stiff leather stock, and coatee buttoned up tight around our neck, with a heavy shako. The weather being warm and roads dusty, we began to get somewhat tired and thirsty. We were halted close to a small village, where we procured some butter-milk from the peasants, who gave it willingly. I went into a house and asked for a drink of water, when the old woman brought me a large noggin of buttermilk, saying, "dhrink this acushla, its bether nar cauld wather for ye on the road." I offered her some coppers, but she refused, saying, "no, I thank ye, sur, do you think I would take pay from a poor sojer for a drop o' buttermilk, the sorrow bit thin, I wish it was bether, it's myself that would give it ye."

After getting refreshed we started on again; we had nine miles more to march before we got to Ballymore, where we were to be billeted for the night; we had frequent halts for a few moments at a time, during the remaining nine miles, when the people brought us noggins of buttermilk; as we resumed the march, the band struck up "Patrick's Day," which well repaid the people for their buttermilk, and several of them accompanied us for miles along the road.

Arrived in Ballymore at two o'clock, when we were told off to our respective billets. This is a very wretched small town, with only three public houses; most of the men were billeted in private houses, the poor people were hard pressed to find room for us; but we were tired and not very particular, as long as we got some place to stretch ourselves. After arriving at our billets, dinner, such as they had, was ready for us; tea and coffee there was none, but instead, we had an abundance of bacon, cabbage, and potatoes, which we washed down with plenty of new milk. After satisfying the cravings of the inner man with these substantials, we felt we should like to try a drop of good Irish whiskey, made up a subscription and sent our host out for the "crater." After partaking of this luxury, so long unknown, in which the landlord joined in a sociable manner, we turned out for parade; when we were inspected by captains of companies and dismissed.

We had supper at six; oat-cakes, potato-cakes, and new milk, and soon after we were in the land of dreams, well tired from our march. Reveille was sounded at five next morning, arousing the hitherto quiet village, when we were all on the alert; got breakfast of bacon, eggs, potatoes and milk; falling in for parade at seven, marching off with the band playing "Patrick's Day," which caused the people to shout and cheer. After a long march of sixteen miles we reached Athlone at two o'clock, dismissed to our billets where dinner was ready according to instructions received in advance.

My wife fared much better to-day than yesterday. I had procured for her a seat on a side-car with the hospital sergeant's wife, by paying half the expense of the car. This is a good sized town, large barracks and strongly fortified on the Shannon, dividing Leinster from Connaught. We fared well here and got good billets; to-morrow will be Sunday; we will halt. We were allowed to indulge in a good sleep on Sunday morning, nothing to do before ten o'clock, only get breakfast of ham and eggs; church parade in front of O'Rourk's hotel, where we were inspected and marched off to our different places of worship, the band playing, causing great crowds of people to assemble and accompany us to church. After dinner the men walked out in full dress; there were crowds of people and plenty of whiskey drunk during the day and night; great excitement to see so many soldiers in the town. At tattoo that night one corporal and six privates were confined; the corporal for being drunk, and the privates for minor offences. In the morning, the six privates were reprimanded, and the corporal sent back for a court martial on arrival at Castlebar.

We were on the march at seven o'clock, the band playing Patrick's Day and Garry Owen, as we marched out of town, cheered by the crowd. We were in good spirits for every fellow had a parting glass with the landlord before parting, besides we were getting accustomed to the march. After a march of fifteen miles we arrived in Castleblakeney at two o'clock. This is a small town like Ballymore. During the march to Castlebar, we always started at seven every morning and paraded at five every evening for inspection.

Next day at two o'clock, we reached Tuam, a fine town, where Archbishop McHale and Bishop Plunket reside, where we were billeted that night, marching as usual in the morning; next night at Holymount, arriving at Castlebar on Thursday, the 18th May, 1850, where we were to be stationed till further orders, accomplishing a journey of about one hundred miles in seven days. On arriving we were shown our quarters; bed-filling at the barrack stores, and cleaning our appointments after the long march, occupied the remainder of the day.

The following day commanding officer's parade in heavy marching order at ten a.m., when we were minutely inspected, and dismissed. We had good barrack accommodation, and easy duty, the men getting ten nights in bed between guards. After we had been here a few days, we became aware of the fact that a contested election for a member of parliament was to take place in about three weeks, and we found great excitement among the people; the committees of each candidate were holding meetings and canvassing for their party, many rows took place between them, the public houses were continually crowded, police were brought here from distant stations, and as the day of polling drew near the excitement increased. On the day of voting two troops of cavalry arrived, and we were under orders to turn out at a moment's notice. On the morning of the election, the grenadiers and light company were drawn up in line on each side of the square fronting the court-house, with the two troops of cavalry; the voting commenced at ten o'clock, the police were all formed ready to pass the voters in and keep the crowd back, the voters were brought in from the country on side-cars, guarded from the mob by a policeman on each side of the car.

The people were very roughly used at first by the police, which raised their wrath, when they rushed with immense force on the police and thoroughly defeated them, forcing them to retreat to the lines of the military for protection. Having effected this object the crowd retained their position, but did not attempt to assault the soldiers, though their shouts of defiance to the police rose loud and long. The police were ordered to advance again and seize the ringleaders; they obeyed very reluctantly, but being assaulted with sticks and stones their individual courage was excited, and they rushed to chastise the mob, who again drove them back in greater disorder than before; and a nearer approach to the soldiers was made by the crowd in the scuffle which ensued. The police were again ordered to charge the mob, when a more serious scrimmage arose, sticks and stones were used with more effect, and the parties being nearer to each other, the missiles intended only for the police overshot their mark and struck some of the soldiers, who bore their painful position with admirable fortitude, although their patience was sorely tried to stand a target for the mob; but a soldier's duty is to obey orders in whatever shape they come from his officers, and therefore they had to put up with rough usage. The mob were now furious, and the magistrate had to read the Riot Act before the soldiers could attempt to quell the disturbance; at last the military were ordered to fire, the captain giving the command, "with ball cartridge, load, ready, present, fire," the men were previously cautioned in an under tone of voice to fire over the people's heads.

This had the desired effect, the crowd dissolved as the muskets were brought to the present, after which they gave three cheers for the soldiers and down with the "peelers."

This act brought the soldiers into high esteem with the populace. The business of the interior was now suspended for a time by the sounds of fierce tumults, which arose after the soldiers had discharged the volley; some rushed from the court-house to the platform, and beheld the mob in a state of great excitement. A popular candidate now stood forward on the platform and was greeted with fresh cheers. He waited till the uproarious cheering died away, and then addressed them in a few words touching their nationality and the honour of their country.

After which the crowd gave him three hearty cheers, and quiet was restored, when the troops were marched into barracks, but kept in readiness should another row commence; but happily all were peaceable afterwards although much excitement with plenty of whiskey continued for several days after, in which several of the soldiers joined.

After the election, our men were highly respected by the inhabitants; the old women brought the men bottles of "poteen whiskey" in their milk cans. The sergeant on the gate not suspecting any smuggling, saw nothing but milk in the can—but if he had searched the can he would have found a black bottle of the real "mountain dew" at the bottom.

After being stationed here three months we got the route for Galway, a town situated at the mouth of Lough Corrib; it is the west terminus of the Midland Great Western Railway, and 117 miles west of Dublin.

CHAPTER IX.

THE MARCH—GALWAY—CAPTAIN BOURCHIER—DETACHMENT—REGATTA—ROW WITH THE POLICE—ROUTE TO GALWAY—MAJOR BOURCHIER EXCHANGES—CAPTAIN CROKER—CLADDAGH—ATTEND A CAMP MEETING—THE CITY OF GALWAY—THEATRE—ROUTE TO DUBLIN.

AUGUST 26th, 1850, at 7 a.m. We marched out of Castlebar, the townspeople accompanied us for some distance and gave us three hearty cheers on parting. We marched sixteen miles that day, and were billeted at Holymount. Previous to this Captain Bourchier had applied for leave of absence for three months, which reached him here, when he started for England after bidding the company good-bye, and handing it over to Lieutenant Coulthurst. We all suspected that he was going to be married during his absence, which proved to be a fact, for on his return to the regiment in November he brought his wife with him.

Next morning we were on the march again, and after fifteen miles, arrived at Tuam, where we were billeted for the night; arriving in Galway at two o'clock p.m. the following day, after a tiresome march of eighteen miles. The grenadiers and light company, with four others, were stationed at the Shamble Barracks, and four companies at the Castle. Most of the officers stayed at Mackilroy's Hotel, in the Market Square or "Green," as it was called, where they remained until their quarters were ready for their reception. After our arrival, we all turned out to fill our beds with straw at the barrack store as usual. Duty here was easy, having only three guards to furnish, which consisted of two sergeants, three corporals and twenty-four privates daily, but we were kept continually at drill, either commanding officer's, adjutant's or sergeant-major's. The only time we had to call our own was from supper till tattoo.

During Captain Bourchier's absence from the regiment he had been promoted to Brevet Major, and on his return about the thirtieth of November, he brought a beautiful bride back with him to share his military honours. He rented a comfortable house in one of the aristocratic terraces of Salt Hill Road, in the suburbs of the town. At Christmas he treated the company to a good dinner and a barrel of ale to wash it down, when we drank towards his and his lady's health and happiness, and wished them many returns of the season.

On the 30th January, 1851, I had an increase in my family, for a boy was born to me. We had him christened Thomas Henry, Thomas after my father, and Henry after my wife's father.

Our company were under orders for detachment at Banagher, a small fortified garrison town on the River Shannon, and thirty miles south of Galway.

May 1st, 1851.—Our company were formed on the barrack square, inspected by the Colonel, and after a few words of fatherly advice from him, we marched up High Street, accompanied outside the town by the band, playing Irish airs. We had thirty miles to march, which we accomplished in two days. We marched through Oranmore, Athenry, and were billeted in Balinasloe one night, passing through Eyrecourt, arriving in Banagher next day at three p.m. These barracks are sufficient to accommodate about one hundred and fifty men, situated within a fortification which commands a bridge that spans the Shannon, and connects King's County with the County Galway. This part of the country is celebrated for fishing, shooting and boating, and Portumna Lake, about fourteen miles from here, is famous for regattas, which our three officers, viz., Major Bourchier, Lieutenant Coulthurst and Ensign Williams, availed themselves of during our time of duty at this station. They purchased a yacht, a four-oar gig, and a duck boat, from their predecessors. They also hired one Jack, the boatsman, to take care of the yacht and boats, and accompany them when required. They frequently took a man or two of the company with them when on sailing excursions to work the yacht, which we enjoyed very much.

The Major, Ensign Williams, "Jack" and myself, went to a regatta at Portumna; a distance of fourteen miles, in the four-oared gig; we rowed down the river very fast, arriving there at twelve o'clock, in time for the first race. The officers were invited on board one of the gentlemen's yachts, which was to sail in the match, I and "Jack" were left in charge of the gig. After the race the officers returned at nine o'clock, p.m., when we started to row back to barracks; after we got eight miles, we came to a lock which was open as we passed through going down in the morning; but now it was shut, and we had no alternative but carry our boat to the other side of the lock. This being done, we took a drink of "poteen" which we had in the boat to cheer us up. After refreshing ourselves we started again with renewed vigour. In going down in the morning we thought nothing of rowing fourteen miles with the stream, but now going back against it, was quite a different affair, the stream ran so very swift, and we had hard work to make headway against it. However, with good pluck and a drop out of the bottle of "poteen," now and then, we braved the stream and reached barracks at two o'clock in the morning. Scarcely a day passed without a boating, fishing, or shooting excursion of some kind. This makes it a very pleasant station, and besides the town has a clean, neat and tidy appearance, compared with some towns we have seen in Ireland, and can boast of one decent hotel, "Mann's Hotel," besides several public houses with skittle allies attached, which place of amusement several of our men patronized. Two of the company had an altercation with two or three of the police at one of these places, when the latter tried to take the two soldiers to the police station, this the soldiers objected to, whereupon a row ensued, then several more police joined and were forcing the soldiers off, when their comrades in barracks having been warned of the row by some person, rushed out of barracks with naked bayonets in hand, rescued the two soldiers and beat the police, driving the whole force out of the town and chasing them through the country where they skedaddled and hid in the potato fields. Several of the police got hurt, but not very seriously. Our company and the police never could agree after that row, but they never again attempted to take any of our men to the station-house. About a month after the row with the police, we got relieved by No. 6 company from head-quarters.

On the 27th October we marched out of barracks at two o'clock, p. m., as the relieving company marched in. After a march of sixteen miles we arrived in Balmastor at seven o'clock in the evening, where we were billeted for the night. The railway, which was in course of construction as we passed here *en route* to Banagher, being now finished and the trains running on it, we took the train at eleven o'clock, a. m., arriving at Galway Station at twelve, where we were met by the band, which marched at the head of the company down Main Street, playing the "British Grenadiers" as we marched into the Shamble Barracks. One month after this, Major Bourchier had exchanged to the 54th Regiment, which were in the East Indies. The night previous to his departure his brother officers of the regiment entertained him as their guest at the mess, where they all expressed deep sorrow at his leaving and his loss to the regiment. After bidding the men good-bye, he left for India, taking with him the best wishes and prayers for his future welfare, especially of his own company the grenadiers, to whom he had ever been a father during his command. Many of the men accompanied him to the railway station to see him off; need I say we lost a friend.

Captain John Croker, a Limerick man, not only the tallest officer in the regiment (height 6 feet 4 ins.) but now the senior captain, who formerly belonged to No. 8 company, now got command of the grenadiers, vice Captain Bourchier promoted. Galway has a population of about 25,000; the old town is poorly built and irregular, and some of its old houses have the Spanish architecture, easily accounted for by the great intercourse which at one time subsisted between Galway and Spain. The new town consists of well planned and spacious streets, built on a rising ground which slopes gradually towards the harbour; its suburbs are very wretched, collections of wretched cabins, inhabited by a poor class of people; one of these suburbs called the Claddagh, is inhabited by fishermen who exclude all strangers, and live perfectly amongst themselves, electing their king, etc., and ever marrying within their own circle. These fishermen still speak the grand old Celtic language, and the old Irish costume is still worn by the women, open gowns and red petticoats.

They annually elect a mayor, whose functions is to administer the laws of their fishery, and to superintend all internal regulations. One of these fishermen's sons took a great liking to the soldiers, and frequently came into the barracks to see us at drill. He was about 6 feet 4 inches in height and a powerful built young man of eighteen years old. He applied to the sergeant-major to enlist. He took him before the Colonel, who approved of him. When he was enlisted in the 17th Regiment, his name was Paddy Belton, His father came and tried to get him off, but it was no use, he had his mind made up, and wished to be a soldier. After getting his uniform on, he invited a comrade and myself, to a "camp" in his village; which is a contest of skill, or, competition for priority—a display of female powers at the spinning of yarn. It is indeed a cheerful meeting of the bright fair girls; and although strong and desperate rivalry is the order of the day, it is conducted in a spirit so light-hearted and friendly that I scarcely know a more interesting or delightful amusement in a country life. When a " camp " is about to be held the affair soon becomes known in the neighbourhood; sometimes young women are asked, but in most instances, so eager are they to attend that invitations are unnecessary; in winter time and in mountain districts, it is often as picturesque as pleasant.

The young women usually begin to assemble at four o'clock in the morning; and as they always go in groups, accompanied besides by their sweethearts, or some male relative,each of the latter bearing a large torch of well dried bog-deal, their voices, songs and laughter break upon the stillness of the morning with a holiday feeling, made five times more delightful by the darkness of the hour. The spinning wheels are carried by the young men amidst an agreeable volley of repartee. From the moment they arrive the mirth is fast and furious, nothing is heard but laughter, conversation, songs and anecdotes, all in a loud key; among the loud humming of spinning-wheels, and the noise of reels, as they incessantly crack the cuts in the hands of the reelers, who are perpetually turning them from morning till night, in order to ascertain the quantity which every competitor has spun; and who ever has spun the most wins the "camp," and is queen for the night. At the conclusion of the "camp" we all repaired to a supper of new milk and flummery, which was most delicious. This agreeable meal being over, we repaired to the dancing-room, where Mickey Gaffet, the piper, was installed in his own peculiar arm-chair of old Irish oak; a shebeen man, named Barney O'Shea, had brought a large jar of poteen to cheer the boys' hearts for the occasion, of which they freely partook, when the dancing commenced. It is not my intention to enter into a detailed account of the dancing, nor of the good humour which pervaded amongst them, it is enough to say that the old people performed cotillions and the young folks jigs, reels, and country dances; hornpipes were performed upon doors (the floor being of earth) with the greatest skill. My comrade and myself enjoyed the dance, which was kept up all night, taking a drop of poteen between the dances, to keep our spirits up by pouring spirits down. Our leave was up at six o'clock in the morning, and we had to report ourselves not later than that hour to the sergeant of the quarter guard, so we left the dance at four o'clock, got to barracks before six, gave in our passes to the sergeant, and were just in time for morning drill, when we drilled till a quarter to eight o'clock, I can assure you with aching heads after the poteen.

The principal buildings in Galway are, the Queen's College, which was just opened a year before our arrival there ; among the other edifices are three monasteries, and five nunneries, Smith's College, the court-house, and barracks, with the grand old church of St Nicholas. It has numerous flour, and other mills, also breweries, and distilleries. Extensive salmon and sea fishing are carried on here.

The bay is a large expanse of water about eighteen miles broad at its seaward extremity, diminishing to about eight miles inland, and being about twenty miles long. It is protected from the swell of the Atlantic, by the Arran Isles. South-west from Galway to the sea is the district called Connemara, which contains vast bogs, moors, loughs and marshes, which present a bleak and dreary aspect. Galway abounds in ancient remains of Celtic as well as of the Norman period ; cromlechs and monastic ruins are found in several parts of the county.

A very fine specimen of this class is that of Knockmoy, near Tuam, besides several round towers. The officers amused themselves both fishing and shooting when off duty, they frequently could be seen with rod and line landing a large sized salmon, on the banks of the river, and another officer coming into barracks in the evening with his dog and gun, with his bag well filled with game, after his day's sport.

Besides these enjoyments they organised an amateur

dramatic company, with Lieutenant Lindsay, Lieutenant Coulthurst and Ensign Williams at its head, with the band and a few smart non-commissioned officers and privates; which was well patronised by the officers and their ladies, besides several of the nobility and gentry of the town and any of the soldiers who wished to attend. This brought round the best of feeling between the regiment and inhabitants, and produced excellent results.

We had been for some time looking out for an order for Dublin. Our expectations were fulfilled on the fifteenth of March, by the colonel receiving a large official envelope containing the route for the 17th regiment to proceed by rail on the 28th March, 1852, to Dublin, there to be stationed and do garrison duty till further orders, to be quartered in the Richmond barracks. The order having been read to the regiment, the news soon spread to the creditors in the town, when could be seen tailors, shoemakers, hatters, bakers, grocers and liquor merchants, all rushing into the barracks looking for their debtors.

Notwithstanding the credit of the regiment having been cried down on our arrival, many trades people had given credit to several parties, which they now were trying to collect; but, all those who cannot collect it now, the first tap of the big drum will pay them, when we march out of town.

> "How happy is the soldier who lives on his pay,
> And spends half a crown out of sixpence a day."

We had fifteen days to get ready, which were occupied

in cleaning barracks, filling nail-holes, and white-washing, to obviate as much as possible that curse, barrack damages, which always follow a regiment from one barrack to another.

CHAPTER X.

THE MARCH — RAIL TO DUBLIN—ARRIVAL — GARRISON DUTY — CASTLE GUARD—THE OLD MAN'S HOSPITAL—DIVINE SERVICE—TENT-PITCHING—DEATH OF THE "IRON DUKE"—THE FUNERAL—THE QUEEN VISITS DUBLIN—BUILDINGS AND INSTITUTIONS—THE ROUTE.

MARCH 28th, 1852.—The regiment was formed on the Barrack Square, at six o'clock, a.m., in heavy marching order, full kits in our packs; the companies minutely inspected and told off by their respective captains; reports collected by the adjutant, when all reported present to the Colonel, who then gave the command "fours right, quick march," when they stepped off, the companies wheeling to the right out of the gate, the band striking up "Patrick's Day," playing up the main street. During the inspection the barrack-gate had been besieged by a large crowd of town's people, who accompanied the regiment to the railway station, where we were joined by the two companies from the Castle. While getting the regimental baggage, women and children on the train the band discoursed some sweet music, causing frequent cheers from the crowd. At length all was ready, when a wild scream from the engine was heard, and the train moved out slowly from beneath the vaulted roof of the station, amid cheer after cheer from the populace, who were assembled in large numbers to see us off; the band playing during the slow departure of the train from the station, and the men waving their handkerchiefs, in response, from the carriage windows. At last the train quickened the speed, and soon station and crowd faded from our view. We were scarcely an hour in our seats, and viewing the country as the train sped along, and admiring the beautiful green fields, hills and valleys, interspersed with running streams, the peasantry gazing in wonder, and the country girls waving their handkerchiefs as the long train of soldiers passed them by, when a shrill whistle from the engine was heard, and then, with much noise, and many a heavy sob, the vast machine swept smoothly into the station at Ballinaster.

There were, formed in line on the platform, the companies from detachment at Banagher and Portumna, waiting our arrival to join head-quarters. The train stopped at this station twenty minutes, when the two companies came on board. All being ready, the train moved off again, soon reaching Athlone, where we stopped fifteen minutes. Here we got refreshments—a glass of beer and a biscuit, which we enjoyed, having breakfasted at five that morning. About an hour after we were in Mullingar, stopping fifteen minutes, when we started again. We are rapidly leaving Mullingar behind. The fields gradually assume a green and spring-like aspect. This part of the country is highly cultivated. Occasionally a small village in the valley, by some running stream, or upon the hill side, give life and charm to the landscape. The Royal Canal runs alongside of the railway all the way from Dublin to Mullingar, and unites the Liffy with the Shannon in the west.

As I was viewing the beauty of the landscape, the engine gave a loud and long whistle, which reminded me we were close to the city. Now we can see Wellington's monument, in Phœnix Park; arriving at the station at one o'clock, after a ride of one hundred and thirty miles, when we were met by the band of the 39th Regiment, who played at the head of the regiment to Richmond Barracks. On arrival we were told off to our different barracks.

These are splendid large, airy barracks, sufficient for two regiments, with good officers' and staff quarters, but bad for married soldiers, who have to rent apartments outside.

The military force in Dublin then consisted of the 11th Hussars, Island Bridge Barracks; 17th Lancers, Royal Horse Artillery and Foot Artillery, Portobella; 2nd Dragoon Guards, 27th Regiment, Royal Barracks; 32nd Light Infantry, Ship Street and Linen Hall Barracks; 39th and 17th Regiments, Richmond Barracks; besides depôts at Beggars' Bush; the whole under the command of Major-General Sir Edward Blakeley, whose quarters were in the Old Man's Hospital, near Phœnix Park.

The regiments furnish the duties in their turn. In garrison orders of the 30th, the 17th Regiment were detailed to furnish the whole of the duties on the following day, viz :—The Castle Guard, one captain, one subaltern, two sergeants, and twenty-four privates; Lower Castle, one sergeant, one corporal and six privates; Vice-Regal Lodge, one sergeant, two corporals and eighteen privates; Old Man's Hospital, one sergeant, two corporals, and twelve privates; Kilmanane, one corporal, and three privates; Arbour Hill Hospital, one sergeant, one corporal and twelve privates; Magazine, one sergeant, one corporal and six privates; Mountjoy, one corporal and six privates; Island Bridge, one sergeant, one corporal and twelve privates; Picture Gallery, one corporal and three privates; Bank of Ireland, one subaltern, one sergeant, one corporal and twelve privates; Richmond, one sergeant, two corporals and twelve privates.

These guards, with the regimental guards, assemble daily (Sundays and wet days excepted), on the Esplanade, at ten p.m., when they are trooped, the junior officer of the Castle Guard carrying the colours during the trooping. The regiment who furnishes the duties for the day, also furnishes the band, which plays during the trooping of the colours, when crowds of spectators assemble to witness this military review. After they march past in slow and quick time, the guards are formed on their commanders, when they are marched off to their respective guards by the field officer of the day. Relieving the Castle Guard is a very imposing sight, and hundreds of people assemble to witness this military performance, as well as to hear the sweet martial music while the guards are relieving. Before the old guard marches off the new guard plants their colours in the centre of the Castle yard, with a sentry over them. Two sentries are posted at the gate of the Castle yard, and two on the door of the Castle, under the portico. All the sentries of the old guard having been relieved, the guard is marched off by its captain, the subaltern carrying the colours, when the new guard salutes by presenting arms, after which the new guard takes the place of the old; the relief being told off, they are dismissed to the guard-room. The guards take their rations with them, which consist of three-quarters of a pound of beef or mutton, one pound and a half of bread, one pound and a half of potatoes and onions, one-eighth ounce of tea, quarter of an ounce of coffee, two ounces of sugar, with pepper and salt to each man. There being but one pot and pan in each guard-room they are kept, as you may well imagine, in active work until six o'clock in the evening, every relief boiling potatoes and making tea and coffee.

I was detailed for the Old Man's Hospital, which is a large establishment, and consists of the Major General's Quarters, the English Church, where the troops from Richmond attend divine service, as well as the "Old Pensioners," or "Old Fogies," as they are called. There are quarters here for about eight hundred men; any pensioner can be admitted who applies (married men excepted). They are required to pay in their pension for their board and clothes; the latter consists of cloth trowsers, red tunic, which comes down below the knee, and a Napoleon hat. They have no duty to perform, only keep themselves and quarters clean and tidy. They are all well satisfied and seem happy; chatting, and fighting their battles over again. The grounds, walks, avenues, shrubbery, kitchen-garden and flower-beds, around this institution show the taste, cleanliness and discipline of those old veterans whose home it now is, provided by a grateful country.

Being relieved from guard next day, we had kit inspection by the commanding officer, accompanied by Major Cole, who had just joined Sunday church parade. At ten a.m., being inspected, we were marched off, the band playing, through Kilmanam, to the Old Man's Hospital, where the Protestants and Roman Catholics parted for the time. I, belonging to the latter, marched to St. Mary's Church, on Arran Quay. As we marched along the Liffy the sweet strains of music, which re-echoed along the river from the different bands as they marched to church, caused a most pleasing sensation, which raised our thoughts heavenward. It is deeply to be regretted bands do not now play on Sundays, owing to Puritan objections. Strict military discipline, numerous general field-days and reviews, drilling at tent-pitching in the nineteen acres, regimental drills and parades, with five nights in bed, kept our men pretty well employed. But the beautiful walks in Phœnix Park, and driving to the strawberry beds on side-cars with our sweethearts on Sunday afternoons, together with theatres, concerts, museums, picture galleries, and the scenery of the city, compensated us well for all our strict discipline, and we were well pleased with Dublin as a military station.

Now came a sad and mournful event to the army. The Duke of Wellington—the Iron Duke, that noble and illustrous warrior and statesman, whose glorious and eventful life history relates and old veterans remember—terminated this earthly career at the ripe age of 84 years. This event, which took place suddenly and unexpectedly, occurred on Tuesday, the 14th of September, 1852, after a few hours' illness, at Walmer Castle, his official residence. The intelligence of this mournful event was received at the time with the deepest regret by the officers and men of our regiment, and universal gloom pervaded throughout the whole garrison. The hero of Salamanca, St. Sebastian, Quatre-Bras, Ligny and Waterloo, had paid the last debt. November the 1st, a general order was issued directing one officer, one sergeant, and twelve rank and file from each regiment in garrison to proceed, on the 8th inst., to London, to take part in the funeral procession of the late Field Marshal, His Grace the Duke of Wellington. Lieutenant W. H. Earle, Sergeant Plant, and twelve rank and file (I being one of the latter), to parade on the Esplanade, with the detachment from the other regiments in garrison, when they were inspected by the General, and marched off, with a field officer in charge, going on board a steamer at the North Wall, at six o'clock p.m. We had on board about one hundred and fifty picked men from these corps, I being the smallest man of the party, and I was five feet eleven. The men vied with each other in a smart soldier-like appearance. All being ready, the Captain cried out, "all on board," when the steamer moved out slowly from the quay, passed clear of the shipping, and Pigeon House Fort on the right, where detachments of our men assembled, and gave us three cheers, waving their handkerchiefs, the steamer rushing onwards, city and shore fading away, and nothing but heavy clouds and water could be seen. The evening had an angry appearance, darkness closed around, the sailors thought it looked like a storm, but they were mistaken, although the vessel rolled and pitched more than we thought agreeable. After a good deal of rolling and pitching, with a frequent wave breaking over our bow, we steamed into Liverpool docks at six o'clock in the morning, landed, got breakfast, and marched to the railway station, took the train at 9 a.m. for London. The engine gave the warning whistle, and we moved out of the station, and were whirling onward towards London. The morning was bright, invigorating and beautiful, the swift-winged train going thundering along at the rate of forty miles an hour. After a ride of one hundred and eighty miles in nine hours, we were set down at Euston Station. While in London, we were quartered in Regent Park. On the morning of the 13th of November, nothing could be more imposing than the whole line of this melancholy procession; the day was fine, and the appearance of the troops splendid.

The streets were lined with cavalry and infantry, from the station to St. Paul's Cathedral. At twelve o'clock the body arrived by rail from Walmer Castle, escorted by a guard of honour. To detail the order of the procession would occupy too much space here; suffice it to say, that the cortege moved from the station, the bands playing the dead march, minute guns firing, as it marched to St. Paul's Cathedral, where the body was lowered into the crypt, close to the last earthly resting-place of the heroic Nelson, waiting for the trumpet to turn-out. The funeral was one of the most gorgeous and solemn spectacles, that had ever before been witnessed in England.

This solemn duty being performed, we returned by rail next morning to Liverpool, where we took the steamer at six p.m., for Dublin, arriving there at six in the morning, after a rough passage, with several cases of sea-sickness, when we marched to our respective barracks.

The regiments in Dublin are changed from one barrack to another every ten months, ours having been in Richmond the prescribed time, were changed with the 63rd from the Royal Barracks. The first of April we marched from Richmond, meeting the 63rd when the junior saluted the senior; the 17th being the oldest regiment, we had the honour of their salute. On arrival, we were quartered in Palantine Square. The change we hailed with pleasure, as it brought us closer to the amusements of the city. Twelve men of each company were now armed with the Minié Rifle, rather an improvement on Brown Bess, and proceeded to the Pigeon House Fort, to go through a course of rifle instruction on the beach; this course being finished, the rifles were handed over to twelve others who went through a course in the same manner, and so on, until the whole regiment had gone through a course of rifle instruction.

On the 1st of February, 1853, I had another increase in my family, for a daughter was born. We had her christened Jane Stanislaus, at St. Mary's Church, Arran Quay.

In the summer, the Queen and Prince Albert visited Dublin. A message having been received that Her Majesty and the Prince were to land at Kingstown, the grenadiers and light company were ordered to proceed by rail from Westland Row Station, to Kingstown, as a guard of honour. We were formed in two lines facing inwards from the terminus to where the Royal yacht was to come along side, forming a passage which was spread with a red carpet, for Her Majesty and the Prince to walk to the railway carriage. We were standing there an hour when the Royal yacht was descried in the distance, and as she steamed into the harbour, the ships fired a royal salute. The yacht coming alongside the quay, we could see Her Majesty and Prince Albert walking the deck. Her Majesty looked well, and wore a plain plaid shawl, and seemed well pleased with the reception. Soon after arrival, the Royal couple landed. As Her Majesty stepped on shore, the guns of the fortresses belched forth a royal salute; at the same time the bands played "God save the Queen." A special train was in readiness, which conveyed the Royal couple and guards of honour to Dublin, where they went in an open carriage to the Vice-Regal Lodge, accompanied by several troops of cavalry. On the occasion of her Majesty and the Prince landing, many thousands of people were present, and on the streets along the route to the vice-regal lodge, were immense crowds, who cheered and waved their hats, Her Majesty and the Prince most gracefully acknowledging their loyalty. Two days afterwards, the troops in garrison were ordered to assemble in review order at ten a.m., in the fifteen acres, to be reviewed before Her Majesty and Prince Albert. On the day appointed, the troops were marched into the park, bands playing at the head of their respective corps, (accompanied by thousands of citizens) and were formed in line of contiguous quarter distance columns facing the east, with the field batteries on the flanks, and the cavalry in rear at ten a.m.. After waiting a few minutes, Sir Edward Blakeney and his staff arrived, when he deployed the troops into line.

On the appearance of Her Majesty on the ground the artillery fired a royal salute, the infantry presenting arms, the bands playing " God save the Queen." Her Majesty, in an open carriage, drove down the front of the line inspecting the whole, including the boys of the Hibernian School. After the inspection the troops marched past Her Majesty in slow, quick, and double time. The Queen seemed delighted with the marching past; afterwards they were put through several field movements. As the Queen was looking on, the crowd made a rush, determined to take off the horses and to draw Her Majesty in her carriage; this Prince George took for an attempt to assault her person, not understanding the character of the Irish people, when he called out for the cavalry to form up; but when he found that he mistook the people's loyalty, he apologised. This little contretemps caused the Queen to smile at the mistake he had made, when she drove off (well pleased with the review) to the vice-regal lodge, accompanied by an escort of cavalry. The troops were then marched to their respective barracks, with their bands playing. On arrival in barracks the grenadiers and light company were detailed for a guard of honour to Her Majesty during her visit at the vice-regal lodge, and be encamped in front of the lodge in readiness to turn out at Her Majesty's pleasure. After Her Majesty's departure, the regiment was removed from the Royal to Shipstreet Barracks, with two companies at Linen Hall. We also formed a guard of honour on the occasion of the Lord Lieutenant opening the great Irish exhibition. The public buildings of Dublin are famed for their number and grandeur; in the first class may be mentioned the Bank of Ireland, formerly the House of Parliament; Trinity College, the Custom House, and the Four Courts, which, from the chasteness of their design, and the massiveness of their proportions, have a very imposing effect. Here also we find monuments of William the Third, in College Green, of Nelson, in Sackville Street, of the Duke of Wellington in the Park, with several others. There are numerous places of worship; Roman

Catholic and Protestant, monasteries, convents, and a Jewish synagogue. The most remarkable among the Protestant churches are St. Patrick's Cathedral and Christ's Church, and among the Roman Catholic, St. Mary's, St. Saviour's, St. Augustine and St. Kivin's. The squares, which are very numerous, spacious, and well kept, are Stephen's Green, which occupies an area of twenty miles and a mile in circuit; Marrion Square, the most aristocratic; the Trinity College Squares occupy more than 40 acres; Rutland Square, with the Rotunda at the end of Sackville Street. The environs of Dublin are especially beautiful. Rathmines, a southern suburb, is a favourite residence of the wealthier part of the mercantile community. Glasnevin on the north deserves special notice, being the last resting place of the remains of Dan. O'Connell, Curran, and Tom Steele. The Phœnix Park is a magnificent area of nearly 200 acres, having a large amount of timber, which shelter immense herds of deer; it affords scope for military reviews, and is most extensively used by the inhabitants for recreation. The Liffy is crossed by nine bridges, two of which are iron; and throughout the whole extent of the city, the banks of the river are faced with granite walls.

At Christmas, our captain, John Croker, treated the company to a barrel of Guiness's porter; Lieutenants Couthurst and Earle looked after the sergeants and married men in the way of several substantials at Christmas. when we drank towards their health and wished them many returns of the season. Winter here is very pleasant, not much drill, visiting theatres and concerts in the evening. Our term here is short. On the 16th February, 1854, we got the route for Templemore, a town 90 miles south-west of Dublin.

CHAPTER XI.

ARRIVAL AT TEMPLEMORE—THE ROUTE TO CORK—EMBARKATION FOR GIBRALTAR—QUEENSTOWN—THE VOYAGE—STORM AT SEA—GIBRALTAR.

AT ten, a.m., after inspection by Colonel McPherson, C. B., who took command of the regiment, vice Styte who retired, we marched to the great South-western Railway station, the band playing the "British Grenadiers," accompanied by crowds of people, who gave us three cheers, as the train moved from the station, the band playing "Auld Lang Syne," and the men waving their handkerchiefs. After a run of one hundred miles in three hours we arrived in Templemore and marched to our respective quarters. These barracks are built on the same plan as those at Richmond, and large enough for two reigments. The town is small and dull, but the country very pretty. We were here a little over two months when we got the route to proceed to Cork by rail on the 27th April, there to embark on board two sailing transports; the "Dunbar," and "Cornwall," two sister ships, the right wing to go in the latter, and the left in the former.

War with Russia having been declared on Friday, March the 28th, we all agreed that, though ordered to Gibraltar, before many months would elapse we would have the honour and glory of taking the field shoulder to shoulder with those troops who had already embarked for the seat of war in the east.

April 27th, 1854. The regiment took the train at two p.m. arriving in Cork at five p.m. distance one hundred miles in three hours. On arrival we were quartered in Cork Barracks that night, next morning we were conveyed to the transports, which rode at anchor in Queenstown harbour, by two small tug steamers. This harbour is unsurpassed for capacity and safety; it is distinguished into upper and lower, the latter is situated eleven miles below the city, three miles long by two broad, and completely landlocked. Its entrance is by a channel two miles long, by one wide, defended on each side by forts Camden and Carlisle. The upper portion extends for about five miles below the city to Passage; within the harbour are several islands, the principal of which are, Great Island, on which is situated the fortifications of Queenstown, Spike Island, on which is a bombproof artillery barracks, and convict depot, Rocky Island, on which are powder magazines excavated in the rock; each side of the harbour is richly planted with ornamental trees and shrubs, studded with beautiful villas, cottages and terraces; and Queenstown deserves special notice, for its magnificent suburban residences of the gentry, interspersed with ornamental trees, well-kept lawns and promenades, elegantly designed churches and chapels, red brick buildings, splendid shops with large plate glass windows, and clean wide streets, with a fine view of the shipping in the harbour, make it one of the most delightful places in Ireland. The climate being so salubrious, it is much frequented by consumptive invalids.

The right wing were all on board (except some married officers and their families) when each company were shown their berths and mess-tables, after which stowing of knapsacks commenced; the ship's officers were busily engaged telling off the women and children to their berths in the after part of the ship. On the upper deck everything was in confusion; the ship's steward was getting his fresh supply of provisions on board for the voyage, and the sailors stowing away in coops and pens, hens, ducks and sheep; at last the deck was cleared, and things put ship-shape. The rolls being called and all reported present, the watches were then told off. The captain walking the quarter-deck, the sailors and soldiers man the capstan, and the band ready to play, with a stiff breeze off the land. At 3 o'clock p.m. the captain gave the order to weigh anchor, when the band struck up "Rule Britannia," the sailors keeping time to the music, manning the capstan. As the anchor was tripped, the sails were unfurled, and we ran out of the harbour amid cheers from the shore and shipping in the harbour, and were soon bowling along with a stiff breeze on the bow (N. W.) The men were served out with hammocks and one blanket, one tin plate, one panakin to each man, one meat dish, one soup can for each mess; every mess had brought their own pudding clothes. At five the tea bugle sounded, when the orderly men repaired to the cook's-galley for the tea, and served it out to the messes. After tea the men went on deck to smoke, chat and wonder if they were going to be sea-sick. At five thirty the ration bugle sounded, when the orderly men proceeded to draw rations for next day, which consisted of salt pork and beef on alternate days, biscuits, flour, raisins, currants, tea, sugar, cocoa, vinegar, mustard, pepper and salt ; they made the plum pudding for dinner, tied it up ready to boil after breakfast next day—so you see Her Majesty cares for her gallant soldiers. The ship was skimming along with a stiff breeze on the starboard bow, all sails set. At six o'clock the boatswain piped down hammocks, when they were all swung, and as the last post sounded at nine o'clock, they all managed to crawl into them. I was on watch from eight to twelve; the wind had been increasing during the evening. I also observed the sky had an angry appearance; the sailors were all busily at work securing every sail and making all taut. The wind had changed in the night and was now blowing hard in our teeth ; it was a case of tacking, and for landsmen a very trying affair; all night it blew a gale, the wind still from the same quarter; in the night the sailors had to shorten sail several times, each time the ship was brought round on the other tack with a tremendous lurch, and mess tins, water kegs, and tin dishes were dashed to the other side in frightful confusion. My watch being relieved I turned in at twelve, and with all the pitching and tossing I slept soundly until I was awoke by the orderly sergeant turning out the men to get their hammocks stowed on deck. When I went on deck to put my hammock in the place appointed, the wind was still blowing hard; I had to hold on to keep my footing; the whole sea was alive, wave chasing wave and bounding over each other crested with foam. Now and then the ship would pitch her nose into the waves even to the bulwark, and dash the billows aside, and buoyantly rise again, bowling along at ten knots an hour though under moderate sail. Breakfast at eight o'clock of hard sea biscuits and cocoa; but many were on their backs in sea-sickness. After breakfast all hands were ordered on deck except the orderly men, who kept the mess in order and prepared the meals. The wind was still very high and the long swells began to tell on the men; the figure-head plunging as usual deeply into the water, and the heads of some of our men hanging in agony over the gunwale and portsill, in the horrors of sea-sickness.

At the sound of the grog bugle at twelve, they all sprightened up, and very few were absent from their half-gill of rum and two waters. When the dinner of salt-beef and plum pudding was served, most of them made appearance. After dinner the sun had shown through the clouds, and the men gathered in groups on deck to smoke and chat. The progress of the ship was a subject of interest; it was the first thing in the morning and the last at night; and all through the day the direction of the wind, the state of the sky, the weather, and the rate we were going at, were the uppermost topics of the conversation. The ship was bounding along very fast, and it was a fine sight to look up at the clouds of canvas bellied out by the wind like the wings of a gigantic bird, while the ship rushed through the water, dashing it in foam from her bow, and always dipping her figure-head into the waves, sending up a shower of spray. There was always something exciting in the ship, and the way in which she was handled astonished us soldiers; for instance, to see the top-gallant sails hauled down when the wind freshened, or a stay-sail set as the wind went round to the east. The hauling in of the mainsail on a stormy night was to be remembered for a life-time; twenty-four sailors on the main-yard at a time, clewing in to the music of the wind whistling through the rigging. The sailors sing out cheerily at their work, the one who mounts the highest or stands the foremost on the deck usually taking the lead, thus—they cheer up—

> "Haul in the bowlin',
> I love you, Mary Nolan,
> Haul in the bowlin',
> Rollin' yo, heave ho."

In comes the rope with a jerk until the "belay," sung out by the mate, signifies that the work is right. Then there is a rush on the deck when the wind changes, and the yards are to be squared as the wind comes more aft. Being relieved at twelve I turned in and slept well until four o'clock, when I was awoke by the watch holystoning the deck, under the charge of the officer of the watch. I need scarcely explain that the holystone is a large, soft stone, used with water for scrubbing the decks. It rubs down with sand; the sand is washed off by water from the hose, the pump being worked by four men, a man directing the nozzle of the hose into every crevice; the force of the water washing every particle of dirt from the hen-coops, sheep-pens and decks. The watch always wash decks in their bare feet, their trowsers turned up above their knees. After the decks are well washed down with water from the hose; they are dried with swabs, and the deck looks as white as a table-cloth; the boards brighten with the work, not a grease-mark or spot of dirt is to be seen; all polished off with hand-scrapers; the ropes all neatly coiled man-of-war fashion, not a bight out of place, and the brass-work polished and shining—hard work before breakfast. By six o'clock the decks are all clean and dry and everything looking neat; at nine o'clock the doctor ordered all the women and children on deck; the sun shone through the clouds and all was pleasant; the ship running along with close-reefed canvas. At sundown the wind changed round on our larboard quarter from the north-west, and we were making good progress across the Bay of Biscay; we were getting accustomed to the motion of the ship, and many of the officers and men assembled on deck until a late hour watching our course and looking for our port. On Sunday morning the wind was blowing a gale; during the twenty-four hours we made 190 miles.

At ten o'clock we were all assembled on the main deck for Divine service, which was read by the captain of the ship; the day was fine with a stiff breeze; we were running before the wind at the rate of ten knots an hour; we had slept well all night; going on deck next morning, I found the wind strong from the north, and the ship going through the water at a splendid rate; as much sail was on her as she could carry, and she was dashing along, leaving a broad track of foam in her wake. There is no resting, but a constant pushing onward; and, as we look over the bulwark, the waves tipped by the foam which the ship has raised seem to fly behind us at a prodigious speed. At ten next morning we found the ship's run during the twenty-four hours had been 200 miles, a grand day's work, nearly equal to steam; we ran well before the breeze all night until about six in the morning, when the wind changed to our starboard bow, and heavy dark clouds appeared in the distance, and the wind dropped almost to a calm, the sails flapping against the mast all day and night.

Next morning the sailors were busy securing ropes and getting every thing ready; they said this calm was but weather breeding and predicted that we were to have a change. The glass was falling, and we were to look out for squalls. They were not disappointed in their morning's expectations of a gale. Before morning we had it in earnest.

We, novices in sea life, thought we had a severe storm on Friday night; but the sailors only laughed at us when we spoke of it; in our hammocks below we knew that the wind was blowing a gale, that the ship was pitching and tossing about fearfully, and could hear the boatswain's whistle, and the sailors aloft reefing sails, and the waves breaking clean over the deck above us. At two o'clock in the morning, a heavy sea struck our starboard side. The concussion seemed like striking against a rock, some were thrown clean out of their hammocks, women and children thrown from their berths, crockery smashed, and boxes rattled, trunks, water kegs, tin dishes, plates, pails, and every movable article, were dashed with violence from one side of the ship to the other.

Women and children screamed with fright, and men jumped from their hammocks; for a few moments the ship stood perfectly still, as if stiffened with the stroke, then she shivered from stem to stern, and the timbers groaned and quivered; in a few moments more she was dashing headlong onwards through the mountain of waves. I should think if there were any on board who had never prayed before, they must have prayed now. Both men and women vied with each other in the exchange of good offices and friendly words.

Envy was subdued, passionate wrath and revenge were forgotten, all acted as men and women who were soon to stand in the presence of their God. There was the pure steady and charming light of Christian hope and love shining beneath the very shadow of death. It was a solemn and touching thing to hear so many strong men acknowledge, in that hour of peril, their utter helplessness, and praying Him who once lay on a pillow asleep "Lord save us we perish," praying Him to abide with us. The hatches were all canvased and fastened down, so that none but the sailors and the soldiers on watch could go on deck, the sea was washing over the deck; that was indeed an awful night, dark, chilling, and drenching; hour after hour passed as we momentarily expected our doom. The deck was continually washed over by great seas. As soon as morning light appeared I managed to get on deck, though with extreme difficulty, both from dizziness and the motion of the ship. I was determined to enjoy the fresh air and see how the ocean looked lashed into a tempest. I had to cling fast to keep my footing; the ship was pitching up and down, tossed like a feather in the wind. We rode on huge mountain billows of dark leaden colour, capped with molten glass, and tipped with silvery caps of foam. As I hung on to the rope, meditating on the vastness of the ocean, and waves mountains high, my soul was deeply impressed with the omnipotence and infinity of the God who scooped out this mighty abyss, and filled it with those powerful waters. He hath set them their bounds and says to them in their wildest commotion, "thus far, and here shall thy proud waves be stayed." This dreadful storm raged all day, and the night was terrible; there was no more distance or space; the sky was turned into blackness, and shut itself down upon the ship, nothing was any longer visible on this the race-course of the wind; we felt ourselves delivered over to a merciful providence. The men, women and children had their second attack of sea-sickness, even the sailors were sick. The storm raged all next day (Sunday), and night, no one on board could get anything cooked as the fires were all put out from the sea washing over the ship; even if they could, few could eat, they were all so sick.

THE VOYAGE TO GIBRALTAR.

On the wide expanse of the stormy seas,
Our noble ship swept before the breeze,
Our gallant captain when twelve days had run,
Tried with his sextant to take the sun.

The heavy fog seemed still much worse,
Scarcely knowing where to lay his course,
And tried and tried the stormy main,
While heavy fog seemed to kiss the plain.

The clouds they broke and showed the sky,
Placing the instrument to his eye,
The howling wind our course had fixed,
And marked the latitude at forty-six.

An eastward course he then did try,
While billows they rose mountains high,
The captain's orders were to haul yards back,
And set the sails on starboard tack.

The storm it rose a furious gale,
Which caused the landsmen's hearts to fail,
With deathly sick, as then the heaving ship,
Rode high on billows, then her prow would dip.

On the wave-washed deck with deep dismay,
The dizzy soldier feels the deck give way,
And tries in vain a last resource,
To catch a rope to stay him in his course.

Rushing with nausea to the side,
Where the starboard watch at him did chide,
He holds on taut, while feet give way,
And clings like death to portsill stay.

But now the western winds the sails expand,
And soon the "look out" reports he sees the land,
Where there before us in the vapours rolled,
The African mountains looming out so bold.

T. Faughnan.

Monday morning at four o'clock the wind changed on our larboard quarter, and suddenly dropped. The boatswain piped all hands to square yards and make sail; this order was hailed by the men, and it soon reached the women, when they all offered up prayers and thanks to God for their deliverance.

The wind dropped considerably, and by twelve o'clock all was quiet, the ship running steadily before the wind.

The usual grog bugle sounded at twelve, when every man made his appearance. At six in the evening the wind fell away altogether. This repose after that fearful storm was an unspeakable blessing; all that had been fury was now tranquillity; it appeared to us a sign of peace; we could let go the rope or stay we were holding on by; the women and children could stand upright and straighten themselves, and walk and move about; we felt ourselves inexpressibly happy in the depths of this heavenly change. All night was almost a dead calm, and it was a blessing; we all slept well after the awful pitching and tossing we had had the last three days. In the morning when I went on deck the sails were flapping, and not a breath of wind. After breakfast the women and children were ordered on deck, when the lower decks were thoroughly scrubbed and cleaned, and when dinner bugle sounded they were allowed to go below. After dinner the upper deck was washed and cleaned. Toward evening the wind changed to our starboard and began to freshen; towards morning we were running before the wind at nine knots an hour. At ten o'clock, a.m., I was agreeably surprised when I heard a sailor from the mast-head cry out, Land, ho! I found by the captain's eyes that the land lay off our weather beam, but though I strained my eyes looking for the land, I could see nothing. It was quite an hour before I could find it, and then it looked more like a cloud than anything else. At length the veil lifted, and I saw the land stretching away to the eastward, as we neared it and saw it more distinctly. It looked a glorious object to us soldiers, though we were then ten or twelve miles off, yet the highest peaks, which were above the clouds, some hundreds of feet high, were so clear that they looked as if they had been stolen out of the "Arabian Nights," or some fairy tale of wonder and beauty.

The bluff and lofty headland of Cape St. Vincent, with its sharp detached rock, white light-house, and adjacent convent skirting the edge of the precipice, was the first land that I saw, as the ship bounded upon our glorious waters of Trafalgar Bay. All on board were quite recovered of their sea-sickness, as the ship glided across wide bays and along the indented coast of Spain. The ship had soon studding-sails set, and she swept onward like some large bird of prey towards the straits. Tarefa, famous in martial story, with its low flat-roofed houses, backed by barren-looking, sun-scorched hills, was passed, and all eyes were turned on the tremendous scragged outline of the African coast rising several thousand feet above the sea. The hazy morning light added to the effect, throwing out in relief the broad stone face and picturesqure form of Ape's Hill, streaked with shadowy fissures, crevices, and indentations, which the scorching sun failed to touch. But the Spanish side of the straits, through which the blue Mediterranean now became visible, engrossed the larger share of our attention. There stood the bold rock of Gibraltar, rearing its bald crest to the sky, a fit sentinel at the gate of those waters which lave the shores of fallen, but once mighty empires, now the key and glory of Old England. The ship now hoisted her flags which were immediately noticed at the signal station, on the loftiest part of the range, where a flag-staff is visible against the sky. Some of our officers who were on the rock before with the help of their telescope could trace many an old haunt. They knew every path on those craggy heights. There was the town behind the old Moorish walls looking the same as ever; there was the Alameda, the convent, and many other familiar domiciles, peeping from amongst shrubberies and gardens.

At five p.m. we cast anchor in the harbour of Gibraltar, when the ship was besieged with bumboats of vendors in oranges, dates, lemons, figs, and luxuries of almost every kind. Soon after a boat with a yellow flag approached the ship; it was the health officer, who made inquiries of our doctor as to sickness on board, and was answered "All right. No sickness but sea-sickness," when he returned to shore, and afterwards a staff officer appeared who informed the captain that he had got "pratique," when the order to disembark at once was given.

CHAPTER XII.

THE LANDING—BARRACKS—GARRISON DUTY—OLD NORTH FRONT—SMUGGLING—MARKET—QUEEN'S BIRTHDAY—THE DINNER—SPEECHES—THE ROUTE—THE MARCH—EMBARKATION FOR THE CRIMEA—THE PARTING—THE VOYAGE—ARRIVAL AT MALTA.

MAY 13th, 1854.—At 6 p.m., the right wing formed in open column of companies, right in front, on the New Mole, after a very rough passage from Queenstown, and considering how the men were knocked about, they looked remarkably clean and well. The band and pipers of the 92nd Highlanders met us at the New Mole, and played alternately during the march to the Casemate Barracks, where we were quartered, followed by a crowd of Rock Scorpions, a motley crowd of English, Irish, Spaniards, Italians, Jews and Moors. Several soldiers from the garrison welcomed us, and seemed pleased to see a fresh regiment arrive to share their military duties. By two o'clock next day, the "Dunbar" arrived with the left wing. They landed at three o'clock and joined head quarters at the Casemate Barracks, number six company proceeding to Catalan Bay on detachment.

The regiment was exempt from garrison duty next day, in order to get their baggage in order, and settle down in their quarters. The following day we found the whole of the garrison duties. The guards with their colours are trooped every day at ten a.m. (Sundays excepted), on the Alameda, under the field officer, assisted by the brigade major. I was detailed for the Old North Front Guard, which consisted of one captain, one subaltern, one sergeant, two corporals, and twenty-four rank and file, the soldiers take their rations with them on guard. The officers get their meals sent from the mess.

This guard furnish a chain of sentries across the neutral ground, which divides the Spanish from the British lines. Gibraltar is a free port, and a resort, in consequence, of Spanish smugglers, who drive an amazing trade, by running contraband goods into Spain, and *vice versa*, which the British authorities endeavour to stop by all means possible. Notwithstanding all their exertions, this fraud is still carried on under cover of dark nights. I, being posted on No. 6 post along the Spanish lines from twelve till two, my orders were to make prisoners of any smugglers who attempted to pass through. As I walked up and down my post, I heard some slight noise in the long grass. I stooped down and saw two men crawling along the grass. I advanced, and challenged, "who goes there?" when they stooped down and tried to get away. I then advanced nearer, and threatened to fire if they did not answer my challenge, at the same time brought down my musket to the charge, and full cocked. When they saw I was about firing, they stood still and answered me saying, "Bono Jonny, me good man, here me gib you plenty bacca, me gib you plenty gin, him good gin, me gib you plenty eberyting, you let me pass, mit dem tings to garden, you plenty big good man, come from Inglas, you von good man, plenty drink gin, him good for you." They took some stone jars of gin, and some tobacco, to give me for letting them through; but true to my orders, when I saw the smuggled goods they had, I made them prisoners, telling them if they moved, I would shoot them. At the same time I passed the word to the next sentry to send for the sergeant of the guard. They begged off very hard, and finally offered me all their stuff if I would let them go. As soon as the sergeant came, I handed him the prisoners, with six large, square blocks of tobacco, and six large cases of gin. This smuggling is ever carried on, and the sentries have all they can do to prevent it. Some sentries, I am sorry to say, compromise with the smugglers, tobacco and gin being too strong temptations for them. The guard being relieved, we discharged our muskets into the sea, all our guards being loaded. The climate is warm and pleasant throughout the year, and yet we can see the perpetual snow-capped mountains of Andalusia, towering heavenwards in the distance. The troops have bathing parade twice a week, at five o'clock in the morning; and several times during the day, may be seen soldiers and civilians besporting themselves like porpoises in the water of the Old Mole. There is a market every morning which opens after gunfire. The Spaniards cross the neutral ground from Spain with their mules, loaded with all sorts of provisions, vegetables and fruit, standing outside the drawbridge, waiting for the gate to be opened. The market place is fenced in, and divided into square stalls, which are rented by the vendors, who consist of Moors, Spaniards, Jews and Italians.

The Moors squat down behind their stalls with their Fez cap, and turbans, big breeches and a long loose gown open in front, yellow slippers and smoking a long pipe. Oranges, grapes, figs, lemons, dates, olives, and fruit of almost every description are sold here very cheap.

On the 24th May, the Queen's Birthday, the troops in garrison, consisting of two batteries royal artillery, two companies sappers and miners, and four regiments of infantry, were drawn up in line on the North Front at twelve o'clock, each man furnished with twelve rounds of blank cartridge; as the clock in the tower struck twelve, a gun fired from the Sky Battery was the signal for a Royal salute; then the batteries on the rock as well as the men-of-war in the harbour fired twenty-one guns each, and the line of soldiers with the field artillery on their flanks, fired a feu-de-joie. After the smoke cleared off, the men waved their shakos in the air, then gave three cheers for Her Gracious Majesty. This was a grand sight for the spectators, more especially the Spaniards, who assembled in thousands to witness this military celebration of Her Majesty's birthday.

The troops then marched past, in slow, quick, and double time, they were then divided into two armies, and put through a sham-fight, which lasted till four o'clock. We had those fights frequently, and a general review once a week during the summer months. On the 15th November, I had another increase in my family, a girl was born, and she was christened Elizabeth.

On the 20th November, 1854, we received a letter of readiness to prepare for active service in the east. Then came the usual packing of baggage, and creditors, Jews, Moors, and Gentiles, flying round the barracks with pieces of paper in their hands, looking for what was not easily found just then.

The evening before embarkation our company was entertained at a supper by the grenadiers of the 39th Regiment, whom we had often met, and done duty with in the same garrison, and a friendly feeling had sprung up between the officers and men of both companies, both captains and officers were present to see the men enjoy themselves. After the cloth was removed the president proposed a toast to the Queen, which was drunk with a hearty good will, and three cheers for Her Majesty. The captain of the 39th stood up to propose the health of their guests. "Brother officers and soldiers," he said, looking down the two rows of faces, one on each side of the long table, with a cheerful frank smile, "in the name of the grenadier company, which I have the honour to command, allow me to extend to you, our brothers and comrades in arms, a hearty welcome, I think as this garrison, which has been so jolly, and is about to be broken up by the gallant '17th Royal Bengal Tigers' going to join the army in the Crimea, I must say that we are heartily sorry that it has not come to our turn to share the honours of our comrades in a brush with the Muscovites; but we hope ere many days pass, we will have the gratification of joining you in the east, and there share the glories of the British Army in fighting for our Queen and country, and leading such men as I now see before me at this hospitable board against the Russians. We tender to you frankly the hand of military comrades, and instead of fireing a feu-de-joie of compliments, it is the duty of those who remain to drink the health of those who are proceeding on active service in the east, a bumper then, let us say good health and God bless them." With three times three the glasses were drained; whilst the band struck up "The British Grenadiers."

Captain John Croker was then called upon to respond. He said, "Brother officers, and soldiers of the 39th Regiment, this cordial reception and courtesy of the officers and privates demand our warmest acknowledgments, which I, in the name of my company, have the honour to acknowledge, and I propose a health to the grenadiers of the 39th Regiment with whom we are about to part,—charge your glasses;" and the toast was drunk with all honours, to the appropriate tune of "Auld Lang Syne," the company singing, "They are Jolly Good Fellows."

December 2nd, 1854, at 8. p.m., the 17th Regiment "Royal Tigers" paraded in the square of the Casemate Barracks for the last time, and having been called to attention, and inspected by the commanding officer, Colonel McPherson, C. B., he gave the word of command, the men stepped off, preceded by the bands of other regiments, through the main street of the town playing the "Girl I Left Behind Me," followed by a motley crowd of friends, sweethearts, and curious spectators, as we marched to the New Mole, where the steam-ship "Tamar," was lying along side the wharf to convey the 17th Regiment, two batteries of royal artillery, and two companies of sappers and miners, to the seat of war in the Crimea. Our parting with our wives and children was a very affecting and trying sight, officers and soldiers taking the last farewell (some of them, perhaps, for ever) of those nearest and dearest to them, whom they were now leaving behind on that barren rock; many hundreds of miles away from friends or relatives, and not sure whether we would ever return again, to our loved families. I had left my wife and three children, one of them only sixteen days old, trusting in God.

But our Queen and country requires us to meet the despot in mortal combat, and defend the honour and glory of that old flag "that braved a thousand years the battle and the breeze," therefore we must sever all family ties, though hard to give up our feelings, when our Queen and country calls us to the front. Let it not be supposed that the officers are wanting in sympathy towards the private soldier; very superficial has been the observer, who can believe that the officer and the private possess little in common with each other; or who can persuade himself that the private soldier is only a machine, moved only by the command of his superiors. Should such a casuist exist let him remember that men are men, whether the scarlet on their backs is of the finest or coarsest texture; and that if the advantage of birth and the refinement of superior education have done nothing for the officer, the private soldier who makes a good use of such talent as he may have received, occupies a higher position, be his ever so humble. There were some private soldiers in the regiment who, at the parting moment, felt as deeply the separation from wife and children, as the more aristocratic members of the same profession, nor were incidents of a romantic interest wanting, though the tearful young girl who saw with anguish her true lover's departure was only dressed in calico. Doubtless in these latter times, when England has sent forth so many of her sons to fight for the honour of her flag, there are few who have not seen something of the display of the varied emotions, which such departures call forth; it will therefore be unnecessary to say that though the sad time of parting had come it was visible in the tearful eyes and blanched cheeks of many in the crowd. The loud cheers which greeted the 17th Regiment, as it passed through the gate of the drawbridge leading down to the wharf where the ship lay; showed the chivalrous emotions of the stern British soldiers who lined the ramparts and along the docks, with crowds of people, whose hearts beat with sympathy as the regiment embarked.

At eleven o'clock all being ready, the captain gave the word and the steamer moved out slowly from the wharf, the band playing in slow time "Auld Lang Syne," amid cheer after cheer, and handkerchiefs waving from the people, and returned by the crowds of red coats who assembled on deck to wave their handkerchiefs and wipe away the tears, which were fast running down their cheeks as they gazed on their little ones left behind on the wharf.

As the steamer rounded the New Mole her speed increased, and the music also changed time; at length Europa point, with its barracks and batteries, was turned, and the reverse side of the rock, still more bold and barren, with "O'Hara's old Tower," rearing its lofty weather-beaten ruined spire, on the highest summit of the Wind-mill Hill. Favoured by a beautiful sunny day and a westerly breeze, the "Tamar" swept rapidly past the gigantic sentinel whose watch-word is the roar of the signal gun, on the summit of the telegraph station; and when the evening sun was gilding the snow topped mountains of Africa with a streak of gold, the good ship had proceeded many miles to the eastward, and, though the mountains of Africa reared their bright summits above the horizon, the "Old Rock" was no longer to be seen.

Then our attention was directed to the white-capped mountains on the south coast of Spain; and when these faded from view, time was passed in looking out for African capes or sun-burned islands.

After tea the men assembled on deck, indulging in all sorts of games to pass the time. A comic soldier dressed up like a baboon grinned and jumped round the decks, up the masts, and through all the performance of a monkey, causing roars of laughter from all around. After this, dancing was introduced, several of the men being musicians had brought their fiddles, we were at no loss for music; at the other side a group were singing comic and sea songs; in this way the evening was passed until the bugle sounded at nine o'clock, when we turned into our hammocks. We have much better accommodation than we had on the old "Cornwall," although we have three times the number on board.

Next morning decks were washed by the watch at four o'clock; at ten a.m. commanding officers parade, when the men looked in excellent spirits. Now came in view something to call their attention, a grampus had blown a shower of water in the air fifty feet; the men all rushed to see what it was, several gave their opinion as to what caused the eruption of the water, some thought it was a volcano that broke out, some said it was an infernal machine the Russians had placed there to destroy our shipping, and many various opinions were brought forward to explain the cause of the wonderful blow; a sailor, however, came along and told us that it was a grampus. Now we see plenty of flying-fish, whole shoals of the glittering little things glide along in the air, skimming the top of the waves; they rise to escape their pursuers the bonitos, which rush after them showing their noses above the water now and then; but the poor flying-fish have their enemies above as well as under the water, for they no sooner rise than they risk becoming a prey to the ocean birds which are always hovering about ready to pounce upon them; it is a case of "out of the frying pan into the fire." They fly farther than I thought they could, I saw one of them fly at least one hundred yards, and sometimes they fly on deck some fifteen feet from the surface of the water. The weather was all that could be wished for, and our splendid ship making rapid progress through the blue waters; the sea is almost a dead calm, hardly a ripple on the face of the deep; an occasional whale is seen blowing in the distance, and many grampusses came rolling and blowing about the ship. One thing that struck me most is the magnificence of the Mediterranean sun-set; the clouds assume all sorts of fantastic shapes and appear more solid and clearly defined than I have ever seen them before; toward evening they abound in colour, purple, pink, red and yellow, alternately, while the sky near the setting sun seems of a beautiful green, gradually melting into the blue sky above, the great clouds on the horizon look like mountains tipped with gold and fiery red. One of those sun-sets was a delightful sight; the sun went down into the sea between two enormous clouds, the only ones to be seen, and they blazed with brilliant colours which were constantly changing, until the clouds stood out in dark relief against the still delicately tinted sky. I got up frequently to see the sun rise, but it is not near so beautiful as at setting. After sun-down the officers chose out a few of the best talent among the men, who assembled on the quarter-deck and sang some excellent glees, comic and sentimental songs, with great applause; at nine o'clock the bugle sounded when we turned in and slept well, the ship running as steady as if she was in a canal.

Next morning after parade the officers amused themselves with their revolvers shooting at porpoises which came in shoals close to the ship. After dinner the band played on the quarter-deck to the delight of all on board, more especially the ship's officers and sailors. The weather was beautiful and the sea like a mirror.

At seven next morning the sailor on the look out on the mast head cried out, "land ho!" when all eyes were strained looking for the desired object, but none could see it for some time afterwards—at last we saw it in the distance, like a dark cloud lying on the waters; as we neared the land it appeared to us a rocky, barren-looking island, Malta. Yet the cultivated strips here and there were so green and flourishing, they presented a most charming and beautiful appearance. Those who had not before visited the place were struck with the imposing appearance of this remarkable city. Tier upon tier of batteries upon all sides showed bristling rows of guns, daring intruders to enter the harbour with hostile intentions. To the right the principal part of the town was to be seen, terrace above terrace, dome and spires, towering above the houses, all looming darkly against the sky. The air was sultry, and the reflection of buildings, rocks and shipping, in the almost still water were only agitated by the little boats which were moving about in all directions. The harbour was crowded with shipping, and as we moved into our moorings at ten o'clock, we were cheered by the sailors and soldiers on board the men-of-war in the harbour, as well as from the batteries on either side. We had a splendid passage of nine hundred and eighty miles in four days.

CHAPTER XIII.

MALTESE—DEPARTURE—A CAPTAIN COMMITS SUICIDE—THE FUNERAL—SMALL-POX—RETURN—RESUMED THE VOYAGE—GRECIAN ARCHES—DARDANELLES—GALLIPOLI—TURKISH SENTRIES—CONSTANTINOPLE—TURKISH LADIES—THE BOSPHORUS—VOYAGE ACROSS THE EUXINE—ARRIVAL.

SOON after our arrival in the harbour, a coal-barge came alongside, and about fifty Maltese commenced to coal our ship; they carried the coal on their heads in round, wicker baskets; passed each other on the gangway after depositing their load in the ship's bunker. The coaling lasted about two hours, during which time the officers and men were amused by divers who came along in little boats; a boy managing the boat, while the diver was left free to exercise his strange employment. His dress consisted of a light pair of drawers short at both ends, and a loose shirt; bringing his little craft alongside, where we were looking over the railing, and divesting himself of his upper garments, he commenced in a supplicating tone of broken English; "sixpence, me dive for sixpence, me get him quick; me get him sure." Some of the officers tossed a sixpence into the water where it was very deep, supposing he was going to the bottom for it; but experience taught him an easier mode of catching it.

Watching it with the eye of a hawk he saw it strike the water, and poising himself, he sprung head first in the sea; the water was so clear we could follow him with our eyes. Down he went like an arrow, outstripping the sixpence in the race for the bottom; before it had sunk twelve feet he had his hands under it in the form of a bowl, the shining piece dropping into his hands; he then clapped it between his teeth, rose to the surface, climbed into his boat and exhibited the prize with the air of a conqueror. This was repeated several times and with unerring certainty he caught the prize every time. He then asked for some one to throw a sixpence the other side of the ship, which was done, when he sprung under the ship and brought it up in his teeth on the other side. The Maltese had finished coaling at twelve, when our steamer moved slowly from her buoy; dense masses of people lined the batteries and yet larger crowds of soldiers in the forts St. Angelo and St. Elmo, cheered as our steamer moved along, the cheers from one fort being taken up by the troops on board, as well as the sailors and marines in the harbour, and joyously responded to by our troops who assembled on the deck to give our last hurrah for the East. The Town of Valetta with its strong forts, batteries, terraces, domes and houses grew smaller by degrees as the gallant "Tamar," ploughed her onward course through the blue waters of the Mediterranean, the island looking like a little blue cloud in the distance gradually fading away; we have the trackless expanse around us; in the distance Mount Etna looms up in the north-west. The ship was making rapid progress through the waters, the captain says, "if this breeze lasts, we will reach Constantinople on the 8th," but our expectations were frustrated; "man proposes, but God disposes," which we found to be true; for on Saturday, at 8 a.m., a very melancholy occurrence happened which threw a deep gloom over all the troops on board; the captain commanding the detachment Royal Artillery had cut his throat in his cabin; no person could ever find out what was the cause which led him to commit this dreadful act.

How deeply touching is a burial at sea! replete with reflection, striking and sublime, as should always be the spectacle of a funeral; the tree falling as it must rise again, with no leaves or flowers of repentance or prayer, or office to alter its final doom, ever to bloom again on that cut down stem; far more deeply does the service and the sights and the sounds of a funeral on the ocean always move one. The clouds had cleared and it was intensely hot; the funeral took place at two o'clock; we saw the body sewed up in a hammock with a round shot at its feet, and borne by the men of his battery from his cabin and laid upon the deck. We had no clergyman on board, therefore the painful duty of reading the service devolved upon the captain of the ship, which could not have been performed by a clergyman. As he began to read, not a sound, not a breath broke the solemn silence; nothing but the noise of the rolling swells against the smooth side of the ship as I stood close to the gangway while the service was read, in deep thought, and gazing on the bright and glorious shining sea, now nearly calm, looking so intensely sunny and blue; it seemed to some a mocking at the king of terrors, whose victim was about to be committed to its keeping. To me it looked like the gemmed and crystal gate of that heaven through which the Son of God had promised the faithful Christian who believe and trust in Him to wing its happy way, there to learn many a marvel that he had striven on earth to trace and explore.

Earnestly and solemnly he read, and, when he uttered the last words, the sailors raised the body to the edge of the gangway and let it slide, feet foremost into the sea "and so we commit his body to the deep." You who think it a solemn thing to hear the bell of some country church at home echoing through the rich woods or flowery valleys, telling of the death of some one who will never return home again, cannot form any idea of the awe which strikes into the heart at sea. I do not think there were many dry eyes among the officers and men of his battery, as they saw the body splash into the deep sea and sink straight down, with the heavy round shot at his feet. After this painful event the doctor reported two cases of small pox, which had broken out amongst the troops, and immediately, the captain and officers held a council to know what course they would pursue. It was decided to return to Malta, and put the sick men into hospital there; and prevent taking the infectious disease out to the Crimea amongst the troops. The ship was headed for Malta where we arrived at six p.m. next day; as we entered the harbour unexpectedly, from one of the upper forts, at the end of the harbour, there came a flash, followed by a loud report, which was echoed back and forward against the rocks, and buildings, till the roaring sound at last died away, and the wreath of white smoke slowly ascended into the sky. It was the evening gun, which is fired at sun down. After handing over the two patients to the proper authorities we again steamed out of harbour. There were crowds of people again assembled along the batteries to witness the departure of our noble ship, with the living cargo of redcoats on board, of course wondering what caused our return. As we got out to sea, a breeze sprung up, on our larboard quarter, when all sails were set, and soon the island faded again away in to the distance, and once more our ship was going through the waters at 15 knots, under the influence of wind and steam; next day at six p.m. we had run 240 miles in 24 hours. Sunday at ten a.m. parade for divine service, which was read by the captain of the ship; at sun-down the wind wheeled round right in our teeth, which obliged us to take in all sail. The men were paraded at ten a.m. next day, and between various duties, and the sharp appetites brought on by the sea air, we managed to get over the time very pleasantly; the band played on the quarter deck in the afternoons, when the weather permitted; towards evening the wind veered round on our starboard bow, and the boatswain piped all hands to make sail; but we were doomed ere long to experience a change of weather, for as the sun went down, in a clear but stormy sky, the wind piping, snoring, and howling through the blocks and rigging, the waves thundering against our starboard, the ship had to struggle with a south-easterly gale of such fury, that it reminded me of a Levanter, which the Mediterranean is famous for; at day light the land was made, a heavy cloud-like line just perceptible. It was the Morea, and the men rushed on deck to see the land. As we ran up, the snow covered mountain peaks with cold, rocky, barren edges, villages of white houses dotting the declivity towards the sea, became to us perfectly distinct.

At 8 a.m. we passed Cape Matapan; although the old reputation of this cape was not sustained by our destruction, still the sea showed every inclination to be troublesome, the wind kept rising every moment. At ten a.m. we were passing between the Morea and Cerigo, we had a proof that the Greeks were nearly right about the weather. Even bolder sailors than the ancients fear the heavy squalls off those snowy headlands, which gave us but a poor idea of sunny Greece.

The ancient Greeks always considered a voyage round Capes Matapan and St. Angelo fraught with great danger. As we rounded the angle of the cape the wind rushed at us with much fury, we saw the sea rushing with crests of white foam right on our starboard bow. Its violence was terrific, the sea was rolling in wondrous waves towards the ship; she behaved nobly and went over them with the greatest ease. The gusts came down furiously between the little islands, which we could not make out or did not know the names. The men bore up well against this furious storm, although they were all sea-sick, but never absent when the grog bugle sounded at twelve o'clock.

The night came upon us and the ship labouring on, dashing the sea into white spray in the darkness. At day light next morning the sight was most discouraging, the clouds were black and low, the sea white and high, and between them on the horizon was a mass of a broken character so that one could not be known from the other. We passed Milo at 6 p. m., and the gale increased; afterwards at ten a. m., when the wind changed one point aft, and the ship rolled very much, the deck was inclined to so sharp an angle that we could only hold on by a tight grip of the stays and ropes. The sea breaking over the ship swept several of the horse stalls loose about the deck, and the poor animals lay helpless against the bulwarks. About twelve o'clock the wind went down and the sun burst forth, sending his golden, warm rays through the clouds, when the artillerymen picked up their horses and put every thing in its place again. We passed the Greek coast trending away to the left, showing in rugged masses of mountains capped by snowy peaks, and occasionally some good sized towns were visible on the dark brown hill side, with several wind mills along the beach. With some exceptions the isles of Greece rather disappoint the lovers of the picturesque; seen from the sea they are more or less bold and barren, abounding with sterile rocks almost entirely devoid of wood, except a stunted olive tree here and there, and clothed with a kind of reddish brown grass. The Candian mountains are perhaps the most striking features which we encountered in our progress through what the sailors call "the arches." As we swept through the "Thermian Passage," accompanied in our course by several ancient looking craft with little white sails stretching outwards, resembling the wings of Icarus, and others of no less ancient model, with lofty prow and solitary square rigged mast. On the left lay the Gulf of Athens, on our right rose the snowy heights of Mount Ida, 5,400 feet above the level of the sea, to the north the lofty Lemnos. At three p.m. we passed the castles of the Dardanelles and the Hellespont; we were not stopped nor fired at as in days of yore. As we passed Gallipoli about seven p. m., we could see a collection of red-roofed houses, with tall minarets rising up amongst them. From the entrance of the Dardanelles to Gallipoli the straits are very narrow, not more than a quarter of a mile in some places. We ran along close to the bank on the European side; its breadth opposite the town of Gallipoli is about four miles, and it expands towards the Sea of Marmora. As the ship run along the banks we could see large herds of goats and small black sheep, feeding on the high rocks along the edge of the river. Night was closing on us and, as we passed the numerous forts on the European side, the sentries yelled out strange challenges and burned blue lights, and blue lights answered from our ship in return, so that it looked to us a strange spectacle. The lights were put out and our eyes are as blind as owls in day light, but our eyes soon recover, the stars at last begin to twinkle and we see a little around us. All night we were crossing the Sea of Marmora with a strong current against us.

Next morning, after breakfast, we came in sight of Constantinople; at ten a.m. we passed the Seven Towers on our left, with Seraglio Point just before us; at ten thirty we cast anchor with hundreds of other vessels at the mouth of the Golden Horn. Steam ferry-boats of the English kind were passing to and fro, and caiques flitted in and out with the dexterity and and swiftness of a sea-gull. As we cast anchor, a small brig coming down stream ran foul of us on the starboard bow, snap and crash went her bowsprit and yard, causing considerable damage to our bulwarks and stays; this accident detained us two hours. The stream runs so swiftly down the channel that vessels frequently run foul, sometimes causing serious damage. We notice, passing back and forward from Stamboul to Pera, caiques with Turkish women wearing white cloths, and staring at us out of two black holes in their yashmak. At twelve o'clock we weighed anchor and continued our course through the Bosphorus. The scenery is of almost unrivalled beauty, and the panorama of which Constantinople forms the principal part, is such as is perhaps nowhere else to be seen in the world.

As we proceeded up the stream and looked back, the view of the Marmora, as we leave it behind, is very fine. On the opposite Asiatic shore Mount Olympus, 8,800 feet high, with its snow-crowned summit fades away into the blue of the heavens, while the Imperial Palace of the Seraglio, St. Sophia's Mosque, and others of less proportions, stud the banks in unbroken lines from the very foot of the forts which command the entrance up to the crowning glory of the scene, where the Imperial city of Constantine, rising in many coloured terraces from the verge of the Golden Horn, confuses the eye with its numerous gardens, cypresses, mosques and palaces, its masses of foliage, red roofs surmounted by snow-white minarets, with golden tops. The residences of the Pashas, the Imperial palaces of the Sultan, and the retreats of opulence line these favoured shores. As the ship ran along we could see the Turks sitting cross-legged like tailors on their verandahs smoking away and looking as like each other as if they were twins. The windows of these houses are closely latticed and fastened, but here and there can beseen a white faced lady with gay coloured robe, peeping through the jalousies, showing that the harem is occupied by the fair sex. These dwellings succeed each other the whole length of the Bosphorus, and at places such as Buyukdere, they are numerous enough to form large villages, provided with hotels, shops, and lodging-houses.

The Turks delight in sitting out on the platform over the water while they smoke their chibouque, and the greatest object of Turkish ambition is to enjoy the pleasure of a residence on the banks of the Bosphorus. These waters abound in fish, and shoals of porpoises and dolphins disport on its surface, splashing and playing about with ease as they swim against its rapid stream.

I noticed the Turks never took the least notice of us as we arrived, so we departed in silence, and as far as the Turks were concerned, in solitude. The boatmen scarcely turned their heads to look at the majestic steamer with her deck covered with British troops crossing the broad, rough and stormy seas to fight for these lazy, indifferent orientals who would scarcely turn their heads to look at us, much less give us a cheer as we departed from the Sultan's Sublime Porte.

As we pass the batteries which mark the opening of the Bosphorus into the Euxine, we cheer the Turkish sentries as we shoot past them into the Black Sea; and soon the land is shut out. A fog, a drifting, clammy, mist, cold and rain fall down on us like a shroud, and as the night closes in it damps out the stars and all the light of heaven, and steals down yard, mast, and stays, this is genuine Black Sea weather.

In the morning the same haze continued with drifting cold wind, after breakfast we commenced to sharpen our swords and bayonets, in order to have them ready to serve out to the Russians in a professional manner, and with as little pain and torture as we possibly could; the grinding-stones were furnished by the sailors, this occupied the whole day. The morning dawned, the sun red and stormy glared from an angry sky, over a rugged outline of coast not more than twenty-five miles distant, and lighted up by white-capped waves, which plunged athwart the ship's course; as we neared the land the captain and officers stood forward with their telescopes in hand: where was the desired haven? was now the subject of conversation, not a sign of an opening was distinguished in that formidable rock, which the telescope scanned from end to end; but at last the captain sighted a ruined tower upon a cliff somewhat lower than the rest with a union-jack flying.

It was not long before the masts of a man-of-war just visible above the high rocks which marked the narrow entrance into Balaklava harbour, was seen; up went our number, but in vain we looked for an answer. We entered the small deep harbour through a very narrow passage which was crowded with shipping. We ran up close alongside the ledge of a steep rock on the left side of the harbour, in twenty fathoms of water, and made fast to iron hooks fixed in the rock for that purpose.

CHAPTER XIV.

DISEMBARKATION—FIRST BIVOUAC—THE MARCH—ARRIVAL—SEBASTOPOL—THE TRENCHES—FIRST MAN WOUNDED—RETURN TO CAMP—AN ALARM—LORD RAGLAN—SORTIE—FORAGING—THE OLD BRIDGE—COLONEL COLE—THE SIEGE.

DECEMBER 15th, 1854, at 2 o'clock p.m. the regiment disembarked, in heavy marching order, at Balaklava, having been served out with the following articles of camp equipage previously, which we carried to the front, consisting of one circular tent complete to every sixteen men, one camp-kettle, frying-pan, axe, hand-saw, spade, shovel, and two billhooks to each mess, one blanket to each man, with three days' ship rations.

The command being given we marched, distributing the camp equipage amongst the men of the company. The rain poured on us, as we waded knee deep through the mud, making the best of our way among the heaps of forage and stores, which lay under the rain and exposed to the weather, without cover of any kind, all around Balaklava. We were obliged to halt outside the town, on account of the heavy rain, and pitch our camp on the side of Kadikoi Hill for the night. Before we got our tents pitched we got saturated with rain to our very skins. We had cold comfort that night, in wet clothes and blankets, lying on the damp ground ; everything wet except our ammunition which we always managed to keep dry. We had not even a light in our tents ; at 9 o'clock, after posting the picquet sentries around our camp, we lay down. This was a good receipt for rheumatism, and it required a strong constitution to bear up. At reveillé next morning, we were on the alert, eat some biscuits without water, alas, there was no water near our camp, and marched oft. After marching four miles through a slough of Balaklava mud, which it is impossible to describe, we pitched our camp on the most favourable spot we could find, and close to a stream of water ; having indulged in the latter beverage very copiously, with some hard biscuits, we turned into our tent, always placing sentries around our camp. The flashes from the guns of Sebastopol lighting up our camp, we lay down as we did the night before, in our wet clothes, overcoat and blanket. Our slumbers were frequently disturbed during the night by the thundering of the guns of Sebastopol. At 6 a.m., we tried to make a camp-fire, and get some hot coffee previous to our departure, but we failed in the attempt ; several foraging parties scoured the neighbourhood searching for some wood or brambles, to make a fire with, but could not find any ; so we drank plenty of water from the stream, and filled our kegs with the blessed fluid. After eating some hard biscuit, we struck our tents and resumed our march to the front. As we proceeded through the "slough of despond," we marched through the French camp, when the French soldiers turned out and cheered us, their bands playing "God save the Queen" as we passed their camp, which we responded to in a most friendly manner. We arrived at the 4th Division, to which we were posted, at two p.m., after wading through slush and mud the whole way, sinking knee-deep at every step, and were shown our camp grounds on Cathcart's Hill, with the honour of being the front regiment of the 4th Division.

Before we had our tents pitched, two-thirds of the regiment were detailed for the trenches that night; several men reported themselves sick, having caught severe colds from sleeping in their wet clothes on the damp ground the two previous nights, together with the heavy fatiguing march from Balaklava, on, I might say, an empty stomach, for we had nothing to eat or drink from the time we disembarked, except cold water. We could not eat raw pork just then, this told on the men's constitutions; although their pluck was good they had to give in, they were sent to the hospital tent. After we had finished tent-pitching, I was anxious to see Sebastopol and its surroundings; I went to the top of Cathcart's Hill, where I had a splendid view along the whole line of trenches from Kamiesch Bay to the Tchernaya River enclosing Sebastopol, which shone white and clear in the sun. I could see a large Russian camp defended by earth-works on the north side of the harbour, and large masses of Russians on parade outside the camp. At sun down the covering party were paraded on the brigade grounds, and after dark, marched for the first time to face the Muscovite, a field officer in charge, each party with their officers. Marching down, the Russians opened a heavy fire, at every flash we all lay down, until the round shot passed over, in this way we dodged them until we relieved the party in the trenches; during the time of relieving, the enemy always opened a heavy fire; they knew the time our relief took place after taking charge of the trenches. One hundred men were told off to build batteries in the second parallel, and cutting advanced trenches. We were formed into gangs of twelve men, each in charge of a non-commissioned officer, with officers superintending the whole, the work having been laid out by the Royal Engineers. We worked hard under shot, shell, grape and carnister, until twelve, when the grog was served; each man getting a half gill of rum, which gladdened our hearts and gave fresh strength to proceed with our work. While we were working, a man was placed on the look out for the flashes of the guns, and when he saw one, gave the word "down," when we lay down in the trench, if it was a shell, got behind the traverse.

The flashes from our guns and mortars gave us light to carry on our work when the night was dark. In the morning we felt hungry, but had nothing to eat or drink except biscuit and cold water, unless we eat raw pork, which some could not do then; a man does not know what he can eat until he is driven to it, which was shown afterwards. The Russians kept up a steady fire during the night from the Garden and Crows' Nest batteries, which our batteries responded to with a powerful fire. During the day we tried several shots with the "Old

Brown Bess" at some working parties, who were throwing up earth-works about 800 yards distant, but could not reach them. Oh, how I wished to have a good Enfield rifle then instead of the smooth bore which we were armed with. A Russian shell burst close to us, a splinter of which struck one of our grenadiers, named Chas. O'Maley, causing a deep wound in his head, this was the first blood shed in the regiment; his wound was dressed by the doctor who was in attendance at the Green Hill trench. Being relieved by a fresh party at sun down, we marched to camp under the darkness of the evening. There we indulged in our usual meal of raw pork, biscuits and cold water. Several parties had been foraging for wood, or roots, or any thing to make a fire, but could get nothing; therefore we had to lie down in our tent, our feet to the pole, knapsack under our head, and fully accoutred, with our blankets round us on the wet ground, without a fire or any warm food. We were never allowed to take off our accoutrements at night. During the night an alarm was given that the enemy had advanced on our trenches in large force, when we turned out and marched down. As we advanced on the trenches the cracking of musketry and roaring of cannon was deafening, the flashes lighting up the way as we doubled to the trenches. When we reached the Green Hill trench, the enemy had been repulsed with great loss, several Russians lay dead and wounded on the field, and in the trenches our loss was comparatively light, four men killed and nine wounded. We then returned to camp and lay down in peace till morning, wet and tired. At eight a.m., next morning, Lord Raglan and his staff visited our camp, when the men turned out; he inspected the camp and was well pleased with the appearance of the men. After the usual breakfast of salt pork and biscuit, all available men, after furnishing the trenches, were employed in carrying round shot and shell from the divisional depôt to the trenches.

This was very hard work; each man carried a round shot in a biscuit-bag on his back, sinking deep in the usual mud at every step; this and dragging big guns into position occupied the whole day. The sortie last night was not on our trenches alone, on the left the enemy did more damage; in front of the left attack there are some trenches which run down the edge of the ravine from the harbour which divides the town from the military barracks; the continuation of this ravine divides the third division from the French lines. In order to guard this ravine the sentries of the French and English ought to be in communication. The Russians followed this ravine and got past our sentries, who took them to be French, as their officers commanded their men in French to throw our men off their guard; in this way they succeeded in getting past our sentries on the extreme left, bayoneted them and got into the trenches before they were recognized as Russians, killing and wounding a major of the 50th among the latter, taking two officers and sixteen men prisoners. When their treachery was detected they were soon driven back with considerable loss; there were several Russians found dead and wounded in the ravine. Next morning a small party of six started off on a foraging *reconnoissance* to the valley of the Tchernaya River in search of wood, taking our water-keg straps with us; as we passed down a deep ravine beyond Inkerman heights we saw lying in the bottom of the ravine over twenty dead Russians who were buried there, the little earth which they had been covered with was washed away by the heavy rains; they were lying in their clothes as they were shot, presenting a most ghastly spectacle. We proceeded to an old bridge, climbing up the side of a steep hill, on the top of which was a Russian battery. We commenced cutting the trees and bushes which grew on the hill side and throwing them down to the bottom. We were not long cutting as much as our straps would hold. We tied up our bundles and quietly escaped along the edge of the ravine lest the Russians might detect us; if they did, it was the last of us, we were close under their batteries, but we got away safely. When we got to our camp there were glad faces when they saw the loads of wood; it was soon chopped up by the men, while others lit the fire and filled the camp-kettles with pork and put them on the fire. The smoke from the fires caused many of the officers to come and see what was up, they were agreeably surprised to see the fires and the camp-kettles boiling. After we had cooked a sufficient quantity of salt beef and pork and prepared coffee, we invited the officers to use the fire, which invitation they most thankfully accepted. We had plenty of hot coffee, salt beef and pork that day, skimming the fat and stowing it away for future use. When the cooking was over we put out the fires; collecting the embers together with the wood we had left to cook our breakfast; this was the first hot food we tasted since our disembarkation at Balaklava. We had hard frost last night and were employed getting up guns and mortars to the front; if this frost continues we will soon have all the guns and mortars in position.

The Russian batteries were nearly silent last night on our attack; but a brisk fire was kept up on the right. Colonel McPherson, C. B., has been promoted to Brigadier in the 4th division, and Colonel Cole takes command of the 17th Regiment; Sir Edmond Lyons has taken command of the fleet, vice Admiral Dundas who proceeds to Constantinople. Our regiment is hard worked; we find two thirds of the regiment for the trenches every night; the others of the division being reduced by sickness and death, and ere long we will have many sick too, if things go on as they are at present. Parading for the trenches yesterday evening, ten men reported sick with dysentery, brought on by exposure and lying on the wet ground in damp clothing, and want of warm food; they were admitted into the hospital tent.

All the Russians seem to think of, is getting up guns in position in every possible direction along our approaches. Last night in carrying earth to a battery on the left of second parallel, I picked from among the rocks something from a hole and thought it was a stone; in attempting to lift it, I stuck my fingers into a dead man's eyes; my sense of smell detected the mistake, I stepped back to wheeling distance, the smell was abominable; ever since, when I think of it, I fancy I smell it. I was orderly next day; an orderly from each tent collects the water kegs of their tent, and takes them down to a ravine near the Worongoff road where a small stream of water, the thickness of a ramrod, springs from a fissure in the rock; this spring supplies the 2nd, 4th and 8th divisions, as well as a division of the French and Turks with water; and as the orderly men arrive, they fall in rear of each other, forming a line waiting for their turn, and not unfrequently the French and English fight for the first turn; the Turks sitting on a stone, at a distance, looking on, and waiting till the last. I saw one of our men and a big French Dragoon, fighting with their fists, when the soldier beat the Frenchman, of course, knocking him down several times; afterwards the French kept away until our men got served.

Little was done in camp to-day, the state of the roads presented the greatest obstacles to the transport of shot and shell, and all that could be effected was to get up scanty supplies of pork, beef, biscuit, and rum, to our camp; the rain, sleet, and snow, fell heavily. The cold wet and slush in and round the camp is truly fearful.

A captain of the Royal Artillery was found dead in his tent, suffocated by the fumes of a charcoal fire he had lighted.

Christmas and New year's day are passed, and we have had a cold, dreary, sloppy, wet and hungry Christmas and New Year; many of our men going to hospital and dying there. Their illness has been caused by hard work in bad weather, and by exposure to wet without any protection. Just think what a tent is, pitched on wet muddy ground, with the rain beating through the canvas, into which sixteen hungry men, drenched to the skin, have to creep for shelter, after twenty-four hours in the trenches up to their knees in slush, and then reflect what state we must be in, after a night spent in such shelter, lying down without any change of clothing, and as close as we can stow, in wet blankets, covered with mud. It rained in torrents all last night and to-day, and floods of mud are flowing through the floors of our tents making their way down the hill-side; the roads are so bad as to cut off supplies to the camp, and we are accordingly placed on half rations; the horses and mules get stuck in the mud, bringing up provisions from Balaklava, and there they lie and die, and the men are dying off faster than the horses, and the Turks dying by the dozen.

Hostilities are almost at a standstill in the trenches, the men are too feeble to work the guns. It is reported the Russians are suffering still more than we are; but they are more numerous and can afford to lose twenty to our one.

THE CRIMEAN WAR.

When from Balaklava to the front we go,
The Chersonese are covered with mud and snow,
Where the horse, the mule, and the Turk have stuck,
Transporting provisions for our British pluck.

Where the tents are blown down with the furious blast,
And the rain pours down immensely fast,
And the shivering soldier in the trenches stood,
With his dripping clothes to chill his blood.

And the noble officer brought up with care,
In his wet and dismal tent, without dread or fear,
Or a covering party with their rifles in hand,
Marching to the trenches a melancholy band.

Or, when in camp without fire or mill,
To roast their coffee or to grind it still,
The commissariat to economise expense,
Issued the troops green coffee ! to show their sense.

To roast and grind as best they could,
Issuing neither mill nor wood,
Or lines of soldiers marching rank entire,
Beaming shot and shell too, at the Russians' fire.

Or the distant Cossack over the hills doth glow,
As winter wraps the Tchernaya Valley with snow,
And Prince Menchikoff in the Great Redan he stood,
Giving the Muscovites orders for to shed our blood.

And Sir Wm. Codrington on Cathcart's Hill,
Giving forth his orders to his gallant men,
Yonder the British Navy riding in the gale,
Idly waiting orders to spread sail.

T. FAUGHNAN.

CHAPTER XV.

MARCH TO BALAKLAVA—RETURN—MEN GO BARE-FOOTED—SNOW FIVE FEET DEEP—LONG BOOTS—HARD FROST—CAVALRY DIVISION—BURIAL GROUND—SOLITARY PROCESSION—MEN FROZEN—I BUILD A HUT—GREEN COFFEE — WINTRY APPEARANCE—DEAD HORSES—63RD REGIMENT —CARRYING PROVISIONS—FRENCH SICK.

JANUARY 6th, Captain John Croker, with six men of his company, went down to Balaklava for some cooked pork, which had been kindly sent out from England to us. The captain took a mule to carry back a bag of charcoal. After we got the pork from the steamer, and the captain his charcoal on the mule's back, we started for camp. We had proceeded about three miles when we got faint with hunger, weary and wet, the mud being knee deep and the load sinking us into the mire at every step. We requested the captain to let us have some of the pork to eat, this he willingly complied with, as he was hungry himself. We opened the bags and divided a four pound piece between every two men, the captain taking his share also; this gave us new strength to accomplish our task and also to help the muleout of the slough. Sleet, snow and rain beat in our faces all the way; we did not reach camp until twelve o'clock that night. This was the hardest fatigue, up to our knees in mud with a heavy load on our backs, I ever performed. After we got to camp the captain gave us each a glass of Hennessey's brandy from a case which he got out from Ireland as a Christmas-box. I believe that brandy saved us from a severe illness, as we had to lie down in our wet clothes. As we were coming up from Balaklava, we saw the 39th Regiment which had just landed, preparing to join the camp before Sebastopol. They were well provided against the severity of the weather; they had all received warm clothing, and looked comfortable in their fur caps and long boots; but the 17th Regiment had not received a single article of warm clothing yet. Our old clothes are in rags and tatters, even our boots are scarcely any protection, the leather having shrunk with the continual wet, and the men's feet having swelled with the cold, that some men could not get their boots on and had to go in the trenches and about the camp bare-footed; this is hard to believe, but nevertheless it is true. January 9th. It had been snowing for the last three days, and this morning the whole of the mountains over Balaklava and along the valley of the Tchernaya River are clothed in a sheet of white, the snow being on the ground to the depth of three feet and in some places over five feet; the cold was increased by a piercing high wind which blew into our very marrow-bones. If we were only well clad this weather would, however, be far more healthy than the wet and storm we have had recently, but, alas, we are not properly provided with outer garments to resist the severity of the Crimean winter. I cannot conceive greater hardship than to stand in the trenches twenty-four hours, then return cramped and nearly frozen, to our damp, cheerless tents to find that there is no fire or wood to cook any victuals, or even a drink of warm coffee. What we require most of all are long boots to protect our feet and legs; most of the officers have got long boots, and find them invaluable. Our mitts are worn out and unserviceable; I made a pair out of a piece of my blanket, which I find answers the purpose admirably, of course it was robbing Peter to pay Paul; it shortened my blanket somewhat. Several men, however, have followed my example.

It has been freezing extremely hard these two last nights, and this morning a man was found frozen in my tent. His name was George Murphin, he was a good soldier; he lay down, as we all did, and went to sleep—and never woke. When the orderly was rousing the men, this man was found frozen stiff in death. There has been over one hundred men admitted into hospital from the trenches these last twenty-four hours, seized with cramps and nearly frozen—all from the want of clothing. The cavalry division lost about fifty horses within the last three days, and I dread to think of the number of men who will die if this weather continues long. The commissariat mules and horses are dying off very fast, and the men seem likely to follow, if there is not something done soon to protect the army from the inclemency of the weather, of which we are more afraid than of the Russians. It is the wish of every officer and man in the camp that Lord Raglan would march the whole army against Sebastopol, and let us take it or die in the attempt—we had better die in battle than die with cold, starvation and sickness. We are of opinion that we would not lose so many men in taking it as we are now losing daily by sickness and the want of food and clothes. A new burial ground having been opened about two hundred yards to the right front of our regiment, on the side of the hill, frequently may be seen passing our tents, every day, four soldiers slowly winding their way towards this grave-yard, with a corpse, sewed up in a blanket, carried on a stretcher on the men's shoulders; no person accompanying the solitary funeral; and buried without the ordinary military honours of three rounds of blank fired over him. The burials are too numerous to pay the usual honours; besides, we have not the men to spare, all available for duty are either in the trenches or carrying shot, shell or provisions. The men's spirits are broken down, and they march along with a load on their back, in solemn silence, regardless of anything, not even looking to the right or left, resigning themselves to death which they daily expect, who is following quickly in their footsteps, not by shot from the Russians, but by a slower and surer torture—starvation and cold. When I saw so many men freezing to death, I began to talk to myself thus, "Tom Faughnan, are you going to make no exertion to save yourself from being frozen to death, as some of your comrades have been, and are now buried yonder, on the hill-side? If you get shot by the enemy it is what you expected when you came out here, and is a soldier's death, fighting the battles for the honour and glory of your Queen and country." As I was walking round the tent-pole to keep my blood in circulation, the temperature being many degrees below zero, I held the above soliloquy. A happy thought struck me, and I carried it out, which I believe saved my life. I took a pick-axe and shovel and commenced to build a hut in rear of of the company's tents. I worked at it every spare moment until I had a hole dug nine feet long by six wide, and four feet deep, cutting the inside walls straight down, and facing them with stones to a height of two feet above the ground; which left the inside of the hut six feet high; building a fireplace and chimney in the end. I then got my comrade, Dandy Russell, to accompany me to the old bridge at the Tchernaya River, where I climbed up a steep hill, close to a Russian battery; where we got wood on a former occasion; and there I got enough of wood to roof my hut. having filled our straps with the best I could find, we started for our camp, escaping the Russians who were just above us on the hill. When we got to camp I commenced to roof the hut; cutting the rafters and laying them at the top with some gads made out of willows cut for that purpose. Having the rafters secured along the top, I stretched some small sticks along the sides of the roof, securing them also, and then laying branches over all. I then cut sods in a ravine, carried them to the hut, laid them on the top of the branches, and covered the whole with earth; smoothing it over with the back of the spade, as I would a potato pit in Ireland, to throw off the rain;

cutting a trench round it, to cary off the water. I made steps going down and I got a flag to fit the door, so my Irish experience stood to me here. We frequently went to the old bridge for wood, but ran the risk of being shot by the Russians every time; by this means we managed to get wood enough to keep a fire in our hut, and were comfortable while the men were freezing to death in their tents. Dandy and I managed to get on trench duty alternately, so as to leave one of us to look after the hut, and prepare the meals for the other, after coming off trench duty.

Having been served with green coffee by the commissariat, and having no means of roasting or grinding it, we had accumulated a large bagful; now we procured the half of a large exploded shell, and with a nine pound shot we ground the coffee in the shell, after roasting it on a frying pan; most of the men threw their green coffee away having no means of roasting or grinding. There has been a good deal of firing going on between the French and Russians on the right attack, and the Grenadier Guards had it very hot last night, from a new masked battery. The Russians opened on the right near Canrobert's Redoubt. There are three large columns of Russians visible opposite Inkerman on the north side of the Tchernaya and their movements are very mysterious. They have sent a large body of cavalry to the east of the valley of Balaklava and at the same time a body of infantry moved off towards the north. The scenery of our camp-ground and the country has now assumed a truly wintry aspect. The lofty peaks and ridges which close up the valley of Balaklava are covered with snow, which gives them the appearance of great height; in the valley and plateau the snow is over three feet deep, and streaked by lines of men and horses carrying up provisions to the camp. The number of dead horses on the wayside increases daily, every slough across the path is marked by a dead horse or mule. At the present rate of mortality the whole division, which can only muster about 600 horses, will be almost extinct in one month more. I went over to the camp of the 63rd Regiment to see a first cousin of mine, named Philip McGurn, I was sorry to learn that he had been severely wounded in the thigh, by a piece of shell, and was sent down to Scutari hospital. The regiment could only muster twelve men for duty, the remainder were either killed or died from sickness in hospital. The 46th regiment have only about fifty men fit for duty; the Scots Fusilier Guards have lost, since they came out, upwards of 1000 men, and can now only muster about three hundred on parade; and many other regiments in a like proportion.

The duty of carrying provisions and rum from Balaklava to the front is very trying on the men; every two men carry a beaker of rum, biscuit or pork, slung from a pole between them; they march about six miles in this manner, from Balaklava to Head Quarters; horses cannot do this trying work, for they cannot keep their legs, and almost every hundred yards along the way is marked by the carcass of one of these animals. I passed through the French Camp, on my way foraging for wood, and went into several of the men's tents, and was surprised to see the misery they were in. It must not be inferred that the French soldiers are healthy whilst we are all sickly. I was astonished to see so many lying sick in their tents and dying with dysentery, diarrhœa, scurvy and pulmonary complaints. Their men were allowed to lie sick in their tents, which differ from us very much; when our men get sick they are sent to hospital at once and there attended by a doctor.

January 14th.—It is thawing fast to-day and the roads are resuming their former sloppy state, which has increased the difficulties of supplying the men considerably.

The cavalry are getting up sheds for their horses, and sheep skin coats have been distributed to some of the men. I wonder when the 17th Regiment are going to get any warm clothing, or sheep-skin coats? Some officers, it is true, have got some warm jackets, and not before they wanted them This week large quantities of clothing were served to some of the regiments. It must not, however, be imagined that the supplies sent up are equal to the demand; several regiments have not received a stitch yet, although large quantities have been sent out by England—whose fault is it? The sick in the hospitals on the hill tops suffer severely from cold, and the snow blows into their very blankets. However, such supplies as the men have had, prove of the greatest service and have saved many lives. Consider what men suffer with snow three feet deep about the tents. The men scarcely know what fuel is in many regiments; they break up empty pork barrels and anything that will burn to cook their meals, or grub into the earth for roots and stumps to make a fire. This is enough to make the poor, worn-out, exhausted soldier despair before he sinks to rest; sighs that he cannot share the sure triumph and certain honour and glories of the day when our flag shall wave from the citadel of Sebastopol! Although our patience is sorely tried, yet there is no deep despair here among the troops, no one for an instant feels the slightest doubt of ultimate success.

If British courage, daring, bravery and a strong arm in the fight, contempt of death and love for our Most Gracious Sovereign Lady the Queen and our country; if honour and glory could have won Sebastopol, it had been ours long ago, and may be ours at any time. We are prepared for a dreadfnl sacrifice, and not one of us for an instant has the least misgiving as to the result. But let our country at least feel that the soldiers now lying on the wet ground before Sebastopol, starving and in rags, deserve at her hands the greenest and the brightest laurels and rewards, and we trust that she may be prepared to award those gallant noble officers and soldiers, who in such a position deserve the highest honour she can confer upon them. Let England know them, as the descendants of that glorious army (led by their illustrious chief His Grace the Duke of Wellington) who thwarted the great Buonaparte in Spain and Portugal, who fought at Quatre-Bras, Ligny, and Waterloo; and let England recollect that in fighting her battles against a powerful enemy at that time, we have now to maintain a struggle with foes still more stubborn and barbarous, with a terrible climate, and if they triumphed over the one she may rest assured, as we are, that we will triumph over the other.

With regard to the prospects of the Russians, there can be no doubt that means of communication exist between Inkerman and Sebastopol along the south banks of the estuary of the Tchernaya. It is necessary that more decisive steps be taken to intercept supplies for their garrison, or, to harass them more in their attempts to bring in provisions to the city. After we seized the Woronzoff road, it was thought that no other means of approach, except by a mountain path, existed between Simpheropol and Sebastopol, on the south side. There can be no doubt that another road has been found out, which enables them to go from Inkerman along the base of the heights on the southern side and traverse the ravines which lead along the banks of the river into the city.

Waggons can be seen every day coming down from the heights over the Tchernaya river towards Sebastopol, and large bodies of the enemy are visible, passing frequently and disappearing mysteriously into a subterranean passage leading to the citadel.

CHAPTER XVI.

TRENCHES—CANAL OF MUD—RUSSIAN NEW YEAR—HEAVY FIRE—ON SENTRY—THE SORTIE—OLD BROWN BESS—SORTIE—ARRIVAL IN CAMP—NEW STYLE OF CANDLE—FLINT AND STEEL—MAKING COFFEE—HEAVY SNOW—NO FIRE—WARM CLOTHING—SHOT AND SHELL.

JANUARY 16th.—A strong party of the 17th Regiment marched to the trenches yesterday evening, and in going down got wet to the skin. A heavy thaw set in, and the trenches became a canal of mud; when we arrived, we remarked that the Russians were very active inside the town, and had lighted watchfires on the north side, and illuminated the heights over the Tchernaya with rows of lights, in the form of a cross, which shone brilliantly through the darkness of the cold, wet, and damp winter's night. They were evidently celebrating their new year; light shone from the windows of most of the houses and public buildings. Our lonely sentries lying on the ground in front of our advanced trench, our muskets loaded and capped, with a watchful eye on every embrasure in front of us; we fancied that the Russians in Sebastopol tried to annoy us with their lights and gaiety. At midnight all the church bells in the city began ringing, it was evident that a solemn religious ceremony was about to take place. We were all warned to be on the alert, and all our advanced posts were strengthened accordingly. After the people came out of their churches, about one o'clock in the morning, they gave a loud cheer, our sailors and artillery who manned the guns in our batteries, responded by opening a heavy fire on them; as did also the French on our right and left. When the Russians in return, began one of the fiercest cannonades along their position that we have yet heard; their batteries vomited forth floods of flame which broke through the smoke as lightning through the thunder-cloud, and we could see distinctly the houses and buildings in the city, and their batteries crowded with soldiers. The roaring of round shot, whistling and bursting of shells, filled the intervals between the deafening roll of big guns. The round shot passed over our trenches rapidly, ploughing up the ground into furrows as they passed us by, or striking into our parapet with a thud. Our "Blue Jackets" and artillery had to shelter themselves closely under their batteries, and could barely reply to the volleys which ploughed up our parapets, knocking sandbags, gabions, and fascines all about the men's heads, and not unfrequently knocking some of them off; nevertheless they always laid their guns correctly, sending the destructive missile into the embrasure with a vengeance. While the firing was going on a strong body of the enemy had been pushed up the hill towards our works in front, on the flank of the left attack. I was one of a chain of sentries, at twelve paces apart, lying down fifty yards in front of our advanced trench. When we saw a strong column of Russians coming out of their batteries and advancing up the hill, we passed the word to each other, when the line of sentries fired on them and retreated into the trench; giving the alarm to our men. The field officer in charge sending back to the other parallels for reinforcements, which arrived in good time to assist us in driving the Russians from our works. In the meantime, the enemy had advanced into our trenches, notwithstanding we kept blazing at them during their advance, and standing against them, on the escarpment of our trench, with our bayonets at the charge. They forced into our trench in large numbers, when we had a desperate hand-to-hand fight; we were completely jammed together, so that as we pulled the bayonet out of one we knocked another over with the butt end of our musket.

The officers fought bravely, cutting the Russians down with every stroke. One officer in cutting a Russian broke his sword, which nearly cost him his life, only for one of our men guarding off a stab from a Russian bayonet, he would have been *hors-de-combat.* He soon picked up a musket, however, and fought bravely with it. I was close to him as he floored the Russians all around him. I can assure you, gentle reader, that we all fought as becometh British soldiers, though the odds against us were ten to one. When the enemy saw the reinforcements coming, they began to retreat by odd ones, until at last the whole of them retired towards their outworks in double time. We fired rapidly after them, giving them chase up to their very batteries, and engaging with them again in the grave-yard close to the careening battery, where we had a very hard fight amongst the tombstones. Oh! if we had the Enfield rifle, instead of the "Old Brown Bess." However, we closed around them in the grave yard, dislodging them from behind the tombstones, where they took refuge, cutting off three of their party whom we took prisoners, besides wounded men we picked up on the field and in the trenches, sending the latter to the hospi tal, and the former on board the fleet. In this affair, two officers and eighteen men were wounded, and six men killed.

The French had also to resist a strong sortie at the same time, and drove them back with great loss, and in pursuit got inside the Russian advanced batteries, where they had a hand-to-hand fight, and by great valour succeeded in fighting their way clear of the enemy, and returned to their own trenches. At daylight all was quiet, except an odd shot now and then as a reminder. Having been relieved that evening by the 21st Fusiliers, we arrived in camp completely exhausted with hunger, wet and hard fighting, our clothes being saturated, it having thawed in the night, and now turned round to freeze, stiffening our clothes with icicles, the noise of which, as we marched along, reminded us of the ancient warriors in coats of mail. When I reached my hut, Dandy was there, but no fire, our wood had been used up; he had been roused up in the night to reinforce the trenches, and carrying shot during the day, he was as weary as I was. How to get a drink of hot coffee was the next thought which troubled me, I wanted it badly indeed. What did I do? I tore a strip off the nether end of my shirt, set it on an empty blacking-tin with some pork fat, and lit it with a flint and steel which I always carried in my pack (our matches being too damp to light, and besides they were very scarce), set my canteen over the blaze with a little water in it at first, making the coffee after the water boiled, then adding more water; we then fried some biscuits in pork fat over the blaze. This new invention proved very useful afterwards, not only to Dandy and myself, but to the officers and men of the regiment; you can scarcely imagine how quick water will boil over a blaze of this kind.

January 19th. Frost continues with frequent showers of snow, which enables us to get up provisions. The artillery were employed to-day with their waggons carrying up shot, shell and powder to the depôt.

January 20th. We had a heavy fall of snow during the night, it is now four feet deep over the plain. The preparations for a general bombardment are progressing rapidly; upwards of seventy big guns and mortars, with sea service siege guns are all up at the depôt, and if this frost lasts, will be in the batteries very shortly, if the frost and snow enable us to get up heavy guns and mortars. Several men have been frozen in their tents, and several men have been sent to hospital from the trenches with severe frost bites, and suffering from bitter cold wind and frost. When a path has been once broken through the snow, men and horses can get along much more easily than to wade through the deep mud as heretofore, but the temperature is very trying in the tents, particularly when we have no wood to make a fire. Many regiments have been served out with fur coats, long boots, mitts, guernseys, and flannel waistbands and socks. But alas, none of these needful articles have reached the 17th Regiment yet, except the men in hospital, who have received a few articles of warm clothing. It is a most melancholy subject for reflection to see our present army. There is scarcely a regiment to be recognised now, save by its well known camp-ground. The officers cannot be distinguished from the privates, unless when they wear their swords. What a harvest death has reaped, and many more are ripe for the sickle. It is sad to see the noble officers who have been brought up in luxury sharing the same fate as the private soldiers. I went into an officer's tent the other day, and I was sorry to see him (Lieutenant Bunkman), sitting in his tent shivering with cold and trying to cut out a pair of leggings off the end of his blanket. As I helped him to cut them out, he says: "Faughnan, they may talk at home about us noble officers of the British army, and imagine us sitting in a snug tent with warm clothing and gorgeous uniforms, partaking of the fare that England has generously sent out here to her gallant officers and soldiers, but which none of us have yet received, and I am afraid never will, if this weather lasts long. It would be more comfortable to be a sweep in London than an officer out here."

We had 400 men employed to-day, January 29th, carrying

shot and shell from the depôt to the trenches. The snow fell during the night and covered the ground four feet deep, but the cold wind drifted it to the depth of six feet in some places. The wind blew so bitterly cold that the mules and horses refused to face it; but the men came trudging along in a dreary string, and there was something mournful in the aspect of the long lines moving across the expanse of glittering snow. When these men came back to camp they had very blue noses and pale faces; and as to their clothes, what would the people of England have thought if they beheld their gallant army; most of the officers as ragged as the men; and many officers have been crippled by frost and obliged to go on leave with their feet badly frostbitten. Several men go about barefooted, up to their knees in snow, they could not get their frozen boots on their swelled feet. There was very severe frost last night, January 23rd.

The activity of the heads of departments which has been recently observable, is becoming more developed every day. Our quartermaster has received to-day, among other useful things for the regiment, a supply of Enfield rifles, to replace the "Old Brown Bess;" they will be served out to the men to-morrow; also a quantity of sheepskin jackets, long boots, guernseys, flannel waistbands, mitts and fur caps. We are hard worked bringing these articles up to camp; we are doing the work of commissariat mules. As we were coming up we passed a large number of sick and dying men who were sent down to Balaklava on mules and bat horses; they formed one of the most ghastly processions that could be imagined; many of these men were all but dead; with closed eyes, open mouths and pale haggard faces, they were borne along two on each mule, one on each side, back to back. One of them died on the way down, his corpse looked most ghastly. Strapped upright to the seat, the legs hanging down stiff, the eyes staring wide open, the head and body nodding with frightful mockery of life at each stride of the mule over the broken ground. As the dead man passed, the only remarks our men made were, "there is one more poor fellow out of pain at any rate." There were several cases of frost-bite among them, but they all seemed alike on the verge of death. We arrived at the front by six p.m., the road being hard, we made rapid progress to get to camp by daylight. Next morning, January 24th, we handed over to the quartermaster the old Brown Bess, and received a splendid Enfield rifle in its stead; we also received one pair long boots, one fur cap each, and several received sheep-skin coats, mitts, guernseys, flannel bands, and socks, with a few large overcoats for the sentries. It would astonish a stranger to go from Balaklava to the front to see the number of dead horses and mules along the wayside; in every hole are the remains of these animals torn by dogs and vultures. The attitudes of some of the skeletons were curious, some have dropped dead, and are frozen stiff as they fell; others seem struggling to rise from their miry grave; most of these carcasses have been skinned by the Turks and French; who use the hides to cover their huts. About five miles of the country are dotted all over with these carcasses, in every stage of decay. Were it summer time, around Balaklava would be a great pest-house, full of festering carcasses of dead mules and horses. The evening after we were served out with new rifles, long boots and fur caps, the 17th Regiment furnished 400 men for the trenches. The weather was clear, dry and cold, but we do not care now for cold, since we got our long boots, fur caps, and warm clothing to protect us from the sharp biting frost. We were in splendid spirits, and felt comfortable during the night in our new boots and fur caps. After we arrived in the trenches, the Russians opened a storm of musketry on us, as if they knew we were armed with the Enfield rifle, and were anxious for us to try it, which we soon did, to their astonishment, the Russian fire was particularly directed against our works the whole night; after daylight the firing recommenced with great vigour, all along our lines. There could be no less than 3000 men engaged on each side, firing as hard as they could pull a trigger; the lines were marked by thick curling smoke. The fire slackened on both sides about ten o'clock. Not a night now passes without severe rifle-shooting from behind the parapets, and between the lines. Our works are pushed almost within one hundred and fifty yards of the Russian batteries, and on the left almost into the town, and its suburbs; but the ruined houses of these suburbs, are turned into defences for their sharpshooters, and the town itself is almost one formidable battery, from the glacis to the ridge over the sea, on which the south side of the town is situated. Our batteries are in good order, and ready for the heavy siege-guns, which can be put into them in a few days, as the ground is hard we can easily get them into position. In the skirmish last night, one Russian officer was taken prisoner on the right attack by the 47th Regiment, who manned the trenches. We have received several deserters from the Russians within the last week, who give a fearful account of how the Russians are suffering from cold and hunger; they showed us some hard black bread they brought with them, in their haversacks. It is evident that the struggle between us and the Russians will soon be renewed with greater vigour than before; the clear frosty days, and nights have given heart and spirits to our men; but the Russians have also derived advantage from the improved condition of the roads and country. We hear they have thrown large quantities of stores into the garrison recently.

When I returned from the trenches Dandy had plenty of hot coffee and fried biscuits ready for me, as well as an extra gill of hot rum. We find our hut very comfortable these cold frosty nights, and we now get two nights off trench duty. Notwithstanding the clear frosty weather, the transport of clothes, fuel and provisions entails considerable hardships on our men; the sick make little progress towards recovery, and the number of them sent down to Balaklava every day is a proof of the unsatisfactory condition of the health of our army. Mules and horses have been sent down to Balaklava for warm clothing for those regiments whose men are nearly all sick. The coffee, for the first time, has been issued to us roasted, which we find a great luxury compared to how we have been getting it; vegetables, however, are greatly needed, picks, spades, shovels and billhooks are in much request and are greatly needed to clear the camp, dig graves and chop wood, when we get any, but we have got none as yet.

CHAPTER XVII.

THE RAILWAY—LORD RAGLAN—COSSACKS—THE NAVVIES—RUSSIAN DESERTERS—THE RAILWAY.

THE railway from Balaklava to the front, under Mr. Doyne, C.E., is making rapid progress; about two miles of rails have been laid down. It winds its way from the post office in Balaklava towards Kadikoi, passing by Mrs. Seacoles' well known door, (the half-wav house,) and is graded as far as the 4th division. The sleepers are on the ground, and will be laid in the course of two weeks. A stationary engine has been placed on the hill above the Kadikoi, which pulls the trucks up from Balaklava; the Turks are astonished by the puffs of steam from its iron lungs, and its shrieks and screams as it is put in motion by the engineers, to their great wonder and astonishment.

Lord Raglan visited Balaklava to-day and inspected the railway, with which he was well pleased; he was accompanied by several staff officers. After inspecting the progress and condition of various departments in the town, he went on board a man-of-war in the harbour, to visit some sick soldiers, who were going down to Scutari. He returned to Head Quarters at six o'clock. I am sorry that sickness does not diminish, dysentery and diarrhœa seem on the increase every day, and I am afraid that scurvy is beginning to show itself among the troops. It is no wonder that the men get scurvy, living on salt rations and hard biscuits without any vegetables, sleeping in their clothes without a chance to wash themselves or change their clothes; water being so scarce we cannot wash our linen. I refrain from describing the state of the army for the want of clean linen or water to wash with; suffice it to say that several new flannel waist bands served to the men were thrown away, and can be seen on the camp ground, occupied by a large army in skirmishing order. I took my canteen, water-keg and soap down to the spring one day to wash my linen, I waited two hours for my turn, after which I filled my canteen and water keg, I then washed my clothes on a flat stone, then waited two hours more for water to rinse them, making four hours in all I had to wait. The reader can understand what difficulty the men have to keep themselves clean.

February 21st. The Russians made a strong sortie on the British lines last night, and were repulsed with considerable loss; the light division had six men killed and ten wounded.

The Cossacks, on the hills beyond Inkerman, have nearly disappeared and there are no indications that they intend to occupy the hills again, or construct batteries there as was supposed. The greatest secrecy is observed respecting our future operations; strict orders have been given that officers and others are not to give information regarding our works or movements but to those entitled to demand it. I was on trench duty last night when it froze hard, with bitter cutting wind, drifting the snow into our eyes and filling the trenches; but the sun shone out in the morning and the wind fell. The day was clear and cold, and the warm clothing and long boots enabled us to bear the severity of the weather, which would have been fatal to many, had we been in the same state as our comrades on whom winter fell with all its rigour, while they had nothing to wear but their old regimental clothing. We are now well secured with long boots, fur caps and warm jackets. As the day was clear, I could see the Russians plainly, in spite of the dazzling effect of the snow and cold. The bridge of boats across the creek, from the government buildings to the other side of the town, was crowded with men, who were busily engaged passing across supplies and rolling barrels to the other side, shewing that there is a centre of supply or depôt in the government buildings behind the Redan and opposite the fire of our batteries. Several lighters under sail and full of men were standing over from one side of the harbour to the other, and boats manned with crews dressed in white were tugging scows laden with stores to the south side of the town. A small steamer was also very active puffing and splurting about the harbour in all directions, furrowing the surface of the water, which was as smooth as glass, so completely is the harbour land-locked—the men-of-war with their white ensigns and St. Andrew's cross, lying in a line at the north side. The masts of three vessels could be seen plainly above the buildings; further away to the right towards Inkerman the white houses and barracks shone brightly in the sun, and the bells of the churches were ringing out clearly in the frosty air; the tall houses running up the hillside, with its massive, public buildings, gave Sebastopol rather an imposing appearance. There was not a soul to be seen in the streets except soldiers running across the open space from one battery to another, relieving guards or posting sentries. Outside the town the eye rests on walls of earth piled up ten or twelve feet high and twenty feet thick, with embrasures, in which I could see the muzzles of the guns pointing towards our batteries; those works are of tremendous strength, with a very deep and broad ditch in front. Round the suburbs of the town are broken-down white-washed cottages, the roofs of which are all gone, the doors off and the windows out, the walls are left standing at a certain distance from the batteries with holes made in them so that the guns can cover their object; they are also used for sharpshooters.

The picture of misery presented by these suburbs is very striking, in most instances the destruction has been caused by our shot, and the houses all round the Flagstaff and Garden batteries have been blown into heaps of rubbish and mortar. There have been a great many shells thrown by the Russians to day, from a mortar battery towards the sea, projecting the shells into the air every half minute or so across a hill in front of it, so as to annoy our working party, who were engaged in throwing up a trench towards the Quarantine fort. The white smoke rushing into the air expands into rings; then follows the heavy dull report; then comes the shrill whistle of the shell travelling through the air as it describes its curve, and descends with great velocity, increasing rapidly every second, till it explodes just as it reaches the ground, sometimes sinking deep into the earth, tearing it up with the explosion to the destruction of those around. It is a most unpleasant reflection when we see a whistling Dick coming in the air, and run out of its way behind a traverse. To how many families have they carried deep sorrow and mourning. The smoke clears away, then men gather round one who moves not, they bear him away on a stretcher, and a small mound of fresh earth marks for a little time the resting place of the soldier, whose wife, mother, children, or sisters, are left destitute of all happiness, save the memory and the sympathy of their country. Who will let the inmates of that desolate cottage in England, Ireland, or Scotland, know of their bereavement? However there goes another shell which does nothing but knock up a cloud of earth and stones.

After being relieved, we marched to our gloomy camp, under a heavy fire from the enemy; but my hut was not so gloomy as the men's tents, it was warm and comfortable, my comrade had a little fire, keeping my coffee and fried biscuits warm, with a cotton rag dipped in pork fat as a substitute for a candle.

February 25th. The 17th Regiment were roused at two o'clock this morning and marched down to reinforce the covering party in the trenches. The Russians commenced one of the most furious cannonades we have heard since the siege began. The whole of the Russian batteries from our left opened with immense force and noise, the Redan, Garden, and Malakoff batteries began firing round shot and shell. Our second parallel and twenty one gun batteries were exposed to the weight of this most terrible fire, which shook the very earth and lighted up the sky with incessant lightning flashes for two hours, under cover of which a very strong sortie was made, and for an hour the musketry rolled incessantly with vigour enough for a general engagement. As soon as the fire opened, an aid-de-camp rode to our lines and gave the order for the 17th, 57th and 20th, Regiments to march to the trenches, and in less than five minutes these three regiments were moving in double time towards the trenches. On arrival, we found that the covering party had succeeded in driving the enemy from our trenches. We then returned to our camp and lay down for a couple of hours. The Russians had made a sortie on the French lines at the same time, and were also driven back with great loss.

At the request of General Ostensacken, an armistice was granted from twelve till one o'clock to-day, to enable the Russians to bury their dead. There was not much firing this morning; at twelve o'clock white flags were run up on the batteries on both sides, and immediately afterwards a body of Russians issued from the Redan, Flagstaff, and Malakoff batteries, and proceeded to carry off their dead; and our men, with the French emerged from our batteries on a similar errand. A few Russian officers advanced about half way towards our batteries, when they were met by our officers and the French, where extreme courtesy, the interchange of profound salutations, and bowings marked the interview. The officers walked up and down, and shakos were raised and caps doffed politely as each came near an enemy; in the meantime the soldiers were carrying the dead and wounded off the field. About one o'clock the Russians retired inside their batteries, and immediately after the white flags were hauled down. The troops had scarcely disappeared over the parapet, when the flash and roar of a gun from the Malakoff announced that the war had begun once more, and our batteries almost simultaneously fired a gun; in a moment afterwards the popping of rifles commenced as usual on both sides.

The Cossacks about Balaklava are particularly busy throwing out their piquets and sentries all along the top of Canrobert's Hill. These sentries can see every thing that goes on in the plain, from the entrance to Balaklava to the edge on which our right rests; not a horse, cart, or man can go in or out of the town, without been seen by these sentries, for they are quite visible to any person, who gazes from the top of Canrobert's Hill. The works of the railway must cause these Cossacks very serious apprehensions. What can they, or do they, think of them? Gradually they see villages of white huts rise up on the hillside and in the valleys, and from the cavalry camp to the heights of Balaklava they can see line after line of wooden buildings, and can discover the tumult and bustle on Kadikoi. This may be all very puzzling; but it can be nothing to the excitement of looking at the railway trucks rushing round the hill at Kadikoi, and running down the incline to the town at the rate of twenty miles an hour. The Cossacks gallop up to the top of the hill to look at this phenomenon, and they caper about shaking their lances in wonder and excitement when the trucks disappear.

About 300 sick men were sent down to Balaklava to-day, on the ambulance mules.

The preparations for the general bombardment are progressing with great rapidity, and arrangements have been made to send up two thousand rounds of ammunition per day to the front from the harbour; about two hundred mules have been pressed into the service in addition to the railway, and the Highlanders, and Artillery horses are employed in the carriage of heavy shot and shell to the front, a duty which greatly disables and distresses them. The Guards are all down at Balaklava; some of them seem in very delicate health; a few old campaigners have attained that happy state in which no hardships or privations can have any effect on them. The silence and calm of the last few days are but the omens of the struggle which is about to be resumed very speedily for the possession of Sebastopol. The Russians are silent because we do not impede their work; we are silent because we are preparing for the contest, and are using every energy to bring up from Balaklava the enormous amounts of projectiles and mountains of ammunition which will be required for the service of our batteries, when we open a general bombardment.

The railway has begun to render us some service in saving the hard labour attendant on the transport of shot and shell, and enables us to form a small depôt at the distance of two miles and a half from Balaklava, which is, however, not large enough for the demands made upon it, and it is emptied as soon as it is formed by parties from the regiments in front, who carry ammunition to the camp depôt, four miles further on.

The navvies work at the railway hard and honestly, with a few exceptions, and the dread of the provost marshal has produced a wholesome influence on the dispositions of the refractory. About 200 men of the Naval Brigade have been detailed to assist in the works of the railway, in order that the construction of it may be hastened as much as possible.

March 4th. I was one of a covering party in the advanced trench, it was a bright moonlight night, with sharp cold frost. The Russians availed themselves of the brightness of the night by keeping up a constant fire of musketry on our trenches. At daybreak the volleys of musketry lasted an hour, mingled with the roar of round shot, whistling and bursting of shells, under cover of which they made a strong sortie on our trenches, and were repulsed with heavy loss; they also made a strong sortie on the French lines at the same time, and met no better success. General Canrobert and staff rode past our camp to-day on his way to visit the British Head Quarters, where he met Lord Raglan and several generals of our army, with whom he held a council of war, but nothing is known publicly respecting the result of the council.

March 6th. Yesterday our first spring meeting took place and was numerously attended, the races came off on a level piece of ground near the Tchernaya River, and were regarded with much interest by the Cossacks on Canrobert's Hill. They evidently thought at first that the assemblage was connected with some military demonstration, and galloped about in a state of great excitement to and fro. In the midst of the races a party of twelve Russians were seen approaching the sentry on the old redoubt beyond Inkerman, the sentry fired and ten of them fled, and when the piquet came up to the sentry they found two deserters had come in from the Russians, one of them was an officer, and the other had been an officer, but had suffered degradation. They were both Poles, spoke French fluently, and expressed great satisfaction at their escape and said, "send us wherever you please, provided we never see Russia again." They stated that they had deceived the men who were with them into the belief that the sentry was one of their own outposts, and as they had lately joined, they believed them, and advanced boldly till the sentry fired at them, when they discovered their mistake and fled. As they were well mounted they dashed towards our lines, the Cossacks tried to cut them off but did not succeed. They requested that the horses might be sent back to the Russian lines as they did not belong to them, they did not wish to be accused of theft. The horses were then taken to the brow of the hill and set free, when they galloped towards the Cossacks. The races proceeded as usual, and subsequently towards six o'clock the crowd dispersed.

CHAPTER XVIII.

ST. PATRICK'S DAY—RIFLE PITS—FOURTH DIVISION—FRENCH LOSS—THE SIEGE—GENERAL ATTACK—FLAG OF TRUCE—BURYING THE DEAD—WOODEN HUTS—TURKISH TROOPS—DIVINE SERVICE.

MARCH 18th. Yesterday being St. Patrick's day, many officers and men were to be seen early in the morning on the hill-side in search of something green to wear as a substitute for a real shamrock, the old symbol of Erin. In the afternoon we had horse races to celebrate St. Patrick's day, and show that Irishmen though far from their native land, had not forgotten the rights and ceremonies, by which this celebrated day was remembered by them. They were in excellent spirits, the day was fine, and the ground dry, both officers and men enjoyed the day's sport; the thunder of the siege guns rose up frequently above the shouts of the crowd in the heat of the races. There has been a fierce struggle between the French and Russians last night, for the possession of the rifle-pits. These pits are situated in front of the Mamelon, and the Russian sharpshooters occupy them every night, and keep up a most galling and destructive fire against the exposed parts of the advanced trenches of our right attack as well as that of the French.

The shot of our batteries make the rifle pits too hot a place for the Russians during the day, but at night they come back and re-occupy them, supported by large bodies of infantry; in these encounters the enemy has had many men killed and wounded. These rifle-pits have cost both armies large quantities of ammunition, as well as the sacrifice of many men; but the French are determined to wrest them from the Russians at any cost, for they are a source of the greatest annoyance to them. They sent a strong force of about six thousand men down close to our second and light divisions, before dusk yesterday evening, and shortly afterwards they were sent to the advanced trenches, on our right, the covering party and riflemen were ordered out to occupy the rifle pits; they advanced but found the Russians had anticipated them, and that the enemy were already in possession of the pits. A fierce battle then commenced, but it was found that the enemy were there in much larger force than was expected; therefore the French could not then drive them from their position, notwithstanding their repeated attempts to do so. The contest was carried on by musketry, and the volleys which rang out incessantly for five hours, roused up the whole camp.

From the roll of musketry, and flashing light in front, one would have thought that a general engagement between large armies was going on. The character of the fight had something peculiar about it, owing to the absence of round shot or shell. About 7.30 o'clock p. m., the 4th division was turned out by order of the General, Sir John

Campbell, and took up its position on the hill near the Green Hill battery, and the light division, under Sir George Brown, at the same time marched towards the 21 gun battery, the second and third divisions were also turned out and marched to the trenches in their front, after the French had desisted and retired from the assault on the rifle-pits. These divisions, after remaining under arms for five hours, were marched back to their respective camps. Had the French required our assistance we were ready to give it; but they are determined on taking these pits, which are in front of their advanced trenches, without any aid from us. The Zouaves bore the heaviest part of this battle; we could distinctly hear their officers between the volleys of musketry, cheering on their men, and encouraging them, and the rush of men generally followed, then a volley of musketry was heard, followed by rapid file firing, then a Russian cheer and more musketry. Between each volley we could hear the officer again giving the command. This work went on for about five hours, when the French at length retired. The French loss at this affair was twenty officers and 200 rank and file killed, wounded, and taken prisoners; the Russian loss was over 600 killed and wounded.

March 19th, 5 p.m. General Canrobert attended by his staff, passed down by our right attack, and examined the position of the rifle-pits, Malakoff and Mamelon. At twilight a strong force of French with a battery of field pieces were moved down towards the advanced works, and another attempt was made to take the rifle-pits; and after a hard fought battle they succeeded in dislodging the Russians, amid a blaze of fire from the forts at daybreak. The French now directed a heavy fire from these pits against the Mamelon and Malakoff, reversing the sand bags and loop holes.

March 23rd. The 17th Regiment furnished a working party of one hundred men for the advanced trenches yesterday evening. At twilight, when we got to the trenches, the engineer officer laid out the work. It was a new trench. Every file of men got a pickaxe and shovel, and were placed at six yards apart, on the open ground, without any shelter from the Russian grape and canister. We placed a man on the look-out for the flash of the guns, while we worked hard to throw up cover. About twelve o'clock the sentries in advance of us gave the alarm, by firing on the advancing Russians, who came so suddenly, we had scarcely time to snatch up our rifles before they were upon us; bayoneting us before we were prepared to receive them. When the sentries first discovered them they were close upon us. Taken at a great disadvantage, and pressed by superior numbers, we met them hand to hand with the bayonet; our men fought like British lions, meeting the assault with undaunted courage. We drove the enemy back at the point of the bayonet, pursued by our shot, they retired under cover of their batteries. The attack was general along the whole line. At ten p.m., our batteries, with the French, began to shell the town, pouring our rockets every five minutes in streams into the city. The sentries in advance of Chapman's battery gave the alarm also that the Russians were advancing in force on the trenches, the 20th, 21st, 57th, and 68th Regiments were the covering parties on the left attack. They were pretty well prepared for the enemy. About the same time the French were attacked by columns of the enemy. As the French were sorely pressed, our troops extended along a portion of their trenches. On the left attack the Russians advanced in great force, through a weak part of the trenches, turning the third parallel; they killed and wounded several of our men, and had advanced to the second parallel, when our covering party came down upon them and drove them back, after a sharp conflict. On the right the Russians came on our men very suddenly. The 34th regiment had a strong force to contend against and as Colonel Kelly, their commanding officer, was leading them on, he got wounded and was taken prisoner by the Russians, and carried off to Sebastopol. After an hour's fight the enemy were driven back to their batteries. During this affair we had ten officers and one hundred men placed *hors-de-combat;* the French had fifteen officers and two hundred men killed, wounded and taken prisoners. On the other hand the enemy lost between seven hundred and eight hundred men. The number of dead Russians lying along the front of our trenches proved that they got a severe chastisement, and that they experienced a heavy loss.

The bodies of one officer and sixteen men remained in our trench until next day, and in front of our trenches the ground was covered with their dead. About one o'clock next day flags of truce were run up from the Redan and Malakoff, and shortly after white flags were waving from the top of ours and the French batteries; previous to the white flags being run up, not a soul was visible in front of the lines. The instant the flags were hoisted, friend and foe swarmed out of the batteries and trenches, the sight was a strange one. The French, English and Russian officers saluting each other most courteously as they passed, and a constant interchange of civilities took place. But while all this civility was going on, the soldiers of both sides were carrying off their dead comrades from the blood-stained ground, which was covered with strong proofs of the recent battle. There British, French and Russian soldiers, lying as they had fallen in their gore with broken muskets, bayonets, pouches, belts, fragments of clothing, pools of blood, broken gabions, fascines, and torn sand-bags visible on every side; and the solemn procession of soldiers, bearing their comrades to their last resting place, looked a most ghastly spectacle. In the midst of all this evidence of war, a certain amount of lively conversation took place between the Russians and our men, such as, "Bono Inglas, Francais no bono, Roosso bono," they lead us to understand that they liked the British soldiers much better than the French, although we always made it hot for them whenever we met, for which they gave us the name of "red devils." It took two hours to bury the dead, at the end of that time the armistice was over, and scarcely had the white flags disappeared behind the parapet of the Redan, before a round shot from the sailors' battery knocked through one of their embrasures, raising a pillar of dust; the Russians at once replied and the roar of big guns drowned all other noise. It is generally believed by the officers and men, that our batteries will open a general bombardment on Sebastopol about the tenth of April. The greatest excitement and activity are displayed in Balaklava, at the railway station, and all round the harbour, with crowds of fatigue parties and labourers engaged in piling up shot and shell, and loading the railway with ammunition, of which immense quantities are being sent up to the front.

The first passenger train from the front to Balaklava was one loaded with sick soldiers, who were sent down to Balaklava.

On the 2nd April five trucks filled with sick and wounded men ran down from the front in less than half an hour; the men of course were much more comfortable than those sent down on mules during the winter. Sickness in camp, I am glad to say, is diminishing every day, instead of sending down a thousand men a week to Scutari, as we did a month ago, we now despatch on an average only two hundred.

April 6th. This evening our mortar battery fired several shells into the Redan, and after the explosion, beams of timber, trunks of bodies, legs and arms of human beings were seen to fly up in the air; and after a time a blaze of fire ran along a portion of the works, which sprang from one of the enemy's mines. The 68th Regiment furnished one hundred men for a working party in the advanced trench last night, and were pounced upon by a working party of Russians, who were throwing up a trench, within sixty yards of them, and a regular hand to hand fight ensued, The men of the 68th who were armed with the new Enfield rifle, could not draw their ramrods, the wood of the rifle, being new, had swelled with the rain and continued dampness, causing the rifle to get woodbound; this has occurred more than once to my own knowledge; therefore after the first volley, they had no resource but to use their bayonet and butt end of their rifle, billhooks, pickaxes, and spades, which they were working with when the Russians came upon them. After the sentries gave the alarm, the covering party from the third parallel came to their assistance, and at last the Russians were repulsed, after a severe struggle. Our loss was about 60 men killed, and wounded; the Russians lost 200 men killed and wounded, out of 800 who were engaged in the affair. I am glad to state that the 17th Regiment have got up two wooden huts at last, one for the grenadiers and the other for the light company; and besides we are now getting a small supply of wood from the commissariat department. The weather is fine, and the camp ground getting dry. We have also got a divisional canteen established, close to the camp of the 57th Regiment. We can now purchase several articles of luxuries, such as butter, cheese, bread, bottled ale and porter, besides several other useful articles, which the men require to nourish and strengthen them, after the hardship they suffered during the severe winter. As regards food and shelter, our men are getting better off every day; we are getting flannel comforters now, when we do not want them. It is a pity that we did not get these things last winter. All the materials we possess now were to be had for moving them, and the thankfulness which the survivors feel for the use of them is tinged with bitter regret that our loved departed comrades can never share again our present comforts. As these neat huts, rise up in rows one after another the eye rests sadly on the rows of humble mounds which mark the resting placc of those who perished in their muddy blankets, under a wet and cold tent. There is not a regiment out here, but has some generous friend in the mother country, whose care and bounty have provided them with luxuries and comforts beyond all price to the sick and declining soldier; some have sent tobacco, cheese, arrowroot and warm clothing. The bounty, kindness and love of the people at home have now most liberally contributed to the wants of the army. About 12,000 Turks have just landed at Kamiesch Bay, they had a long march to the heights of Balaklava. It was astonishing that so few men fell out of the ranks or straggled behind. They had a good brass band which astonished the British soldiers by "Rule Britannia" as they marched past our camp; most of the regiments were preceded by drums, fifes and trumpets.

The colonel and his two majors rode at the head of each regiment, richly dressed, on small but spirited horses, covered with rich saddle-cloths, and followed by their pipe-bearers. The mules, with the tents, marched on the right, and the artillery on the left; each gun was drawn by six horses; the baggage animals marched in rear. The regiments marched in column of companies, most of the men were armed with the old flint-lock muskets, which were clean and bright. They all displayed rich standards blazing with cloth of gold, and coloured flags with the crescent and star embroidered on them. All the men carried a small pack with a blanket on top, a small piece of carpet to sit on, and cooking utensils. As they marched along they presented a very warlike appearance, the reality of which was enhanced by the thunder of guns at Sebastopol, and the bursting of shells in the air. The troops attended divine service on Easter Sunday; the Roman Catholics have erected a small chapel in the 4th division, and a priest celebrated mass outside the chapel, and preached a most eloquent sermon. The troops were formed up in close column by regiments, forming three sides of a square, the chapel filling up the fourth side. It was a very imposing sight; the square of soldiers standing with fixed bayonets and presenting arms at the elevation of the Host, the priest in the centre, bare-headed, and his vestments flowing in the breeze. The Protestants attend divine service in the open air regularly on Sundays, since the chaplains to the forces have arrived. On Easter Sunday the French had High Mass in each of their camps, with all the pomp of military bands. On last Saturday the regiments of the 4th division turned out every man off duty, and dug a deep trench and built a fence round the burial ground, placing a rustic gate at the entrance.

CHAPTER XIX.

BOMBARDMENT—TENTS BLOWN DOWN—SIEGE—LIEUT. WILLIAMS—WOUNDED—SAILORS—GO TO HOSPITAL—DESCRIPTION—SARDINIANS—DISCHARGED FROM HOSPITAL—ATTACK ON QUARRIES—FLAG OF TRUCE—BURYING THE DEAD.

EASTER Monday, at day break, the whole line of batteries simultaneously opened fire on Sebastopol; and as the firing commenced, the overhanging clouds seemed to have burst with the terrific thunder of the big guns and mortars; and the rain poured down in torrents, accompanied by a high breeze; so thick was the atmosphere that even the flashes of the guns were invisible, and the gunners must have fired at guess work by the flashes of the enemy's batteries, as it was impossible to see more than a few yards in advance. A driving sheet of rain and a black sea fog shroud the whole camp, which has resumed the miserable aspect so well known to us already; tents have been blown down, the mud has already become very deep, and the ground covered with slush and pools of dirty water. Our batteries are thundering away continuously in regular bursts, and are now firing at the rate of forty shots a minute; when they first opened they fired eighty shots a minute, but with the down pouring of rain and fog, it is hard work. As it was not necessary to press the gunners they have slackened the fire considerably.

The Russians were taken completely by surprise when our batteries opened fire. The Redan and Garden batteries came into play at once after we opened, but some time elapsed before the Malakoff or Mamelon answered. A sharp fusillade took place in the night between our advanced trenches and the enemy. The piquets were reinforced on the heights of Balaklava, and on the plain at night.

Lord Raglan, Sir John Campbell and General Jones, R. E., as wet and drenching as the day was, posted themselves in their favourite spot at the Green Hill trench, whence they could get a good view along the whole of the batteries. At five o'clock the sun descended in a dark pall, which covered the sky, and cast a pale light upon the masses of curling vapour across the line of batteries. The outlines of the town were faintly visible through the mist of smoke and rain. It seemed quivering inside the lines of fire around it. The ground beneath was lighted up by incessant flashes of light, and long trails of smoke streamed across it spirting up in thick volumes tinged with fire. This glimpse of the batteries, brief though it was, proved extremely satisfactory. The French batteries were firing with energy on the Flagstaff and Garden batteries, which were replied to very feebly by the enemy.

April 12th. The 17th Regiment furnished 450 men for the trenches. After being inspected at sundown by the Brigadier, Colonel McPherson, C.B., we marched down to the

Green Hill trench under the command of a field officer; the 68th Regiment furnished a like number. As we were relieving the 21st and 57th Regiments, the Russians opened fire with tremendous salvoes from their batteries. Our gunners made excellent practice and soon silenced several of their most troublesome guns, and at every shot the earth was knocked up out of the enemy's parapets and embrasures; our shell practice was not so good as it might be, all on account of bad fuses.

The French had silenced ten guns on the Flagstaff batteries, and had inflicted great damage on the outworks. On our side we had silenced half the guns in the Redan, and Malakoff; but the Barrack and Garden batteries were not much injured, and kept up a brisk fire against us of round shot. During the night the firing was very heavy on both sides; there was a continuous roar of big guns and morters. We discharged large quantities of rockets into the town, and our mortars kept up a steady fire on the Redan and Garden batteries. During the night we were greatly exposed to the enemy's fire, for we were employed, as hard as we could work, in patching up embrasures, platforms, and mounting big guns; we had mounted two guns in the second parallel, broken platforms were renewed, and damaged guns replaced by others.

April 13th. At dawn this morning, the batteries on both sides commenced their terrible duel as usual, and it was evident that the Russians had wonderfully exerted themselves to repair damages during the night; for they had replaced four or five damaged guns, repaired broken embrasures, and injured parapets, and were as ready to meet our fire, as we were to meet theirs. The firing has not slackened all day; about three o'clock we were repairing the battery on the left of the second parallel, when the Russians opened a fierce fire of shell and round shot; one of the latter knocked the head clean off the shoulders of one man, dashing his brains into Captain O'Connor's face, and all over the breast of his tunic. As he was getting the man's brains washed off his face and clothing, a piece of shell struck Lieutenant Williams, and cut his eye clean out of his head. As I was gazing with horror at the officer's eye hanging down on his cheek, a piece of shell struck me on the head, cutting through my forage cap and sinking into my skull. This was all done in less than five minutes, the shelling was fearful. I have seen six shells burst in the trench at one time. Lieutenant Williams and myself with several others were *hors-de-combat* for some time after. The doctor in the Green Hill trench dressed our wounds, when we were conducted by a couple of bandsmen to the hospital.

The sailors have suffered severely, although they only work about forty guns in the different batteries; they have lost more men in proportion to their number than any of the other siege trains; at the time I got wounded they had then seventy men killed and four wounded, besides two officers killed and four wounded. The sailors in Chapman's battery silenced five of the best guns in the Redan yesterday; but the Russians replaced them during the night, and opened fire from them in the morning. The Redan is very much damaged on the right and front face, already four of the embrasures are knocked level with the inside of it, but the Russians work hard repairing their batteries during the night; they are so numerous they can spare the men; besides they have not to carry shot and shell as far as we have. When I got to the hospital the doctor examined my wound and dressed it and put me to bed; the first I lay on since I left Gibraltar last year, and the first time I was ever sick in hospital. The change seemed to me a strange one—the doctors were so attentive and unremitting in the care of the sick and wounded men, and so many hospital orderlies waiting on us. I did not think at the time that I deserved such attention and kindness as they were bestowing on me; for I often saw a man getting an uglier wound from the crack of a shillaly at a fair in Ireland, but the doctor made me believe that the wound was much worse than I thought it was at first.

There were many men in hospital with diarrhœa, dysentery, and a few with scurvy; sick and wounded men kept coming in from the camp and trenches, day and night, the worst cases are to be sent down to Balaklava. I am glad not to be one of them, I do not want to go far from my dear old regiment. At the end of three weeks, I was returned fit for duty once more, thanks be to God, and recommended for light duty for a few days.

May 2nd. I was discharged from hospital this morning, the day was warm and beautiful, and a gentle breeze fanned the canvas of the wide-spread streets of tents, for we have only two wooden huts up for the 17th Regiment as yet. I was anxious to have a look at old Sebastopol once more, and see how it looked after the storm of shot and shell, which I have heard roaring and bursting for the last three weeks that I have been in hospital; so I went up to Cathcart's Hill just at the left of our camp ground. As the day was clear and fine the reports of the guns and rifles became more distinct, the white buildings, domes, and cupolas of Sebastopol stood out with menacing distinctness against the sky, and the ruined suburbs and massive batteries seemed just the same and looked as strong as when I saw them three weeks ago.

May 16th. The Sardinians are massing on the hills all round Karanyi daily. Three steamers have arrived yesterday laden with these troops. They have landed all ready for the field, with their transport horses, carts, mules, and vehicles; they looked gay and every one admired the air and carriage of those troops. Our eye was much struck by the large gay plume of green feathers on the top of their dandy shako. The officers wear a plume of green ostrich feathers. They carry very small square tents which are upheld by their lances stuck in the ground, one at each end of the tent, and their encampment, with its flags all round it, has a very pretty effect. We are all very sorry to hear that Miss Nightingale has been ill with fever in Balaklava.

June 3rd. For the last two weeks firing has been very slack, and trench duty has gone on quietly with two and three nights off at a time. The Russians throw an odd shell into our trench to remind us that they are on the alert; we can see the shell black in the shining sun, as it describes its circle high in the air, and at night they are more plainly seen—with a tail like a comet, they are heard whistling, coming through the air, apparently up among the stars.

There has been an unusual languor on the side of the Russians; some say it is due to sickness raging in Sebastopol, others say it is due to the desire of economizing ammunition; but most of us think that it is the warmth of the weather that has dulled their energies. But there is one thing that we do know, for we can see it, that they are working away to strengthen and provision the fortress on the north side.

June 6th. At three p.m., the whole of the batteries encircling Sebastopol have once more for the third time opened a most terrible fire on its batteries. The English and French are now in strength and power equal to any achievement and in the best of spirits, and are anxious to get a good charge at the Russians with the bayonet. Every one feels that the intention of going beyond a vain bombardment is tolerably plain, and we think with some strong defiance of the risk. This afternoon Lord Raglan and General Pellisier, with their staff, rode through the camp, amidst the cheers and acclamations of both their armies. There cannot be any doubt as to the zeal of those whom they command.

Our fire was kept up for the first four hours with the greatest rapidity. The superiority of our fire over the enemy became apparent at various points before nightfall, especially on the Redan, which was under the special attention of the sailors' batteries. After dark the fire slackened somewhat on both sides, but the same relative advantage was maintained by our artillery.

June 7th, at 11 a.m. a shell from the enemy exploded a magazine in our eight gun battery, and a yell of applause by the Russians followed the report. Happily the explosion caused very slight harm; one man killed and one wounded. As the day wore on, it leaked out that something of import was undoubtedly to take place before its close; and that the double attack would probably commence at five or six p.m. The fire on our side which had continued until daybreak steadily assumed a sudden fury at three o'clock, and was kept up from that hour to the critical moment, with great activity. The affair itself came off but little after the anticipated time. It was about 7 o'clock p.m. when the head of the French attacking column climbed its arduous road to the Mamelon. A rocket was thrown up as a signal to our division, and instantly the small force of our men made a rush at the Quarries. After a hard hand to hand fight we drove out the Russians and turned round the gabions and commenced to fortify ourselves in our newly acquired position. At the same time the French went up the side of the Mamelon in most beautiful style, like a pack of hounds trying to rout a fox from his old cover; the Zouaves were upon the parapet firing down upon the Russians; the next moment a flag was up as a rallying point, and was seen to sway to and fro, now up, now down, as the tide of battle raged around it; and now like a swarm they were into the Mamelon, and a fierce hand to hand encounter, with bayonet and musket ensued; and after a very hard contested battle the French succeeded in driving the enemy from the Mamelon.

In the meantime our men fought hard at the Quarries, and repelled six successive attacks of the Russians, who displayed the most singular daring, bravery and recklessness of life, to maintain their possession of the Quarries.

June 8th. Repeated attacks were made on our men in the Quarries during the night, who defended their new acquisition with the utmost courage, and at great sacrifice of life, against superior numbers, continually replenished. More than once there was a fierce hand to hand fight in the position itself.

The most murderous sortie of the enemy took place about three o'clock in the morning; then the whole batteries were lighted up with a blaze of fire, and storms of shot were thrown in from the Redan and other batteries within range. When morning dawned the position held by both French and English was of the greatest importance. The morning brought out on every side, along with the perception of advantage gained, and a prey lying at our feet, all the haste and circumstances of the scene, with its painful consequence of death and suffering. On our side about 400 rank and file and 40 officers were killed and wounded. The French had 1,200 killed and wounded. Next day flags of truce were hoisted from the Malakoff and Redan and Flagstaff batteries, which announced that the Russians requested an armistice to bury their dead; it was a grave request to make in the midst of a fierce bombardment, evidently a ruse to gain time, events hanging in the balance, success, perhaps, depending upon the passing moment; but it was granted by Lord Raglan. I dare not criticise his lordship. From one o'clock until six in the evening, during which time no shot was fired on either side, while the dead bodies, which strewed the hill in front of the Quarries were removed from the field of slaughter. The corpses which incumbered the earth, and were in process of removal, gave out faint tokens of coming putrefaction; fragments of bodies and marks of carnage were interspersed with, as usual, gabions and broken firelocks.

During the five hours' armistice the enemy, with their wonted perseverance, had been making good use of their time, which we knew they would; and when the firing commenced, which it did instantly on the flags being lowered a few moments before 6 o'clock; it was plain that the Malakoff and Redan had both received a reinforcement of guns; so much for politeness, for the Russians were most artful in hiding their working parties during the armistice.

June 11th. We had many men killed and wounded during the night in our new positions, into which the Russians kept firing grape and canister from the batteries which flank the rear of the Redan.

News had reached the camp that Miss Nightingale has

quite recovered from her serious illness, and that she has embarked on board Lord Ward's steam yacht for Scutari. We all pray and trust that she may so improve in health and strength as to enable her to come amongst our wounded men once more at Balaklava hospital; for her presence there is worth all the doctors' medicine. God bless her, prays an honest Roman Catholic. This morning I received, from my wife in England, a letter which conveyed to me the sad intelligence that my youngest child, Elizabeth, had died on the 30th of last April.

CHAPTER XX.

BOMBARDMENT—THE ASSAULT—GREAT REDAN—THE BATTLE—BALAKLAVA—HOSPITAL—MISS NIGHTINGALE—NURSES—PROMOTED—DISCHARGED FROM HOSPITAL—DEATH OF LORD RAGLAN.

AFTER the contest for the rifle-pits and Mamelon, on the 8th and 9th, a temporary lull took place in the siege operations, which was necessary, in order to make preparations for a yet more formidable assault on the Malakoff and Redan, of which the Mamelon and Quarries were mere advanced works. Therefore, on the morning of the 17th June, 1855, the batteries of the allied armies before Sebastopol opened fire from the whole line of trenches, from left to right. The tremendous roar of big guns and mortars was terrible. What a pity that this bombardment had not been kept up until the general assault took place next morning, which Lord Raglan had intended; but in order to suit the wishes of General Pellisier, it was most unfortunate that his Lordship was induced to abandon his intention, instead of which the Russians were allowed to strengthen their batteries and reinforce them with troops, owing to the lull in the firing. By the time the assault was made, they were well prepared to meet us.

June 18th. At 2 o'clock in the morning, the 4th division,

under General Wyndham and Sir John Campbell, consisting of the 17th, 20th, 21st, 57th and 63rd regiments. were marched down to the twenty-one gun battery; thence by files through zigzags to the Quarries, under a galling fire of shot and shell from the Redan, the 17th Regiment leading. As we reached the Quarries, the men got packed closely together in such a small space; and the Russians, having the exact range, threw the shell right amongst our men, tearing them to pieces, throwing their legs and arms high in the air, as we stood there a target for the Russians, waiting for the two rockets which was the signal from the French, when they got into the Malakoff. A shell struck Sergeant Connell of the grenadier company, tearing him to shreds, and throwing one of his legs fifty yards off; which was found afterwards and known by the regimental number on his sock. That leg was all of him that could ever be seen afterwards. Paddy Belton, the third man from me, got struck with a shell and torn to pieces, and several others. We had much better have tried to get into the Redan, than to stand there in suspense, a target for shell and shot. The sailors and 20th Regiment were told off to carry scaling ladders, and wool packs, the latter were placed on the field, as cover for the riflemen, who were told off to cover the advance of the storming party, firing at the Russian gunners, through the embrasures. As the ladder party advanced toward the ditch of the Redan, the storm of grape, canister, rifle-bullets and pieces of old nails and iron were discharged from the big guns of the Redan, besides a cross fire from the curtains of the little Redan and Malakoff, causing great slaughter to the small party of sailors and 20th Regiment. I saw one of the ladder carriers knocked down from one end by a shot, when the weight of the ladder devolved on the other man who dragged it along the best way he could, till he was also knocked over. After hard tugging, several had got as far as the abatis where they had another delay; for during the night the Russians had repaired and strengthened it. This obstructed the advance of the ladder party, who used the greatest exertions to remove that barrier; all who were not shot worked through and deposited their ladders in the ditch of the Redan. Of those who fell, their ladders lay on the ground between the Quarries and Redan. The ladders were barely deposited in the ditch, when Lord Raglan gave the order for the advance of the storming parties, which consisted of the 17th, 21st, 57th and 63rd Regiments, this small party, led by Sir John Campbell, were to attack the left side of that immense and formidable stronghold, the great Redan.

The light division, led by the gallant Colonel Yea, consisting of the 7th, 23rd, 33rd, 34th, 77th and 88th Regiments, the right side, and the 2nd division the centre or apex. On the signal being given, Captain John Croker sung out at the top of his voice, "Grenadiers of the 17th, advance," when the company bounded over the parapet, like one man, led by their captain, followed by the other companies. When the Russians saw us advancing, they opened such a terrific fire of grape, canister and musketry, that it was almost impossible for any man to escape being hit. As we advanced up to the abatis, Sir John Campbell was shot, also my noble captain, John Croker, who was struck with a grape shot in the head, and fell.

LINES ON THE DEATH OF SIR JOHN CAMPBELL AND CAPTAIN JOHN CROKER.

Who fell leading the assault on the great Redan, June 18th, 1855.

Ye Grenadiers ! who fear no foe and scoff at death,
Full well I know that, to your dying breath,
You'll fight like warriors, or like heroes fall,
So now obey your Queen and Country's call.

To crush those Russians with relentless hand,
And scale their ramparts like a gallant band,
Let John Campbell's orders be our guide,
We'll fight and conquer by that hero's side.

Nor will we humble at the Russian bear ;
While God is with us we need never fear ;
Grasp tight your swords for victory's glorious crown,
And share with none those deeds of high renown.

The warriors brave around John Croker stood,
Within the Quarries ready for to shed their blood,
While Captain Croker on the signal given,
Cries: Grenadiers advance ! and trust your fate to heaven.

Stung with desire, they raised the battle-cry,
And rushed well forward to win the fight, or die ;
Our captain waved high his sword and then,
Onward he dashed, followed by all his gallant men.

Who with one loud hurrah, the silence broke,
And charged like Britons through the fire and smoke ;
A moment more and then the bloody struggle came,
With roar of cannon and with flash and flame.

While piled in ghastly heaps the brave soldiers lay,
Filling the trenches with their dead that day,
John Croker's voice was heard above the battle din,
Leading his company through death and slaughter then.

Until at last the fatal bullet riven,
Laid our hero low and sent his soul to heaven;
Deep was the grief and sorrow at his loss we bore,
As that noble chieftain lay weltering in his gore.

While round his ghastly corpse we bravely tried,
To quell the sweeping torrent of the Russian tide
That rushed upon us with such resistless fire,
And levelled our heroes in heaps, there to expire.

But few escaped of the forlorn band,
Of that chivalric company Croker did command;
But those who did, stuck by their leader still,
And laid his corpse to rest on Cathcart's Hill.

T. FAUGHNAN.

At this time, if the commander had supported us, we would have taken the Redan; but the few men who were sent out were shot down. Scarcely a man advanced as far as the Redan but got either killed, or wounded. I got shot through the right arm, fracturing the bone. As I was coming back, covered with blood, for the wound was severe, I saw a man named John Dwyer, who got struck with a grape shot in the thigh. He said to me: "Oh Faughnan I am kilt entirely." He had scarcely spoken, when a round shot struck him again and put an end to his sufferings. I was conducted to the ravine, at the Woronzoff road, by a drummer, where the doctors and hospital orderlies were in their shirt-sleeves, hard at work, amputating legs and arms, and binding up wounds; it was fearful to see all the legs and arms lying around. After the doctor stopped the blood, with a patent bandage, he dressed my wound, and sent me to hospital, on an ambulance waggon, with twelve other wounded men. During the assault on the Redan and Malakoff, the third division, under General Eyre, consisting of the 9th, 18th, 28th, 38th, and 44th Regiments, with a company of picked marksmen, under Major Fielden, of the 44th Regiment, were pushed forward to feel the way, and cover the advance. At the signal for the general assault, the 18th Royal Irish, being the storming party, rushed at the cemetery, and got possession, dislodging the Russians, with a small loss; but, the moment the Russians retired, the batteries opened a heavy fire on them, from the Barrack and Garden batteries.

The 18th at once rushed out of the cemetery towards the town, and succeeded in getting into some houses. Captain Hayman was gallantly leading his company when he was shot. Once in the houses, they prepared to defend themselves. Meantime the enemy did their utmost to blow down the houses with shot, shell, grape and canister; but the men kept close, though they lost many men. They entered these houses about six o'clock in the morning, and could not leave them until eight o'clock in the evening. The enemy at last blew up many of the houses, and set fire to others. When our men rushed out of them the fire was now spreading all over. The 9th also effected a lodgment in some houses, and held their possession as well as the 18th. Why were these men not supported by large bodies of troops, so as to take the enemy on the flank, and round behind the Redan? Whose fault was it? Not the men's! Whose fault was it that the Redan was not breached by round shot, and the abatis swept away before the assault was made? Not the men's. Whose fault was it that large supports were not pushed forward to the Redan, on the assault being made? Not the men's. Nothing can be compared to the bravery, daring and courage of the officers and soldiers of the British army, when they are brought properly into action; but when a handful of men are sent to take a stronghold, like the Redan, armed as it was with all sorts of destructive missiles, and manned by an immense force, it could not be expected that men could do impossibilities. An armistice to bury the dead was granted by the Russians, and at 4 o'clock in the afternoon of the 19th, white flags were hoisted on the Redan and Malakoff; and in an instant afterwards burying parties of the French and English, emerged from the trenches, and commenced to carry off their dead and bury them in rear of the trenches, all in one grave, and in their clothes as they lay, except the officers, who were taken to camp, and buried at Cathcart's Hill. Many wounded men were found close to the abatis, who were lying there thirty-six hours, in their blood-stained clothes, in the scorching sun, without a drop of water to quench their thirst. Several had crawled away during the night, and hundreds had died of their wounds as they lay. After the burial was over, the white flags were lowered and firing commenced again once more. As the ambulance waggons moved along the Woronzoff road towards the hospitals, I could not help regretting our loss in officers and men, more especially Captain John Croker. He was a very strict officer, but a very kind gentleman ; that is, he expected every man to do his duty faithfully and zealously, and beyond that, he was indulgent, generous, and always anxious for the comfort, happiness, and amusement of his company. A better, braver, or more dignified and gentlemanly officer, a kinder friend than Captain John Croker was not in the service, nor one more precise, more exacting, more awake to the slightest professional neglect of duty, and his loss to the grenadier company, I am sure, will be deeply and sorely felt; he was a native of the County Limerick. On arrival at the hospital the doctor examined my wound, and found that the bone was fractured. He then set it, after taking out three splinters, dressed it, put it in a splint, gave me a glass of brandy, and put me to bed. The hospital was getting so crowded, I was one of a party of wounded men who were sent down to Balaklava hospital on mules, next day at ten o'clock. The number sent down from the divisions were two hundred; each mule carried two patients; we sat back to back. On arrival at Balaklava hospital, we were told off to comfortable huts, each containing beds or cots. The wounded men were separate from the others; those very severely wounded were put to bed, and at dinner time one of Miss Nightingale's ladies came round, and spoke kindly to us, and examined our wounds, which we appreciated very much; and at tea time the same lady brought us arrowroot and port wine. Next morning the doctor dressed our wounds, and the lady brought us all sorts of delicacies. How different to the camp rations of salt junk and hard tack; and now we had a real lady to nurse us and attend to our wants. I thought that it was worth getting wounded to have such attendance. Nothing could surpass the kindness and attention which these ladies showed the wounded men; each of them has a certain number of patients under her care; and truly their kindness and unremitting exertions did more good to alleviate the pain and suffering of the wounded men, than all the doctor's medicine. The weather was so very hot, that my arm began to swell, so that the doctor got alarmed and consulted another doctor, when they decided to amputate my arm. I did not like the idea of losing my arm, but the doctors thought the swelling would get into my body; so when the nurse came round with the arrowroot in the evening, after she had washed and dressed my wound, she advised me not to have my arm taken off, but go down to a spring that gushed from a rock at the foot of the hill, and there hold the wound under the stream as long as I could bear it, every day. I did as she told me. I then told the doctor that I would not have my arm taken off. I sat at the spring all day, except at meal times, and held my arm under the cold water that rushed out of the rock, and at the end of a week the swelling reduced. From that time it began to get better; I was in good health and was allowed to walk round the hills during the day. The head surgeon, Dr. Jephson, allowed us every privilege, and our nurse brought us note paper, envelopes and postage stamps, so that we could write home to our friends. The invalids were allowed to roam round the rocks all day between meal times. The hospital, which has been recently established, affords great comfort to our sick and wounded men, who will be saved the evils of a sea voyage to Scutari. It already presents the appearance of a little village with small patches of gardens in front of the huts; and its position on those heights, among the rocks, overhanging the sea and steep crags, which wind up past the old Genoese tower that stands at the entrance of Balaklava harbour, to the height of our camp over the sea, is strikingly picturesque. The judicious surgical treatment of my arm, and the careful manner in which the doctor's directions were carried out by our nurse, together with holding it under the stream of cold spring water, soon restored it to its use again; several other men whose wounds were very severe were fast improving under this lady's care. Her assiduity and skill as a nurse, as well as the gentle kindness of her manner, fully warranted the greatest respect from her patients, who almost idolized her, whose presence in the hut stilled the pain of the wounded men. We often wondered whether she ever slept, as she seemed to be always attending one or another of her charge. Miss Nightingale had left Balaklava for Scutari a few days ago, so I had not the gratification of seeing that heroic lady, whose honoured name is often mentioned among the soldiers of the British Army with the most profound respect—that high born lady Florence

Nightingale, the sick and wounded soldier's friend, whose name will be handed down to future generations, as the greatest heroine of her sex, who left her happy home with all the genial associations, comforts and social attractions, which her birth, education and accomplishments so well enable her to appreciate; going out to a country wherein every turn spoke of war and slaughter; taking up her abode in an hospital, containing none of her own sex, save those noble ladies who accompanied her as nurses; watching and tending the sick from morning till night, among hundreds of wounded, sick, emaciated and hungry soldiers. All these things considered, there has indeed rarely, if ever, been such an example of heroic daring combined with feminine gentleness. Although there is a heroism in charging the enemy on the heights of Inkerman, in defiance of death and all mortal opposition, worthy of all praise and honour, yet the quiet sympathy, the largeness of her religious heart, and her wondrous powers of consolation, will ever be remembered with the love, thankfulness and affection of the soldiers of the British Army, and by no one more than T. Faughnan.

LINES TO MISS FLORENCE NIGHTINGALE.

At the Crimean war, thy life was new;
You left your home, and country too,
To tend the wounded with hands so fair,
To Balaklava Hospital you did repair.

Miss Florence Nightingale, for you is given
The soldier's prayer to God in Heaven,
That you may soar to Him above,
For your right noble valour and Christian love.

If Angels are here, on earth below,
You must be one of them we know;
For flesh and blood can not compare,
Such genuine valour and angelic care

As you displayed, without one thought
Of the sleepless nights on you it brought,
May God His blessings on you descend,
Is a soldier's prayer whom you did befriend.

When you this earthly race have run,
May Angels lead you to the Son,
There to sing with Christ for evermore,
Whom here, on earth, you ever did adore.

T. Faughnan.

After it was ascertained at the regiment that I was not killed, as was reported, but only wounded, and in hospital at Balaklava, the commanding officer had me promoted to full corporal, and my promotion dated back from the 1st of April previous, which left me three months' back pay to draw. This news reached me a few days before I was discharged from hospital. On the 20th of August, I was discharged from hospital, and once more proceeded to join the regiment in camp. After thanking the Sisters for all their kindness and attention to me while under their charge, I bid them all good-bye, and started for the front with six others.

On arrival at camp, the first I met was Major Gordon, who was very glad to see me. He said to me, "Faughnan, we all thought you were killed that morning. I am sorry I did not know that you were only wounded before I sent off the returns; I would have recommended you for the Victoria Cross—but it cannot be helped now, as I have recommended Corporal John Smith for it." I thanked him very kindly, and joined my company, who were all well pleased to see me.

There is a sad feeling among the officers and soldiers in camp, and deep regret evinced, at the loss of Lord Raglan, who departed this life at nine o'clock, p.m., the 28th June, 1855. His death appears to have at once stilled every feeling but that of respect for his memory; and the remembrance of the many long years he faithfully and untiringly served his country, and his frequent cheering visits among the men in camp, had endeared him to the army now before Sebastopol. A military procession was formed at four o'clock in the afternoon of the 3rd of July, to escort the body to Kazatch Bay. As many as could be spared from duty in the trenches and, with safety to the camp, from every infantry regiment, formed an avenue from the British to the French headquarters, and from thence to Kazatch Bay, where the "Caradoc" was ready to receive her melancholy freight. The French troops formed a similar avenue. The cavalry and batteries of artillery were formed up behind the lines of infantry, and bands were stationed at intervals, and played the Dead March as the procession moved slowly along the route marked out by the lines of infantry. The coffin was carried on a gun carriage—the soldier's hearse. At each side rode the four commanders of the allied armies; then followed all the generals and officers who could be spared from trench duty. As the solemn procession moved along, minute-guns were fired by the field artillery of the French. At Kazatch Bay, marines and sailors were formed up on the wharf; the naval officers were in attendance; and the body of Lord Raglan was placed on board of Her Majesty's Ship "Caradoc," and removed from that battle-field where both his body and mind had suffered for the last nine months, and where many hundreds of gallant officers lie in their gore and glory, waiting for the sound of the last trumpet.

CHAPTER XXI.

CAPTAIN COLTHURST—SIEGE—BOMBARDMENT—ASSAULT—REDAN—THE BATTLE—8TH SEPTEMBER—THE EVACUATION—RUSSIANS—BRITISH IN SEBASTOPOL.

AUGUST 25th. Captain Colthurst arrived at camp with a draft of three hundred men, who were posted to the different companies, to fill up the vacancies left by those who fell in battle, or died in hospital, or camp, during the winter. During the month of July and August our loss in the trenches was very heavy, although the achievements were not such as brought great fame and honour to the hardworking army. The outworks had approached so near the Russian batteries that our trenches afforded very insufficient shelter from shot, shell, and rifle-bullets which killed and wounded so many of our working parties; swelling the list of dead and wounded very much every twenty-four hours. Every thing was now reported ready by the engineers and artillery officers for one last and desperate assault on the fortifications.

The labour bestowed by the Russians to strengthen the Redan and Malakoff was almost inconceivable—a formidable abatis of sharpened stakes in front, a parapet thirty feet high, ditch twenty feet deep by twenty-four feet wide, with three tiers of heavy guns and mortars rising one above another. Such was the Malakoff and Redan. The plan of assault was, a vigorous fire to open on the enemy's batteries, by the Allies, on the 5th, 6th and 7th; followed on the 8th of September, 1855, by a storming of the Malakoff by the French, and of the Redan by the British. Generals Pellisier and Simpson arranged that at dawn, on the 8th, the French storming columns were to leave the trenches, the British to storm the Redan, the tricolor flag planted on the Malakoff was to be the signal that the French had triumphed; and the British were then to storm the Redan, for unless the Malakoff was captured first, the Redan could not be held as the former was the key of the position, therefore the Malakoff should be attacked first, and with a very strong force.

Appalling in its severity was the final bombardment of Sebastopol. It began at day-break, as previously arranged by the commanders. The shot and shell shaking the very ground with the tremendous reverberation, raising clouds of earth and overturning batteries along the Russian lines, filling the air with vivid gleams and sparks and trains of fire, burying the horizon in dense clouds of smoke and vapour, and carrying death and destruction into the heart of, and all over, the city. After three hours of this tremendous fire, the gunners ceased for a while to cool their guns and rest themselves; then resumed with such effect that the Russian earth-works became awfully cut up, without however exhibiting any actual gaps or breaches, which would have befallen stone batteries, under such a storm of shot and shell; proving the defensive power of earth-works. Darkness did not stay this devastation; shell and shot continued to whistle through the air, marking out a line of light to show their flight, and crashing and bursting against the defences and buildings. The Malakoff and Redan, when no longer visible in daylight, were brought out into vivid relief by the bursting of shells and the flashes of guns. One of the ships in the harbour caught fire from a shell, and was burnt to the water's edge. All through the night the fire continued; which prevented the Russians from repairing their parpets and embrasures, and with dawn on the 6th, the roar of cannon was only interrupted by a few intervals to cool the guns. The enemy seeing that the hour of peril had arrived used almost superhuman exertions to work their batteries, increased agitation was visible among them, and several movements seemed to indicate the removal from the south to the north side of the harbour of all such persons and valuables, as would not be required to render assistance in the defence. Again did a night of intermittent fire ensue. On the 7th, another ship was burnt in the harbour by our shells; flames broke out in the town, and a loud explosion like that of a magazine took place in the evening.

THE NIGHT BEFORE THE BATTLE, 8TH SEPT., 1855.

To-morrow, comrade, we
At the Great Redan must be,
  There to conquer, or both lie low!
The morning star is up,
But there's wine still in the cup,
  And we'll take another tot, ere we go, boys, go,
  And we'll take another tot, ere we go.

'Tis true, in warrior's eyes
Sometimes a tear will rise,
When we think of our friends left at home,
But what can wailing do,
Sure our goblet's weeping too !
With its tears we'll chase away our own, boys our own,
With its tears we'll chase away our own.

The morning may be bright ;
But this may be the last night
That we shall ever pass together ;
The next night where shall we
And our gallant comrades be,
But—no matter—grasp thy sword and away, boy, away,
No—matter—grasp thy sword and away.

Let those who brook the lot
Of the Russian great despot,
Like cowards at home they may stay ;
Cheers for our Queen be given,
While our souls we trust to heaven,
Then for Britain and our Queen, boys, hurra ! hurra ! hurra !
Then, for Britian and our Queen boys, hurra !

THOS. FAUGHNAN.

On the morning of the 8th, a destructive and pitiless storm of shot and shell continued until noon, when the fire of our batteries ceased, and the storming columns of the French issued forth, preceded by riflemen and sappers and miners. The French had bridges as substitutes for ladders ; the ditch was crossed by the bridges, and the parapet scaled with surprising celerity. Then commenced the struggle, with guns, rifles, pistols, swords, bayonets, and gun-rammers ; but in a quarter of an hour the tricolor flag floated on the Malakoff, announcing that the formidable position was taken.

Although the French had captured it, the Russians so well knew its value, it being the key to the whole position, that they made furious attempts at recapture. But the French General judiciously sent powerful reserves to the support of McMahon, and these reserves maintained a series of desperate battles against the Russians within the Malakoff, bayonet against bayonet, musket against musket, man against man. The contest continued for several hours; but the French triumphed, and drove the Russians from their stronghold.

Anything more wildly disorderly than the interior of the Malakoff can hardly be imagined. The earth had been torn up by the explosion of shells, and every foot of the ground became a frightful scene of bloody struggles; thousands of dead and wounded men being heaped up within this one fort alone. As soon as the tricolor was seen floating on the Malakoff, two rockets gave the signal for the British columns to storm the Redan. Out rushed the storming party, preceded by the ladder and covering party, a mere handful altogether; indeed it appears astonishing that so few should have been told off for so great a work; every soldier had a perilous duty assigned him. The riflemen were to cover the advance of the ladder party, by shooting down the gunners at the embrasures of the Redan; the ladder party to place the ladders in the ditch. As soon as the storming party rushed from the Quarries, the guns of the Redan opened a fierce fire on them, sweeping them down as they advanced. Col. Unett, of the 19th Regiment, was one of the first officers that fell, and Brigadiers Von Straubenzie and Shirley were both wounded, and scarcely an officer who advanced with the storming party but got either killed or wounded. The distance from the Redan to the Quarries was too great, being over two hundred yards, which gave the enemy a good opportunity to mow the storming party down with a tremendous fire of grape, canister, and musketry. The survivors advanced and reached the abatis, the pointed stakes of which, standing outward, presented a formidable obstacle to further progress; however, the men made gaps through which they crawled. Then came another rush to the ditch, when the ladders were found to be too short. However, our men scrambled down, and climbed up, many falling all the time under the shot of the enemy. Officers and men were emulous for the honour of being among the first to enter this formidable battery; but alas too weak in the numbers necessary for such an enterprise. Mounting to the parapet, the besiegers saw the interior of the Redan before them filled with masses of soldiers and powerful ranges of guns and mortars; wild and bloody was the scene within the assailed fort. Colonel Wyndham (afterwards Sir Charles) was the first officer to enter; and when fairly within the parapet, he and the other officers and men did all they could to dislodge the Russians from behind the traverse and breast-works; but the Russians overpowered our handful of men that were sent to take this stronghold, for we had no support to back up those that got a footing in the Redan. The Russians continued bringing up reinforcements and soon overpowered the few British who saw they must either retire or remain to be shot down. New supporting parties kept arriving in such driblets and in such confusion as to render impossible any well-directed charge against the place. If, for a time, a few men were collected in a body, volleys of musketry, grape, canister, and old pieces of iron of every description, fired from their big guns, levelled our men to the dust. The officers and men at last seeing no supports coming to their aid, lost heart and retreated to their trenches.

The embrasures of the parapets, the ditch, and all round the abatis became a harrowing scene of death and wounds, heaps of dead and wounded lay all round the Redan, and piles of them lay at the bottom of the ditch, where they fell by the Russian shot, as they climbed up the scaling ladders. At two o'clock the attack was over, and in these two hours the British loss was very severe. No other day throughout the war recorded so many killed and wounded, which amounted to the large number of 2450 in all. The French loss was three times more severe, it comprised no less than 7550 killed and wounded.

Next day another attack was to be made on the Redan. Sir Colin Campbell sent down a party cautiously in the night to see how the Redan was occupied, it was found to be vacated ; telling plainly of the abandonment by the Russians, of the south side of the town. It appears that Gortchakoff, when the impossibility of maintaining his position became evident, commenced blowing up the public buildings of the town ; the gunners, during the early hours of the night, kept up a sufficient fire to mask their proceedings in the stillness of the night when the allied camps were filled with men, either sleeping or thinking anxiously of the scenes which day-light might bring forth. Lurid flames began to rise in Sebastopol ; explosions of great violence shook the earth, and intense commotion was visible to the men in the trenches. The fires began in various parts of the town, and tremendous explosions behind the Redan tore up the ground for a great distance ; and other explosions succeeded so rapidly that a thick murky mass of smoke and flames from burning buildings, imparted an awful grandeur to the scene. Now came a resistless outburst which blew up the Flagstaff battery ; then another blew up the Garden battery. As day-light approached, Fort Paul, Fort Nicholas Central, and Quarantine Bastion were seen surrounded by flames. We could not withhold our admiration of the manner in which Gortchakoff carried out his desperate plan, the last available means of saving the rest of the garrison.

On the morning of the 9th September, when the troops in camp, heard the announcement that the mighty city had fallen, the city which, during twelve months, had, day by day, been looked at and studied by our generals and engineers, and in front of which 10,000 of our troops had been killed, or wounded on the preceding day. With difficulty was the announcement credited, so accustomed had all been to the dashing of their hopes, and the non-fulfilment of their predictions. I was one among many who hastened into the town and was astonished at the enormous extent of the batteries, and the manner in which our shot and shell, had knocked down and tore up the massive buildings. The French soldiers rushed into the town, peered about the burning houses, and plundered them of tables, chairs, looking-glasses, and countless articles, and carried them up to their camp. The French soldiers always keep a bright lookout for plunder. I must say that our men did not touch a single article, that I ever heard of, except one man, who found a lot of money in a bank. He emptied it into his haversack, and left at once. The bank clerks in their excitement and hurry must have forgotten to take the money in their haste to get out of the city. We had a chain of cavalry all round the town, to keep back stragglers, and stop any person from taking anything out of the town; thus ended the wondrous Siege of Sebastopol. On the 9th of September, when the allied commanders found that the Russian garrison, together with inhabitants, had crossed to the north side of the harbour it became their duty to ascertain whether any traps or explosive mines had been laid by the enemy, before our troops could be allowed to occupy the town, to ward off camp-followers, and divide the spoils of the garrison between the two invading armies; and to take measures for the destruction of the forts, and docks.

The appearance of the town, at the time that we entered it, was fearful indeed. Destructive forces had been raging with a violence never before equalled in the history of sieges; and the whole internal area was one vast heap of crumbled earth-work, shattered masonry, shot-pierced buildings, torn-up streets, scorched timbers, broken guns and muskets, and shattered vehicles. The buildings were shattered into forms truly fantastic; some of the lower stories almost shot away and barely able to support the superstructure; some with enormous gaps in the walls. Proofs were manifold that the Russians intended to defend the town street by street, had we forced an entrance; for across every street, were constructed barricades defended by field pieces. In some of the best houses columns were broken by shot, ceilings falling, which these columns had once supported; elegant furniture crushed beneath broken cornices, beams, and fragments of broken looking-glasses, mingled with the dust on the marble floors. The effect of our 13 inch shells had been extraordinary. These dread missiles, of which so many thousand had been thrown into the town, weigh 200 pounds each, and falling from a great height, have the weight of over sixty tons, descending deep below the foundation of the houses, and when they explode, scattering everything around far and wide. Our army still continued to encamp outside the town; sending only as many troops as would suffice to guard it, and take up the principal buildings among the ruins for guard-houses. Now we have plenty of wood, each company sending a fatigue party daily from the camp to Sebastopol for it. These parties could be seen by the

Russians from the north side pulling down the houses for the wood, and carrying it to camp. While doing so the Russians invariably fired upon us, from the north side of the harbour; where they have thrown up very strong forts, armed with the heaviest guns. They have placed some of those guns with the breach sunk into the ground, in order to get elevation; and throw shot right into our camp amongst our tents; not unfrequently killing and wounding our men.

We have now regular guards and sentries all over Sebastopol. After posting a sentry one day, I happened to go down some steps which led to the basement of a large building, and there I found to my horror fifteen dead Russians. My sense of smell first detected them in the dark vault; they were in the worst state of putrefaction. It was found on removing them, that they had all been wounded and had crawled in there and died from their wounds. We buried them where thousands of their comrades were buried, in rear of the Redan. The army is now quiet, no firing, except an odd shot from the Russians at our fatigue parties in Sebastopol. We have no trench duty to perform, nothing but the regular camp guards; we have plenty of fuel and good rations; any amount of canteens on the ground; so we are making up now in comfort for the hard times we had last winter. The army was now at a stand still, having nothing to occupy their time.

But the commanders began to look forward to a second wintering in the Crimea as a probability. Invaluable as the railway had become, it was inadequate to the conveyance of the immense bulk and weight of supplies required day by day, in the army, and hence it is necessary to do that which, if done in the early part of last winter, would have saved so many valuable lives—to construct a new road from Balaklava to the camp. Therefore the road was laid out and large numbers of our men worked on them daily; but making roads is only child's play compared with making trenches under shot, shell, grape and canister. The whole of the divisions were kept continually at road-making; the road promises to be a splendid one and we were all anxious to make it. We had no less than 10,000 men working on this road, between Balaklava and the front. By the end of October a most excellent road was constructed, including branch roads to the several divisions. The French at the same time constructed a road across the valley which connects their camp with the main road to Kamiesch; and besides they have improved the old Tartar roads.

Our army suffered much last winter from the want of roads. This excellent road which the British army has constructed, will ever remain as a memento of British occupation. During the three weeks of September which followed the evacuation of the south side of Sebastopol, the Russians were quietly but actively strengthening their fortifications on the north side; making all the heights bristle with guns, and firing a shot whenever an opportunity offered to work mischief upon our guards, sentries and fatigue-parties in the town. We had planted a few guns in position so as to bear on the northern heights; but no disposition was shown to open a regular fire on them, except an odd shot to remind them that we were ready for them at any time.

Camp rumours arose concerning some supposed expedition into the interior of the Crimea, but the securing of the captured city was regarded as the first duty.

On the 20th September, 1855, the anniversary of the battle of the Alma, a distribution of the medals for the Crimea, and clasps for Alma, Balaklava and Inkerman, took place among the troops; these decorations were very much appreciated by the officers and men. The day was commemorated with much festivity and amusement in both camps.

CHAPTER XXII.

EXPEDITION TO KINBURN—THE VOYAGE—ODESSA—LANDING—CUTTING TRENCHES—BOMBARDMENT—THE WHITE FLAG—CAPITULATION—THE PRISONERS — RECONNAISSANCE — THE MARCH — VILLAGE—BIVOUAC—MARCH—A VILLAGE—PIGS AND GEESE—DEPARTURE—THE FLEET—RETURN—SIR W. CODRINGTON—RUSSIAN SPY.

AN expedition to Kinburn having been decided upon by the allies, on the 6th of October a squadron of H. M. fleet were in readiness at Kamiesch Bay to convey the 17th, 20th, 21st, 57th, and 63rd Regiments, together with marines, artillery and engineers, under the command of General Spencer. As we marched to Kamiesch Bay the morning was close and sultry. When we got a third of the way private Hanratty fell out of the ranks and reported himself sick, when Captain Smith calls out, "Corporal Faughnan, take Hanratty back to hospital." "Yes, sir," says I, we were then marching down a very steep hill. I marched back to the hospital, although I was badly able, for I was bad with dysentery myself at the time, and for upwards of two weeks previously, and was so weak that I could scarcely march ; but I did not wish to give in and be left behind. After I gave over the sick man I saw the regiment a long way off in the valley. I marched as fast as I was able with a full kit. In the afternoon rain commenced to drizzle, and the regiment halted to cloak. I then gained on them and soon overtook them. When we halted at the beach I could have fallen down from weakness and exhaustion, but I kept up my pluck and never gave in. The troops were embarked on board the fleet by small steam-tenders; the 17th Regiment had the honour of being conveyed to Kinburn by the flag ship "Royal Albert."

On the 7th October, the troops having been on board, and every thing ready, we set sail, accompanied by several line-of-battle ships, small steamers, gun-boats, mortar-vessels, and three French floating batteries, constituting an armament of great magnitude. The English squadron comprised six steam line-of-battle ships, seventeen steam frigates, ten gun-boats, six mortar vessels, three steam tenders and ten transports. The Russians north of Sebastopol were in wild excitement when this large squadron appeared; but the ships soon disappeared from the Crimea.

The admirals signalled to the several captains to rendezvous off Odessa. As we got out to sea the band discoursed music while the officers were at dinner; before dinner they played as usual the "Roast Beef of Old England," which we had not heard for many months before.

We had no hammocks so we were obliged to lie all round the decks in groups during the night. At eight o'clock next morning we cast anchor off Odessa, three miles from the town. It was then the turn for the citizens to be alarmed by this display of force.

The Russians on the heights, in barrack square, and all

round the city became incessantly active in making observations. We could see the old fashioned telegraph on the towers along the coast working, and clouds of Cossacks, infantry and artillery, formed up along the cliffs, ready to defend the place if attacked. All day on the 9th, the fleet remained at anchor; about 80 French and English vessels forming a line six miles in length, eagerly watched from the cliffs by large masses of troops; the rocket-boats, gun-boats, mortar-vessels, and floating batteries might have gone nearer and crumbled the city to ruins; but such was not our orders, and not a shot was fired, and thus was Odessa spared for the third time during the war.

The object of the admirals in making this feint on Odessa, was to draw the Russian troops away from Kinburn; thereby reducing the number of troops in that garrison.

The 10th, and 11th, we were still at anchor, dense fogs giving the seamen a foretaste of the dangers of that coast; and as the 12th and 13th were very stormy, the admirals would not risk leaving until the weather moderated; thus it happened that the citizens had the threatening fleet in view for six days. The squadrons weighed anchor on the morning of the 14th, and cast anchor off Kinburn that afternoon; in the evening some of the French and English gun-boats entered the estuary of the Dnieper, passing the Fort of Kinburn under a heavy fire from the enemy.

On the morning of the 15th, the troops were landed

along the beach out of range of the fort; by the launches of the ships, each being filled with soldiers; and made fast to each other by means of the painter. After the troops were all got into the launches, they formed several long lines of red coats in little boats, each boat was steered by a naval officer.

The front boat of the line being made fast to a small steamer, the whole were then towed in front of the beach, where we were to land. As the steamer ran in towards the shore, she cast off the line of boats, and while they were under way each let go the painter, and headed towards the beach, running in close on a sandy bottom, when the troops jumped ashore and deployed from where we landed to the River Dnieper, while the gun-boats went up the river. By this double manœuvre, the Russians were prevented from receiving reinforcements by sea, while the garrison were cut off by land. In the evening the mortar vessels began to try their range on the forts.

The troops brought no tents and only three days' rations. After posting outlying pickets, we were set to work cutting a trench from the sea where we landed to the river Dnieper, a distance of five miles. While we were digging the trench during the day, the outlying pickets had a skirmish with a small force of Cossacks; but the chief labour was the landing of stores and artillery, tedious and dangerous work over the rough surf, occasioning the swamping of some of the boats. A camp was formed, but without tents. At two o'clock in the morning we had the trench cut and manned ready to receive the Russian reinforcement for the garrison, which were expected from Odessa, but which did not come. However, a large force of Cossacks came along at three o'clock in the morning, when we opened a heavy fire upon them from our new trench, forcing them to retire quicker than they came, we then kept a good look out till morning. Generals Spencer and Bazaine made a cavalry reconnaissance at day-break when the Cossacks retired altogether.

About four companies of the French and English marksmen were placed under cover at a distance of four hundred yards in rear of the fort, and kept up a fusilade on the Russian gunners; while at the same time the artillery opened a strong fire on the fort; at nine o'clock the ships opened fire on the garrison.

The "Royal Albert," "Algiers," "Agamemnon" and "Princess Royal," and four ships of the line approached abreast of the principal fort; the "Tribune" and "Sphinx" attacked the earth-work battery. The "Hannibal," "Dauntless" and "Terrible" took position opposite the battery near the end of the fort, while the smaller vessels directed their attack on the east and centre of the fort. Thus the Russains, from the shape and position of the fort, were attacked on all sides at once. Each ship poured its broadside upon the port and the strand batteries as it passed, and received the enemy's fire in return. From nine o'clock until noon these powerful vessels maintained their terrible fire against the forts, crashing the parapets and disabling the guns, while the mortar vessels set fire to the buildings within the fort. The "Arrow" and

"Lynx," with others, were exposed to much danger. Having taken up a position close to the batteries to discharge their shell upon the fort, they received in return an iron torrent which tried the resolution of the crew.

At twelve o'clock, the Russians hoisted a white flag, when an English and a French officer met the Governor at the entrance of the fort, when he tendered his surrender in military form by giving up his sword, but not without bitter tears and a passionate exclamation expressive of wounded national and professional honour. The officers bore the scene with dignity, but with deep mortification, and many of them were on the verge of mutiny against the Governor, so strong did they resist any proposals of surrender. The garrison laid down their arms, and were marched outside the town and placed close to our camp, with a chain of our sentries and the French around them. The number of prisoners taken were 1,500, besides 500 killed and wounded, several of our doctors were sent to attend their wounded in the fort.

The prisoners were divided, the English half were taken on board the "Vulcan," while the other half were taken on board the French ships. The prisoners having been sent off to Constantinople, the captors proceeded to garrison Kinburn, repairing and increasing the defences, clearing away the ruins, repairing the walls, and embrasures, replacing the damaged cannon by large ship guns, deepening the ditch, reforming the palisades, strengthening the parapets, restoring the casemates, completing efficient barracks and magazines, in the interior of the fort, and depositing a large amount of military stores of all kinds.

When the small garrison, the other side of the estuary, opposite Kinburn, Àczakoff, found that their guns could effect little against the invaders, and that Kinburn was forced to yield, they blew up the St. Nicholas battery, on the morning of the 18th, and retired a few hours afterwards. On the 20th, Generals Spencer and Bazaine set out on a *reconnaissance* with several regiments of both forces, about five thousand strong. After marching on a sandy plain, like a desert, ten miles, we halted close to a village, piled arms, and were allowed to go foraging into the village, which we found deserted by the inhabitants; but they left abundance of pigs, geese, fowls and provisions, bread baking in the ovens, pails of milk and several other most useful articles, besides in the garden we found abundance of potatoes, cabbage, tomatoes, pumpkins, and almost all sorts of vegetables. We divided the town with the French; after tearing down several houses for fuel and making camp fires, we commenced cooking fowls, turkeys, geese, potatoes, cabbage and vegetables; while others were off through the village killing pigs, geese, turkeys and chickens. Others cutting down branches of trees from a wood hard by, for the purpose of making huts to protect us for the night, as we had no tents, and covering them with hay from the hay yards, and shaking plenty of hay inside to lie on; every mess erected one of these huts. After indulging in the good things, which I can assure you we enjoyed, we lay down very comfortable for the night in the hay, and slept most soundly. Next day at two o'clock General Spencer reviewed the troops under his command, with the French general; his soldiers looking on. We were to have the pleasure of another night in this camp. After enjoying boiled fowls, roast turkeys and plenty of fresh vegetables, we lay down among the hay and slept well, thanks be to God. Next morning, after breakfast, we marched to another village named Roosker, ten miles off. We halted outside the village, and sent in foraging parties from each regiment, dividing the town with the French and placing a line of sentries in the centre. As we approached the village, the people fled, leaving everything behind, pigs, geese, ducks, fowls, bread, milk and butter. As we killed the live stock, we placed them on the commissariat waggons and brought the spoils back to camp. It was a most amusing scene, the French and English officers and soldiers shooting geese, ducks and hens, with their revolvers, and the men chasing the pigs and stabbing them with their bayonets. A soldier catches a pig by the hind leg, the animal drags him into the French lines, when a French soldier claims the animal, and a kind of a good natured quarrel ensues about the ownership of the pig. The geese rose in flocks, and the officers had the greatest sport shooting them. These were jolly times. After ransacking the town, we set fire to it, and marched back to our old bivouac, ten miles distant.

After arriving at our old camp ground, lo! and behold! our huts were all demolished, and not a thing left on the ground. The Cossacks had been there during our absence, and burned and destroyed everything. We could see them away in the distance, about 400 strong, watching our movements; however, we bivouacked there as best we could that night. As we marched back, we passed several windmills which we set fire to. Next morning we marched to Kinburn with the commissariat waggons loaded with pigs, geese, fowls, turkeys, potatoes and cabbage, which were served out as rations in the usual manner.

On the 28th October, Generals Spencer and Bazaine began their arrangements for our departure, first shipping all the stores, guns and horses, and selecting a sufficient number of troops to garrison and guard Kinburn during the winter; but to bring away all the other forces. Sir Edmund Lyons and the French Admiral selected the vessels which were to be left to protect the place from any Russian attack across the estuary. On the morning of the 29th, the troops embarked on board the fleet from the wharf at Kinburn.

The 17th Regiment were conveyed to the Crimea, by the "Terrible." It was a most imposing spectacle, this magnificent fleet sailing in line with the two flag ships leading, and signalling their orders to the captains of the other ships; the line extended over ten miles. What must the Russians along the coast think of this immense armament? The fleet cast anchor in Kamiesch Bay, on the 1st November; and the troops disembarked at once, and marched to our old camp on Cathcart's Hill.

This expedition did the troops more good than all the medicine in the hospital could have done. I was a new man when I got back. If Hanratty had braved it out as I did, and had come on with the expedition, he might have been well by this time, instead of which he is yet in hospital. The change of air and fresh vegetables worked wonders in restoring and invigorating the men's health. On our return to camp we found that a quantity of rum which was left behind, with other regimental stores, in charge of a sergeant and twelve men, was all gone; for which the sergeant was tried and reduced, and the privates were severely punished.

During the month of November we had another change in the command of the army, the appointment of General Sir W. J. Codrington, vice General Simpson. This appointment of Sir William was very popular with the army, and brought increased activity among the troops.

Among other improvements, which were made to meet the wants of the army, was a large reservoir in the ravine between the 2nd light, and the 4th divisions, in the construction of which the French took a prominent part. This reservoir is capable of supplying three divisions of the British and three of the French with abundance of good spring water during winter and summer. Everything seems to have been done now to protect and meet the wants of the army during the coming winter. Almost every kind of supplies is in abundance, and the army in the best of health and spirits.

I was in command of a divisional guard, near the Tchernaya valley, when a Russian spy was given in my charge by a cavalry *reconnaissance* party. I immediately posted a sentry to take charge of this prisoner; but he watched his opportunity and slipped out under the fly of the tent. The sentry gave the alarm, when I rushed out after him, calling a file of the guard to follow me. As I gave him chase, I threw off my accoutrements, in order to give me more freedom; he had then about one hundred and fifty yards start of me, and was barefooted, whilst I had heavy boots on; however, I gave him chase. We had run about two miles when I saw that I was gaining on him, and I kept gaining, little by little, for about five miles, when I came up behind him. I was then nearly out of breath; I kept close behind him a good while till I got my wind; then I threw my foot before him with the Connaught touch, and pitched him on his face; then I jumped on him and held him, keeping him down, lest he might overpower me if he got up, as he was a most powerful man, and the file of the guard had not come up to us yet. While I gave him an odd kick, he begged for mercy, which I granted, and marched the Tartar back, meeting the file of the guard as I was returning. If I had let that spy escape, I would have been tried by a court-martial; but my Irish experience in running, before I joined the service, stood to me then; I would have run after him into the Russian camp before I would have lost him. When I got back to the tent, I tied him to the pole with a guy rope, at the same time tying his hands behind his back. I was determined he should not get away again.

The camp followers and speculators have got so numerous that they have a large bazaar formed in the rear of the 4th division. Large shops of almost every description, saloons, billiard tables, restaurants, hotels, groceries, tobacconists, wholesale and retail liquor stores, and in fact almost everything that can be got in any town, can be had here for cash. There is another large bazaar in the French camp. As we assemble in Smith & Co.'s liquor store of an evening, drinking "Guiness's bottled stout," smoking our pipe or cigar with the greatest of comfort, we could but contrast our position with that of this time last year, when the inclement weather commenced. The want of food, forage, huts, clothing, fuel, medicine, roads, vehicles and horses, proved its tragic results. Men lay down in the mire to die of despair, and no commanding officer could tell how many of his poor soldiers would be available for duty next day. But now, towards the close of 1855, we have every kind of supply in abundance, thanks to the people of England! The army is well fed and well clothed, and we are looking out for some active operations against the enemy. The Russians continue to fortify the northern heights without firing a shot, and we occupy the south quietly, without disturbing them, how long this will last will be seen in the next chapter.

CHAPTER XXIII.

ARMISTICE—CESSATION OF HOSTILITIES—EXCHANGE OF COINS—HEIR TO FRENCH IMPERIAL THRONE—TREATY OF PEACE—INVITATIONS—GRAND REVIEW—REMOVAL OF THE ARMY—EMBARKATION—THE VOYAGE—SHIP ON FIRE—ARRIVAL AT MALTA—JOIN THE RESERVE BATTALION—PROCEED TO ALEXANDRIA—THE VOYAGE—ARRIVAL—VISIT PLACES OF RENOWN—VISIT CAIRO—THE NILE—ARRIVAL—THE CITY—BAZAARS.

AT the end of February, 1856, the diplomatists at Paris agreed upon an armistice during the discussion of a treaty of peace. The immediate effect was observable in the Crimea, as soon as the several commanders had received information. On the morning of the 1st March, a white flag was hoisted on the Tchernaya bridge, and near it assembled the Russian commander, a staff of officers and a troop of Cossacks. The English commander with his staff, accompanied by others from the French and Sardinians, descended across the valley to the bridge where they met the Russians with whom they discussed the details of an armistice. The cessation of hostilities was to last one month, during the consideration of the treaty. Through the aid of their interpreters they decided that the Tchernaya river was to be the boundary between the opposing armies. The quietest month spent by the allied armies in the Crimea, was the month of March, 1856. Hostilities were entirely stopped, and yet none could say whether they might not commence again with all its horrors. The diplomatists at Paris had one month to decide the question of peace or war.

The commanders, while maintaining their boundary arrangement, did not prohibit friendly meetings of the opposing armies on their respective banks of the boundary line, where the officers and soldiers frequently assembled to look at each other in peace and try to converse in a friendly manner across the stream, when the exchange of coins and other small articles or mementos took place, and an interchange of civilities such as "bono Johnny," "bono Francais," "bono Roos," beside other complimentary expressions. This intercourse was kept up during the month of the armistice. For the rest, the operations of the month differed little from those of the camp at Aldershot, all the divisions being exercised and reviewed in the open spots all round the camp. Sometimes the Russians held their reviews on the same day as we did, with the glittering bayonets of each full in view of the other, and both alike safe in the conviction that no unfriendly shot would disturb the pageant.

On the 23rd of this month, festivities in the French camp celebrated the birth of an heir to the French imperial throne; bonfires were kindled, guns fired, reviews held, horse-racing on the banks of the Tchernaya, healths drank by the French and their allies, even the Russians participated in the rejoicings, for they lighted fires all along their lines.

April brought with it the treaty of peace. Before the hour had arrived when the armistice would have expired, news was received that the treaty had been signed at Paris. When peace was proclaimed, an interchange of invitations took place between the Russian army and the allies. The Russian soldiers came over to our camp, in small parties at a time, and we did the same to their camp, each party in charge of a non-commissioned officer. I and twelve privates visited the Russian camp and their bazaar, which we found much the same as our own. All sorts of English goods were sold there, even "Bass's bottled ale," and "Guiness's porter," at a dollar a bottle. Their bread was as black as your boot; the coffee-houses were crowded with English, French, and Russian soldiers, drinking, singing, and dancing; and the interchange of any amount of "bono Johnny's," "bono Roos," and "bono Francais," trying to make each other believe that they were great friends.

On the 17th April the British and French troops had a grand review on the heights near St. George's Monastery (at which General Luders, the Russian commander, with his brilliant staff, was present). They were formed up in line of continuous quarter distance columns of battalions, when the commanders of the different armies with their gorgeous retinue of staff and cavalry officers rode along the line, with the bands of each regiment playing in succession; after which they marched past the grand assem-

blage of commanders and staff, in quick time, each regiment marching past in grand division style, with its band playing in front. General Luders returned deeply impressed with the appearance of the allied armies, and expressed himself much gratified at the attention shown him by the allied forces. Duties of a more serious character, however, now demanded the attention of the Generals. Large armies were to be removed from the Crimea, and vast stores of provisions and ammunition; besides all the round shot the Russians had fired at us during the siege, which we had gathered and carried on our back to the railway depôt for shipment to England; with all the commissariat stores brought down from each divisional depot at the front where they had been collected in such immense quantities. Day after day during the summer months did the various regiments leave the Crimea; some for Malta, others for the Ionian Islands, the West Indies, or Canada, but the greater part for England. All the camp equipage and stores for each regiment had to be brought into transport order, and everything brought to Balaklava for shipment.

About the 10th of May the 17th Regiment marched from their old camp on Cathcart's Hill, and embarked at Balaklava, at two o'clock in the afternoon, on board the steam transport "Sir Robert Low." At 3 p. m. we moved slowly out between the rocks which overhang the narrow entrance to the harbour. We were all on deck with tears in our eyes, taking a last sad look towards "Cathcart's Hill" where we had left so many noble comrades behind in that cold, desolate plateau, so far away from friends and relatives; these thoughts filled us with sadness. As our ship glided through the beautiful calm blue waters of the Euxine the land faded from our view. We then turned our thoughts homewards, after giving thanks to God for the great mercy he had shown in bringing us safely through all the death struggles and hardships which our brave troops had suffered; and now that we were returning alive we had every reason to be thankful.

The weather being fine, we made the passage across the Black Sea in 48 hours. The second day, at 2 p.m. we passed the old fortress of Riva which commands the entrance to the Bosphorus, passing Constantinople at 3 o'clock, taking a last look at that strange old city, with its picturesque sights, the tall minarets and the blue waters of the Bosphorus catching the golden light as the sun dipped behind the distant hills. We rounded Seraglio point and steamed down the Marmora, passing the Seven Towers on our right, and slowly the beautiful city faded from our view forever. We had a smooth passage across the Sea of Marmora. Next morning at ten o'clock we passed Gallipoli. On the 14th May, at 9 o'clock in the evening, as our ship was running at the rate of ten knots an hour, an alarm of fire came from the cook's galley. The troops were immediately formed up along the decks, and the pumps manned. After a quarter of an hour's hard work we mastered the fire, and put it out, but not before it had burned a large hole in the ship's deck, and destroyed the galley. We had in truth a narrow escape, the fire nearly getting the better of us. On the morning of the 17th May, we arrived at Malta, where we received orders to proceed to Quebec. The Regiment being over the strength of non-commissioned officers, those who had families at home got the preference of remaining behind, and joining the reserve battalion at Malta. I was one of the latter; after bidding good-bye to the old regiment, with tears in my eyes, I disembarked, with twelve others and joined the reserve battalion. The regiment proceeding to Canada next morning at 8 o'clock, we, after landing, were quartered in Strada Reale Barracks.

The garrison was at this time filled with the soldiers of more than one nation, and the medley of tongues was rather bewildering to the ears, as was the diversity of costume to the eyes. There were the Italian and German Legions, promenading the streets in their gay uniforms, Malta fencibles, English artillery and infantry. The large number of soldiers in such a small place made it a perfect military hot-house.

The Strada Reale, with its lazy moving crowds and singular architecture, was soon entered. Lights were beginning to brighten the shop-windows and streets; occasionally sparkling from the numerous bay-windows above; but though the night was approaching, the air, deeply impregnated with the fumes of tobacco and odour of garlic, was close and suffocating, more especially from the intense heat exhaled from the arid rock, which had all day blazed under a fierce sun. The barracks were so crowded, and the weather so hot, that the doctor ordered the 17th under canvas at St. Frances' Camp. An order detailed your humble servant, Corporal Faughnan, to proceed on June 6th, by one of the Peninsular and Oriental Company's steamers, to Alexandria, there to take over some marine invalids according to written instructions, and take charge of them to Malta.

June 6th. At nine o'clock, a.m., I embarked on board the steamer for Alexandria. As we passed out of the harbour at 9.30, the sky was blue and pleasant, the air balmy and clear. The Island, like a blue cloud in the distance, faded away, and again the trackless waste of waters stretched like a boundless expanse around us.

June 9th. It is now three days since we left Malta. We should have been in harbour to-day, but have been retarded somewhat by head winds.

June 10th. Expecting to enter port this morning, I was early on deck. We were already in sight of land. As we neared the coast, one of the first things that caught my attention was the number of windmills, standing upon an eminence along the shore; at first they reminded me of a line of soldiers in skirmishing order, but as we neared them they lifted their tall, circular form, and stretched out their sheeted arms, like huge sentinels, keeping watch along the coast. The entrance to the harbour is a tortuous and difficult one; vessels cannot get in by night or by day, without a very experienced pilot. We were straining our eyes to catch the first glimpse of the strange land, and there, just upon that projecting point of land we are now passing, where you see an insignificant light-house, stood a famous and costly tower, bearing upon its top, as it lifted its colossal form above the waves, a beacon-light to guide the mariner to his haven. It is said to have been so lofty it could be seen one hundred miles at sea—which, of course, is a mistake. This gigantic tower of white marble was erected by the old Egyptian kings three hundred years before the birth of Christ. It was one of the "seven wonders of the world." But here we are safe at our moorings. How strange everything looks. There are the hulks of a number of great old ships, rotting away and falling to pieces into the water. They were once the Viceroy's fleet. The flags of many nations float from the masts around us. There is a boat approaching with a Union Jack flying, and manned with blue jackets.

After landing the passengers, we had to pass through the Custom House. A liveried servant in Turkish costume, guarding the door, politely bowed us through, and we stood before the receiver of customs. He wore a rich Turkish costume, a magnificent turban on his head, a gold-hilted sword by his side; he addressed us in English and called all our names from a list; as we answered we passed on. No other questions were asked; personal baggage is seldom examined at this port. We had scarcely passed the door before we were surrounded by a crowd of donkey boys in blue shirts and red fez caps. They began pulling and snatching at our baggage, for the privilege of taking it to a hotel. Luckily, an omnibus, a European innovation, from the very hotel we had selected, stood at the entrance, and we made a sudden dash into it. A crack of the driver's whip, and we were whirling through the dirty narrow streets of the Turkish quarter of the city. We soon emerged into the English part of the town, and a magical change came over the scene ; a fine open square ornamented with fountains and surrounded with beautiful stone houses presented a most inviting appearance. A runner from the hotel conducted me to the Marine Hospital, when I presented the order for the invalids to return with me to Malta, when the surgeon informed me that two of the men had had a relapse and could not be removed for some time. This gave me a good opportunity to visit several of the renowned localities, places of antiquity and monumental records, that the ravages of war and the wreck of time have failed to obliterate. During the voyage I had made the acquaintance of two Frenchmen, and after I got back to the hotel they were pleased when I told them that I would have to stop at Alexandria for some time, and did not know how long; they could speak English pretty well and we got quite familiar. The hotel was kept by a Frenchman, and the business of the hotel was conducted on the European plan, but the floors and walls were constantly crumbling; scattering sand and lime upon clothes and furniture and affording plenty of hiding places for bugs and fleas. Of the presence of the latter we had too strong demonstration, but fleas in Egypt are as common as sand on the sea shore, and we made up our mind to pay the tribute of blood demanded by those pests with the resignation of martyrs.

We next visited Cleopatra's Needle, since removed

to London. Of these remarkable obelisks there are two, just within the walls and near the sea shore at the north-east angle of the city—one is standing, the other has fallen down and is now nearly buried in the ground. They are of the same material as Pompey's Pillar, red granite, from the quarries of upper Egypt. These two obelisks stood about seventy paces apart; the fallen one lies close to the pedestal, its length in its mutilated state, is sixty-six feet, and was given, many years ago by Mohammed Ali to the British government, who have lately brought it home. The standing one is about seventy feet high, seven feet seven inches in diameter at the base and tapering towards the top about five feet.

Next day we visited the Catacombs, which are about three miles outside the city; the Frenchmen hired a guide and we all rode on donkeys. The grounds near the entrance were once covered with costly habitations and beautiful gardens. The vast extent of these underground tenements, their architecture, symmetry, and beauty; the more wonderful from the fact that they are all chiselled out of the solid rock, must excite the greatest wonder and admiration. In these tombs, generation after generation have laid their dead; Egyptians, Persians, Greeks, Romans and Saracens have, no doubt, in turn used them, and different nations have here blended in the common dust, at least such is the common opinion. Ancient Alexandria, with all her magnificence and splendour, is now nothing but heaps of ruins. The modern city stands upon the ruins of the past—well may we say the great immortal past. An Egyptian city at night is a gloomy place—business suspended, shops all closed, no amusements, no meetings, no windows next the street to shed even a little light upon the gloomy alleys; all is involved in Egyptian darkness, but silence is not there, for dogs are among the wondrous speakers of this land. They howl about in packs like wolves, owning no master, making night hideous with their row and fights; in addition to this, the watchman's yell rung through the city every quarter of an hour; it woke me more than the guns before Sebastopol; a calm of fifteen minutes succeeds, and again the lengthened shout assures the citizen "all is well." Being disturbed by the watchman's call, howling of dogs, bugs and fleas, we could not sleep, so we were up early and had breakfast at seven o'clock, after which we all agreed to visit Cairo, and at once proceeded to the railway station, which, by the way, has only been lately constructed. The present facilities for reaching Cairo can only be appreciated by those who have been familiar with the former slow locomotion of canal and river. Then it was by the toilsome process of wind and oars. Now a first-class railroad of about one hundred miles connects the cities. At ten a.m. the signal was given, and we struck out into the great delta of the Nile; away to the left is the harbour of Aboukir, where the immortal Nelson with his fleet met the French in 1798. His victory was complete; all the French ships except two were captured, and the victor was rewarded with the title, "Baron Nelson of the Nile."

The immense green plain stretched out each side of us as

far as the eye could reach. Crops of some kind are raised all the year round, except when the soil is covered with water from the inundation of the Nile. There is no cold weather to prevent the growth of vegetables. Look out of the carriage window: do you see that long line of water just by the side of us? It is the Nile. The Nile! The famous Nile, that has a place in history with the Euphrates and the Jordan; for thousands of years sending out a living flood from its mysterious and hidden sources, rolling onward through this great valley, and emptying itself by its seven mouths, into the blue sea. A river which the Egyptians worshipped, and whose waters, by the rod of Moses, were turned into blood.

About 5 p.m. our train came to a halt in the station of Grand Cairo; we landed on the platform amid the strangest crowd of human beings I had ever seen congregated. There was the Turkish official, with his great loose sleeves and flowing robes, gold hilted sword and turbaned head, loathsome looking beggars, wretched women and squalid children. As we emerged from the station, a hotel porter, in English costume, addressed us in English, "Shepherd's hotel, sir? Omnibus just here, all right!" and in fifteen minutes we were in a good European hotel, built in the oriental style, with a large open court and pleasure-grounds; terms only two dollars a day. After tea, which was ready on our arrival at the hotel, we took a walk through the city. The streets are numerous, narrow, and crooked, there being but one in the business part of the town wide enough for a carriage; this public thoroughfare being only about 35 feet wide, many of the others are not more than ten feet. The upper stories of the houses projecting over the lower ones, and the large prominent windows projecting still beyond the houses, the windows of the upper stories are brought so near together, you could easily step from one to the other. The bazaars are very busy places, and are thronged by a mixed and motley multitude of people, camels, horses, donkeys, men, women, and children, mingled together in strange confusion, while the noise and bustle present a wild and striking scene that can be nowhere witnessed but in an Arabic city. Amid this wild confusion may be seen a great variety of oriental costumes. But the turbaned heads predominate, the black of the Copt, the blue-black of the Jew, the green and white of the Moslem are mingled in strange variety. There moves a lordly Turk with loose sleeves and flowing robes, with all the solemn dignity of his nation, the grandee, with his rich flowing robes of silk and lace, loose breeches, white stockings and yellow slippers, the swarthy skinned, half naked fellah, the bare-faced, half-dressed, toil-worn country woman with tattooed lips and eyebrows, and by her side the dignified lady with long close veil, red trowsers, long yellow boots, and dress of richly embroidered cloth. These ladies ride astride on donkeys, the ample folds of their long veils and loose robes almost hide the little animal from view.

CHAPTER XXIV.

THE PYRAMIDS — CROSSING THE NILE—ISLAND OF RODA—ARK OF BULRUSHES—VISIT CHEOPS—HELIOPOLIS—PALACE OF SHOOBRA—PALM GROVES—THE CITADEL—JOSEPH'S WELL — DERVISHES — RETURN.

AFTER hiring three donkeys to take us to the Pyramids next morning at eight o'clock, we retired to rest, and slept much better than we did the night before; the live stock were not quite so numerous as they were in the last hotel. We were up bright and early, had breakfast at seven o'clock, after which we mounted our donkeys and were soon outside Cairo, an old town on the banks of the Nile, founded upon the site of the old Egyptian Baby lon; it is much older than Grand Cairo. Here are the ruins of the old Roman fortress, besieged and taken by the Turks. The solid walls and high towers are yet standing, on the front of which may still be seen the Roman eagle. This fortress has now become a Christian town and is dedicated to St. George, the patron saint of the Copts. There are also three convents here, one is occupied by the Roman, Armenian and Syrian Maronites, another by the Copts, a third by the Greeks. In this Greek convent it is said that the Virgin and the Blessed Child, Jesus, had their abode during their sojourn in in Egypt; here, too, are ancient structures said to have been built by Joseph, and used for treasure houses, in which corn was stored for the days of famine. In an upper chamber over one of the towers is an ancient Christian record sculptured on wood in the time of Diocletian; it is well preserved and of curious device; below is a representation of the Deity sitting on a globe supported by two angels, on either side of which is a procession of six figures representing the twelve apostles. Just on the opposite bank lies Gizeh, from which the Pyramids are named, with a ferry at the upper end of the town. As we approached the ferry, we were surprised at the number of people who thronged the landing place; numerous boats of all sizes were waiting for freight; donkeys and their riders, camels with their huge burdens, ragged men and women were mingled together—antique-looking boats in strange confusion. After securing a ferry boat we gave the boatman an extra sixpence each to land us for a short time upon the beautiful little island of Roda whose grassy banks and shady groves have long been the resort of pleasure parties from Cairo. On this island stands the celebrated Nilometer; this is a square chamber built of stone, in the centre of which is a graduated stone pillar. By a scale on this pillar the daily rise of the Nile is ascertained; this is proclaimed every day during the inundation in the streets of Cairo. By this island, also, tradition fixes the place where a daughter of Levi, under the pressure of that cruel decree, took an ark of bulrushes, daubing it with slime and pitch and put the child therein and laid it in the flags by the river's brink. At this island, the faithful sister, Miriam, half concealed among the banks, watched with anxious solicitude the fate of her infant brother. Are these the waters that went rippling by the ark of the infant Moses, and over which he afterwards stretched his miraculous rod, transforming them into a torrent of blood? Oh Scripture, how wonderful thou art in thy story. Landing from the boat, we were in Gizeh, an old town, the miserable wreck of what it once was in the days of the Mamelukes. Passing along these streets large quantities of oranges, dates and other fruits with bread and vegetables were exposed for sale. We bought some of these things and had some lunch; after a half hour's rest we started again, we had now about four miles to make across the open plain, the huge pyramids all the time in sight; we passed three Arab villages on our way. The appearance of indolence and poverty is everywhere apparent. A dozen ferocious dogs with bristling hair and savage howl, were sure to herald our approach. As we emerged from the last village the gray forms of those great sepulchral monuments lay just before us; their huge proportions seemed rapidly to increase as we neared them. They stand upon a rocky eminence, their base elevated one hundred and fifty feet above the plain just at the foot of the range of hills, behind which lies the vast ocean of sands constituting the great Lybian desert.

The ride was over, and we stood in amazement at the base of Cheops. There are five groups of these pyramids, numbering in all about 40. They extend up and down the valley for ten or twelve miles; most of them have such gigantic proportions as to justly entitle them to a place among the wonders of the world. They all stand upon the brow of the hills opening back into the great Lybian desert. As we stood in deep contemplation, gazing in wonder on this mighty structure we had come to examine, what huge proportions; what an immense labour; what years of human toil! But they were built for all that, and here they stand, and have stood for thousands of years, defying the storms of the desert, and the lightnings of the firmament, how wonderful are the works of men. About a dozen Arabs, with loose trowsers, short jackets, and red fez caps, came up and spoke to us. "Want to go up de top sah?" said the leader of the gang, "me take you up, take you inside, all round." "How much you ask?" said one of the Frenchmen, "He's the sheik" pointing to the best looking, who stood erect, holding the folds of his striped gown about him with all the dignity of a Turk, "he's the sheik, he make de bargains." We agreed with the sheik, for a guide to show us up and down, inside, and all round, for a dollar. We started with our guide, we soon got up half way, and there we stopped to draw breath; the steps are from two to three feet high, corresponding to the thickness of the layers of stone; of these layers or tiers of stone, there are two hundred and sixty-five, the ascent is quite fatiguing especially if one attempts to hurry; it took us twenty minutes to reach the top. A few moments' rest, and I began to look about me, pondering on the magnitude of the stones, and the numerous names in many languages carved upon them. Forty feet of its top has been torn away, and what from the ground looked like a point too small to stand on, is a broad platform, thirty feet wide, I was surprised at the magnitude of the stones even at this height, two to three feet thick, and several feet long, what wondrous labour it must have been to elevate such masses of stone to such a height from the ground, and yet men now say such nations were ignorant and uncivilized.

I looked upon the broad plain that stretched away before me; there was much charming in the air, at this height, I took a survey of the great panorama, which lay in its variety and beauty at our feet. There was the green valley of the Nile, stretching away as far as the eye could reach, welcoming the golden sunlight that came down from the cloudless sky; with the majestic and wonderful river, as it rolled in dignity onward to its ocean home; yonder in the distance were the Arabian hills skirting the vast expanse of the Lybian desert, that lay in bleak sterility beyond; nearer by, a spot upon the landscape was the great city "Grand Cairo," its great gray towering citadel, its mosques and minarets; then I turned and looked down upon the battle field where Bonaparte, with thirty thousand men, met Murad Bey; where the memorable Battle of the Pyramids was fought, and Abercrombie fell; where Bonaparte tried to inspire his men with valour by pointing to these monuments, exclaiming; "forty centuries are looking down upon you from these mighty structures."

The thunder of the battle ceased, the smoke cleared away, thousands were left dead upon the field, and the triumphant Bonaparte camped within the walls of Grand Cairo. Cheops is a travellers' register, and many a visitor has inscribed his name upon the summit. After adding our names (an English barbarism I believe it to be; but it began in our schooldays), to the many already there, we descended in safety. As we approached the base, our guide led the way to the opening that conducts to the interior. This entrance is on the north side, and about fifty feet from the base. It is a low doorway for so magnificent a structure; but who expects anything but a dark and dreary passage to the tomb? for such is the place to where this opening leads, a tomb hidden in the most stupendous pile of stones the skill and labour of man ever erected. The entrance is a low one, and we had to stoop nearly double; we had entered but a few feet when we found ourselves involved in darkness. Luckily we had brought a couple of wax candles with us from Cairo; having lighted the candles we continued to descend the narrow, dismal passage. Our guide conducted us to the King's chamber; this is the great sepulchral chamber of this astonishing structure. Its length is thirty-four feet four inches; breadth, seventeen feet seven inches, and height nineteen feet two inches. The only piece of furniture this chamber contains is a chest of red granite, chiselled from a solid block, its size is larger than the passage leading to the chamber, so that it must have been placed there when the room was built. Was it for this sarcophagus this stupendous pile of stones was erected ? What has become of the lordly occupant ? When, and by whom was it filled, and when did it give up its treasure ? There it stands in mute and mock defiance of every effort to ascertain the history of its owner. Like the tomb of Jesus after the morning of the resurrection, it was empty ; the stone had been rolled away from the door, but no angel sat upon it to give the anxious visitor any tidings of its occupant. We now turned our attention to a few other interesting objects in close proximity. I had often heard and read of the Sphin , but now I had the gratification of looking at this great monster. We are first struck with its peculiar formation, and its immense proportions. It is one hundred and twenty-eight feet long ; from the rock on which it rests its lion-like breast, to the top of the head, is fifty-five feet nine inches. It is in a crouching posture, and it stretches out its enormous paws fifty feet in front of its capacious breast. This unwieldy monster is a monolith, cut from the native rock of the limestone of which it forms a part. This imposing head was adorned with a covering much resembling a wig, the flowing hair of which can still be seen projecting from each side. Time, the driving sands of the desert, and the hand of violence, have left their wasting influence on this noble piece of Art. The horns that adorned the head have been broken off, but there it stands, without them, still grand, noble and majestic.

The whole western bank in this vicinity of the green valley of the Nile, for miles and miles, has been consecrated to the repose of the dead. Here are the sepulchres of kings, mummy pits, ibis tombs and rock-hewn chambers, for the magnificent sarcophagi of Apis bulls. Here countless thousands have been gathered unto their fathers, and the sands of the desert are every year covering them deeper and deeper. In the centre of one of these pits was a large granite chest, cut from the solid block, very much like the one I have described in the king's chamber in the pyramid. This was covered by a lid of the same material. This lid had been carefully lifted off and set on one side. Within the chest lay the sarcophagus. It was covered with hieroglyphical figures and inscriptions, and looked as fresh and perfect as when first deposited. It had not yet been opened. Within that sculptured chest was sleeping the mummied remains of some distinguished personage. For thousands of years he had enjoyed here the quiet sleep of the tomb, among his fathers and kindred; but now his long repose must be disturbed, and in some far off museum, inquisitive strangers would gaze upon the blackened and withered features, and wonder who he was! After seeing those wondrous ancient monuments of Egyptian greatness and idolatry, and paying the sheik and a backsheesh to our guide, we mounted our lively little donkeys and returned to Cairo.

The sun was just dipping his golden disk beneath the western horizon, far over the distant deserts, as we entered the gates and wound our way through the narrow crowded streets of Grand Cairo. We crossed the suburbs, gained the hotel, and enjoyed a good bath. A hard day's toil climbing the pyramids gave additional relish to the smoking viands, and refreshed, we retired to bed, to dream of stone-coffins, mummy-pits and sphinx. We awoke next morning from a refreshing sleep. The sun was shining in at our windows, the songs of the birds were awaking inspiring echoes among the tangled foliage of the Ezbekieh, and the air was fragrant with the perfume of the sweet flowers of the East. The day was to be devoted to an excursion to some place of interest a few miles from the city. Breakfast over, we stood on the steps of the hotel and our three donkey boys whom we had engaged were in readiness; we mounted our donkeys and started off to visit the ruins of Heliopolis, the ancient On, or the city of the sun. These ruins are about six miles from Cairo and the ride a most delightful one, through green fields of corn and various productions of the luxuriant soil. Now an orange grove opens upon our sight, then an extensive vineyard, while all the time our pathway was shaded by avenues of tamarack, fig and acacia, that wove their branches in tangled arches above our head. As we approached nearer, a beautiful obelisk lifts its slender form high into the heavens, standing in solitary grandeur the only monument left to mark the site of the ancient opulent city. It is a single shaft of red granite sixty-eight feet two inches high and six feet three inches broad at the base. This is the oldest obelisk in existence, and here it stands in its original position. Its firm base and towering head have withstood all the assaults of time, the convulsions of the elements and the devastations of war. The wreck and ruin of four thousand years have not prevailed against it. The grounds around and in the vicinity of this obelisk have been cultivated, here the fellaheen sow their seed and gather their harvest, yet here stood one of the oldest and finest cities of the world, and here are buried the remains of some of the earliest temples. The ancient Egyptian name of the city, as interpreted, is the "City of the Sun." The Greeks called it Heliopolis, and the Hebrews Bethshemesh (House of the Sun). This place was one of the most celebrated seats of ancient learning; it was famed for astronomy as well as the worship of the sun. The sacred bull Murvis shared also with the sun, the divine honours of the city, and was one of the most noted among the sacred animals of Egypt. Not far from the obelisk is the beautiful fountain of the sun; the water springing directly from the earth. The people say this is the only living spring in the valley of the Nile. A few yards from this spring a very old sycamore tree spreads broad and thick its massive branches, forming an inviting shade. When Joseph and Mary, with the child Jesus, fled from the jealous and cruel Herod and took refuge in Egypt, tradition says they reposed under the shadows of these overhanging boughs and drank water from the renowned fountain. Here too, was the school of Moses. From the waters of the Nile that flowed but a little distance from here, the daughter of Pharaoh rescued the weeping infant; and she called him Moses, for she "drew him out of the water." In the court of Pharaoh he found a home. Here he became learned in all the wisdom of the Egyptians. How all those recollections forced themselves on me. We next visited the palace of the Shoobra; it is about four miles from the city and near the banks of the Nile. A beautiful avenue, shaded by acacia trees, leads from the city to it; when these trees are in bloom they fill the air with fragrance. The grounds are beautifully laid out, and are frequently open to the public, and large numbers of visitors resort to them. They are beautifully diversified with terraces, walks, towers, flowers and shaded avenues. Many of the walks are tastefully paved with small black and white pebbles, wrought into various designs of Mosaic work. The great attraction of the garden is a noble reservoir of water gushing from marble fountains in the form of crocodiles. From this beautiful place, where the senses are regaled by nature and art, we returned to the city and made a special detour, in order to pass through an Egyptian date palm grove. These groves are planted in rows like our orchards. It is surprising what a variety of purposes the tree serves, and how useful it is made. These trees sometimes grow from fifty to seventy feet high, and are of uniform size from top to bottom. The summit is surmounted by a beautiful crown of leaves. Every part of the tree seems to be of some use; a charming beverage is made from the fruit, used among the natives; wine is made from the sap. The bark and part of the wood are manufactured into mats, baskets, and various other useful articles, the leaves are manufactured into a great variety of fancy articles. But the large crop of fruit is what renders it most valuable, and the failure of the date crop is one of the greatest calamities that can befall the land; the tree is also ornamental as well as useful. They are the most beautiful and striking objects of Egyptian landscape scenery. This grove is very extensive and spreads over several miles of the country. But while we have visited these places of interest the day has rapidly passed, and the evening sun is throwing his parting rays upon the beautiful landscape, and we must hasten to our hotel. Once more we are threading our way through the narrow streets of the city, and our ears are saluted with strange sounds from the vendors of different articles, as they hawk them about. The streets are passed, the din of criers dies away in the distance; we are back to the hotel; a long ride and the delightful air has given us a good appetite for the evening meal which was ready on our arrival. After we had done justice to the delicious oriental viands, prepared for us by our hospitable host, we retired for the night and slept well. After breakfast next morning, we walked out to visit some of the ancient monuments of this wonderful city, The citadel was the first object of our admiration. It is the fortress of the city and tower of its defence, the depository of its munitions of war. It stands upon a hill, its massive frowning walls overlooking the city on one side, and on the other the great barren desert that stretches away towards the Red Sea. From this tower is one of the finest views that can be obtained. First cast your eye towards the great Lybian desert, and see the time-defying pyramids, from the top of which we have before contemplated this land of the Pharaohs. On the other side, the beautiful Nile, slowly weaving his serpentine folds through groves of palm, and along green and flowery banks, and a city of three thousand inhabitants at our feet, with the massive circuitous walls that enclose it; the great mosques and multitude of minarets that crown them all, forming one of the most remarkable and striking peculiarities of a Mohammedan country. Within this fortress stands a splendid palace of the Pasha, and by its side the harem, with beautiful fountains and pleasure grounds.

But what astonished us most, is the wonderful contrivance to supply the citadel with water; it is certainly worthy of the presiding genius of the land. This well is cut into the solid rock to the enormous depth of two hundred and sixty feet, and at the mouth fifty feet wide. Around the wall is a winding stairway cut also into the rock, with a partition wall of the rock left, about three feet thick, between it and the well, with occasional holes for windows to look through into the main shaft. Any one who has seen Dover shaft leading from Snargate street to the heights, will at once understand how this well is constructed. The open passage through the centre of that structure corresponding to the well; the circular stairway winding round it to the descent here, cut in the rock, by which the bottom is reached. One of the most striking things connected with the well, is the manner of elevating the water. A large ox is taken down this winding stairway near to the bottom of the well where a cog-wheel machine for raising water is situated. The food is taken down to him, and he is kept here as long as he is able to work.

This well was found covered up under a wall, by Sultan Yoosef (Joseph) while clearing away the debris when building the fortress in A.D. 1711, hence "Joseph's well." Turning from the well, we next pay a visit to the mosque of Mohammed Ali. It is a gorgeous structure, the finest and most renowned in modern Egypt, standing upon the hill of the citadel and enclosed by its ramparts; it lifts its proud form high above its companions. The whole interior, pillars, walls, and arches is of beautiful alabaster brought from the quarries of upper Egypt.

The mosque is also a burying place. It is the tomb of Mohammed Ali. He built it during his life, chiefly with the design of making it a mausoleum for his ashes when his eventful career was at an end. A conspicuous part of the building has been set apart for his tomb; a railway surrounds it, gorgeous decorations have been lavished upon it, and near it lights are kept continually burning. Here, in pompous state he reposes, and dreams no more of rivals, of conquests, or of power. Such is life! This being our last day in Grand Cairo; after tea we walked round the city to see all we could of this ancient place. and learn the habits of the people.

Here may be seen exhibitions and illustrations of all the passions and affections of the human heart. As we were returning to our hotel, we saw, under the shade of a tree, a company of Dervishes. These are a singular religious sect; they are anxious to obtain a reputation for superior sanctity, and many of them make pretensions to the performance of miracles. They are frightfully superstitious. Their devotional exercises are often of the wildest and most extravagant kind. Taking hold of hands in a large circle round a tree, they commence swinging their bodies backward and forward, jerking the head and shaking the hands, keeping time to a sort of murmuring exclamation, sometimes pronouncing the name of " Allah." As the excitement increases, they toss their hair, foam at the mouth, scream, and seem to give themselves up to the wildest excesses of religious enthusiasm. They let go hands and then commence spinning round like a top, stretching out their arms. By the velocity of their motion, spreading out their loose dress like a large umbrella, for twenty minutes or more, without pause or rest, and continually increasing velocity. These religious devotees will twirl with a rapidity truly astonishing, making fifty revolutions a minute. We are indeed sorry to see their example followed in England by the Jumpers, &c. But we have seen enough of this foolish, useless, so-called religious enthusiasm. It would be well if such energy and devotion could be turned into a more useful channel. This, however, can only be done by God and His Church. Here is our hotel, and our day's excursion is ended.

We were up early next morning and had breakfast at seven o'clock, settled our bill with the landlord, and rode to the railway station in an omnibus, and took our departure by train at ten o'clock for Alexandria.

CHAPTER XXV.

THE HOSPITAL—MOHAMMEDAN SABBATH—DEPARTURE—THE VOYAGE—MALTA—DEPARTURE—VOYAGE FOR ENGLAND—PORTSMOUTH—VOYAGE TO DUBLIN—ARRIVAL AT LIMERICK—THE 6TH ROYAL REGIMENT—PROMOTED—ALDERSHOT—ROUTE FOR GIBRALTAR—THE VOYAGE.

ON my arrival at Alexandria, I went to the Hospital, where I was informed that I would have to wait a few days longer. The men were fast improving, but were not yet sufficiently recovered to warrant the doctor's confidence of their strength, or to survive the trials of a long voyage.

When I returned to the hotel, the two Frenchmen were waiting my return for dinner. Next morning they were to leave Alexandria by steamer for Jaffa, *en route* for the the Holy Land. After breakfast, I accompanied them to the steamer, and there we parted, perhaps for ever. They were jovial, decent fellows, and we enjoyed each other's company very much during our short acquaintance. Their names were respectively Napoleon Pomponnet and Joseph Belair.

It being Friday, the Mohammedan Sabbath, I visited one of their mosques, which is always open and made a place of public prayer. Here the devout come at all times of the day to perform their devotions; but the child of the Prophet does not abstain from his ordinary work on the Sabbath, except at the hour of prayer, about mid-day, and then the mosques are crowded. The mosque is built round a central square; around this square a portico is built, and in the centre of it is a fountain of water for ablution. A good supply of water seems to be considered indispensable among Mohammedans to purity for worship. The side of the building facing Mecca is the most important one. The portico on this side is more spacious, and has one or two extra rows of columns. This side of the mosque is the place of prayer, A niche in the wall marks the direction of Mecca, and in that direction the faces of the worshippers are always turned—Christians always turn to the east. To the right of this niche stands the pulpit, and on the opposite side is a raised platform, supported by small columns, on which is a desk, upon which is kept a volume of the Koran, and from it a chapter is read to the congregation. The floors have no seats, and are covered with matting, to accommodate the worshippers; the rich and the poor pray side by side. Females scarcely ever go to pray to the mosque; if they go at all they go at different hours to the men, and by themselves —but they are taught that it is better to pray in private. Indeed, it is said, women seldom, if ever, pray at all! One little ceremony, however, must not be forgotten. Do not attempt to enter a mosque with your boots on. Recollect that, O, Englishmen! These devout attendants would lift up their hands in holy horror, and send you back as a dog. Stockings are not generally worn, except by the best classes, who wear cotten socks in very cold weather; the only covering for their feet ever worn are a low kind of slipper, made of yellow morocco leather, sharply pointed and turned up at the toes. As these are always slipped off when one enters a mosque they are turned down at the heel. The Mohammedan Sabbath comes on Friday, the Jews' on Saturday, and the Christians' on Sunday—the Lord's day. Here I am, where the Sundays come in succession, so that extremes meet, for we have no Sunday at all, although five periods are set apart in each day as special seasons of prayer. These every good Mohammedan is expected to observe, but they are neglected, and many persons, it is said, do not pray at all. But this neglect does not arise from the want of an admonition. From the minarets of their mosques the call is regularly made. One of these calls is just after midnight, another about the break of day. At the appointed hour, the muezzin ascends to the gallery of the minaret, pitches his voice to a monotonous chant, and commences, "God is great! God is great! Prayer is better than sleep! I testify that there is no deity but God! I testify that Mohammed is God's prophet! Come to prayer, come to prayer!" Sometimes quite long exhortations are given. The Mohammedan Sabbath is but little regarded. The bazaars are all open, and labour of every description is carried on. The mosques are opened an hour at noon, and yet but few take any notice of the call to prayer. Here are several Christian places of worship—both Roman Catholic and Protestant—besides several Greek chapels.

Monday morning, at ten o'clock, I went to the hospital, when the doctor informed me that the men would proceed by the steamer which arrived from the east yesterday afternoon on her way to Malta. I then returned to the hotel, settled with the landlord, came and received the invalids from the hospital, and marched them on board one of the Peninsular & Oriental Company's steamers. At two p.m. we moved out from the harbour, the sky was of a deep blue, not a cloud or film of vapour as big as a man's hand to cast a flitting shadow on the calm blue waters as they glistened in the summer's sun. I stood upon the promenade deck, my eyes intently fixed upon the receding shore, and as it faded from my view I bade farewell to Egypt. "Adieu, thou strange and wondrous land! land of the old wonders, the phœnix, the pyramids, and sphinx, I shall never see thee more! Egypt, what a treasure book of history and of study thou hast been! Once thou wert the pride and glory of earth, but now how changed and fallen! Thy temples and gods have crumbled into dust! Plundered even of the remnants of thy former greatness! The occupants of thy tombs have been borne away, thy obelisks removed, and what remained of thy statues, altars and images, stolen to adorn the parks and enrich the museums of modern cities. But, though thou sittest in silence, solitude and degradation, the traveller will still come and muse among thy ruins, and thou will ever continue to be teacher among the nations!" Such were the reflections that passed through my mind as the dark line of shore grew fainter and fainter, blending with the rolling billows of the deep blue sea, till all was out of view. I looked about me, there was the ship on which I stood, the deep blue vault of the heavens over my head, the vast expanse of waters that encircled me, and all the rest had disappeared. We have about four days sail from Alexandria to Malta. The attention, civility and politeness with which the passengers were treated during this voyage by the captain and crew deserve our warmest gratitude. After a delightful voyage of nearly four days, we entered the harbour of Valetta, about eight o'clock on the morning of the 25th June, 1856. After landing I reported myself at the brigade office, and handed over the invalids at the general hospital, marched out to St. Frances' camp and joined my battalion there. While stationed in Malta we were exercised by the general commanding the garrison, with a battalion of the German and Italian legion, twice a week on Flori-Ann Square. Except these general reviews, we did very little drill, duty was very easy, and the rations, to us, after the hard-tack we were used to in the Crimea, seemed excellent. We got a generous supply of smoking warm goat's milk in our coffee every morning and also for our tea in the evening. The milkman brought his flock of goats round to our tents, crying out, "milk! Johnny me change milk with mungey for the goat." We traded pieces of bread for goat's milk.

The houses are built of grey stone; the streets are steep and narrow; many of them have stone stairways cut in the solid rock, and some of them are arched over head. One of the most venerable and interesting structures in this ancient city is the old church of St. John, which was built in honour of the patron saint of the knights; it is 240 feet long by 60 feet wide. The most curious part of this church is the floor; beneath it many of the old knights are entombed, and above them the armorial bearings of all the Grand Masters of the order are inlaid in Mosaic of various and beautifully coloured marbles. The hand of time has faded the fine fresco paintings of the dome of this venerable structure, but the elaborate Mosaic work of the floor is still the wonder and admiration of every visitor. The climate is warm and exhilarating, the air salubrious and invigorating, and many invalids come here from colder latitudes to restore their health during the winter months. But our time at this delightful station is short; we embark for England on the 18th July.

At last the long wished for day (by some) has arrived, and we embarked on board H.M.S. "Simoon," in Valetta harbour at ten o'clock a.m. the 18th July, 1856. All being ready, at two p.m. we steamed slowly out of the harbour amid cheer after cheer from the citizens and soldiers who crowded the batteries along the harbour to give us a last cheer and wave of their handkerchief; we all stood on the deck returning the cheers and waving our handkerchiefs also until the island, like a little cloud, vanished from view in the distance.

The sky was blue, the air clear and invigorating, and scarce a ripple on the face of the deep. As our noble ship glided smoothly through the clear blue waters of the Mediterranean, our hearts were glad and our joy was great to think that we were returning to our homes, our families and our friends, who were anxiously waiting our return. The afternoon was occupied in swinging hammocks and drawing blankets and provisions from the ship's steward; the men were in the best of spirits, and amused themselves during the voyage in singing, dancing, and all sorts of amusing games. We had excellent rations during the voyage, plum-pudding and pea soup on alternate days. On the morning of the fourth day we sighted the old rock of Gibraltar, rearing its lofty crest to the sky. As we rounded Europa point our transport hoisted her number (every ship that passes the rock must show her colours) which was answered from the signal station, which stands on the loftiest point of the rock. At twelve o'clock we cast anchor in the quarantine harbour where we had a delay of two hours, during which time we were surrounded with bumboats, selling all sorts of delicious fruits, oranges, lemons, cigars, tobacco and pipes to the men. At two p.m. we weighed anchor and steamed down through the straits, soon leaving the rock of Gibraltar far behind. As our ship glided swiftly before a beautiful breeze, with studding-sails set, sweeping onward like some huge bird of prey through "The Gut," we could not help noticing the contrast of scenery between the Spanish and African sides of the straits; the former beautifully clothed in a mantle of green, with herds of sheep pasturing along its undulating banks down to the water's edge: while the latter with its barren-looking and sun-scorched hills, and tremendous precipices, rising several thousand feet above the sea, looked more wild and picturesque. The evening was so delightful, we all sat on deck till a late hour enjoying the sublimity and grandeur of the scene; the moon shone so clear and brilliantly from her celestial throne, and the stars twinkling bright and shining in the clear blue firmament, throwing a pale light through the face of the deep, watching at the same time our noble ship, as she glided swiftly through the smooth clear waters, dashing the sparkling spray and foam from her bows. On the morning of the fifth day from Gibraltar, we sailed round the green shores of the Isle of Wight, on the one side, while the low sandy coast of Hampshire, indented by the roadstead of Portsmouth, that showed a perfect forest of masts towering above its sea defences, made the beautiful island look most lovely, recollecting it was the place where Her Majesty lived and which she loved. We passed through the stately ships of war, as they rode majestically at anchor; an interchange of signals took place between the flag ship and ours, directing our captain where to anchor, we supposed, and soon we cast anchor off Portsmouth harbour, and shortly after the troops disembarked and marched to Anglesea Barracks, where we were quartered *pro tem.* Soon after our arrival, my wife and two children joined me; we rested here a week when we embarked on board a mail steamer for Dublin, landing at the north wall on the 6th August, after a rather rough passage; all the women and children were sea sick; marched to Kingsbridge Station where we took the train for Limerick; arriving there at four p.m. we joined the depôt in the New Barracks. I was here about three months when my oldest child, a boy six years old, took sick with the scarlet fever, and on the 23rd November, 1856, he died. I was very happy previous to this, but the death of this only boy made me very sorrowful.

On the first of March, 1856, I was appointed assistant school teacher at the garrison school, where I continued until the 22nd November, 1856, when I volunteered with several other non-commissioned officers to the 2nd Battalion 6th Royal Regiment, which was then being raised at Preston by Lieutenant-Colonel Fraser. Our depot being over the strength of non-commissioned officers, we were allowed to volunteer to this new battalion. At ten o'clock a.m. on the 22nd November, after signing our accounts, and receiving our pay up to that time, we took the train for Dublin, thence by steamer to Liverpool, where we landed at 7 o'clock on the morning of the 23rd, had breakfast at a hotel, and proceeded by the ten o'clock train to Preston, arriving there at two p.m., marched to barracks, and reported ourselves at the orderly room of the 2nd Battalion 6th Royal Regiment. Next morning at ten o'clock, Lieutenant-Colonel Fraser, with Adjutant Kitchener inspected us at the orderly room, and posted us to our respective companies. That evening my name appeared in regimental orders thus :

"REGIMENTAL ORDERS BY LT.-COL. FRASER, COMMANDING 2ND BATTALION, 6TH ROYAL REGIMENT.

"PRESTON BARRACKS, 24th Nov., 1857.

"1085 Corporal Thomas Faughnan to be Color-Sergeant from the 22nd instant, and posted to No. 5 Company.

"By order,

"(Signed,) H. KITCHENER,

"Lt. & Adjutant 2nd B., 6th R. Reg't."

Next day Lieutenant Kelson, who commanded No. 5 company, appointed me his pay-sergeant. The company were 150 strong, and not one of them had yet received their uniform or kits. Between the drills and parades which were long and frequent, I drew the recruits' uniforms, knapsacks and kits from the quartermaster's store marked them myself, and had their clothing altered and properly fitted at the master-tailor's shop. I must say the Crimea was nothing to what I went through in Preston. After the battalion had got organized, clothed and fairly drilled, we got the route for Aldershot.

On the 26th February, 1858, at 10 o'clock in the morning we proceeded by rail to Aldershot; arriving at Farnham Station at 4 o'clock in the afternoon, and marched to South Camp, where we were quartered in the huts of L. lines. During our term at Aldershot, the battalion was put through a strict course of drill. On the 15th of April, H. M. the Queen and H. R. H. Prince Albert received the troops in camp when we marched in grand divisions. They were much pleased at the manner in which the movements were performed by the young battalion, and H. R. H. Prince Albert expressed himself in a highly complimentary manner to the general, who conveyed it to the troops in orders. After the review was over, Her Majesty and Prince Albert drove round the camp in an open carriage as the men were at dinner; when the band of each regiment played " God Save the Queen " as they passed each respective regiment. That was the last time I ever saw H. R. H. Prince Albert, for he died, deeply lamented by the British Army, on the 14th December, 1861. On the second of May, we received a letter of readiness for Gibraltar. On the 12th, the colonel received the route to proceed by rail on the 18th inst. to Portsmouth, there to embark on board of H. M. Ship "City of Manchester" for Gibraltar. On the morning of the 18th May, 1858, the 2nd Battalion 6th Royal Regiment marched from South Camp to Farnham Station, where we took the train for Portsmouth. The signal being given, the train moved out of the station with its living freight of redcoats, rattling steadily on over the beautiful green landscapes. Trees seem to go rushing past, still on and on, panting in its rapid course flies the long train clattering past walls and bridges with a crash, whistling shrill to warn the unwary of its approach, and howling like a demon pursued, as with hiss and roar it plunges into the tunnel. To describe all the incidents which came under my notice at the station might be thought tedious. Suffice it to say that we arrived at Portsmouth at 2 p.m. and embarked on board H.M. Ship " City of Manchester," in the main dockyard. At 4 p.m. all being reported present and correct, the captain gave the signal and we moved out from the wharf amid loud cheers from the spectators, which were heartily returned by the red coats on board, and we passed down the bright sparkling Solent, glistening in the sunshine of a beautiful May day.

The spectacle was not lost on many of us, as our ship passed through the crowds of magnificent men-of-war and transports, with their sails glittering like silver in the summer sun. After we passed through the Needles, late in the afternoon, the wind being favourable, we spread our wide canvas to the evening breeze, and now the sun went down leaving a pale glare over the dark horizon, the wind began to freshen and the sea to rise. The beacon on the Eddystone lighthouse faintly faded like a little spark and disappeared; on went the good ship bounding beneath a starry firmament, the dim trackless ocean stretching before us like the undiscovered realms of the future; and I once more bade farewell to England. At nine o'clock the last post sounded, when those who were not already in their hammocks now turned in. I stopped on deck watching the sailors reefing sails and handling the ship, and when tired of listening to the piping of the wind through the rigging, and the shrill sound of the boatswain's whistle, I followed the example of my comrades and turned into my hammock. I was wakened in the middle of the night by a tremendous noise on deck. Footsteps rattled, shuffled and stamped above my head, and every now and then, amidst hoarse shouting, whistling and yells of "Aye, aye, sir," there was a sound of banging down upon the deck of heavy coils of rope. The ship was tilted over very much on one side and at times shivering from bow to stern as a heavy sea struck her on the beam. Several of the recruits on hearing this uproar, jumped from their hammocks with fright; some thought the mast had gone overboard, or that the ship was on fire, or had sprung a leak and was fast going to the bottom; but I divined the cause at once, and told them that the wind had changed and the sailors were reefing topsails, when they all turned into their hammocks again.

The motion of the ship now heading against a heavy sea became very unpleasant; she heaved, jolted and pitched so, that I found it in vain to sink again to sleep, but after a couple of hours I again sunk into the arms of Morpheus, where from a heavy and dreamless slumber I was once more aroused between five and six o'clock in the morning by the orderly-sergeant rousing the men to stow away hammocks and wash decks, and a hard job he had of it, for most of them were very sick.

The men were soon up and busily engaged, the pump and hose were set going, and the inundation and swabbing went on briskly; all hands were at work with swabs, scrubbers and scrapers. The ship was still heaving, although the warm sun had burst through the heavy clouds. When the breakfast bugle sounded at eight o'clock, many of the recruits were absent through sea sickness. Time will not permit me further to detail the distresses of landsmen who encountered at starting a gale of wind which lasted nearly two days; I only wish, good reader, you may never experience it. I shall simply record the satisfaction experienced by many of the red-coats on board the "City of Manchester," when the wind changed and sent us flying at the rate of ten to twelve knots an hour, as we shaped our course across a well-known bay of tempestuous character, which, however, on the present occasion was found quiet enough. It was, however, a joyful moment when the rocky and precipitous coast of Cape St. Vincent, loomed up distinctly through the hot mist of the early morning; and before many hours had elapsed our transport was bounding before the breeze through the straits of Gibraltar. The men were now perfectly recovered from sea-sickness, and they assembled on deck looking out for the long wished-for haven, and gazed on the much-talked of "old rock of Gibraltar," which was to be our present home. At three o'clock, p.m., 25th May, 1858, we moved into our moorings at the new mole, and in half-an-hour disembarked and marched to the Town Range Barracks, and part to the Wellington Front and King's Bastion.

CHAPTER XXVI.

ARRIVAL—SPANISH BULL-FIGHTS—LIEUT. JACKSON—CHANGE QUARTERS—THE ROCK—MONKEYS—CAVES—GARDENS—WAR IN ALGIERS—CORFU—VOYAGE—ARRIVAL—SANTA MARIA—DESERTION—THE MARCH—GREEKS.

THE 2nd Battalion 6th Royal Regiment was stationed in Gibraltar four years, during which time we were changed from one barracks to the other, about every twelve months. In the summer of 1859, H. R. H. the Prince of Wales visited Gibraltar, when the troops gave him a right royal reception. St. Michael's Cave, all the caverns and subterranean passages, as well as the city, were illuminated on the occasion, with a grand military ball at the convent, and a public one at the theatre. The inhabitants turned out *en masse*, and gave him a hearty welcome as he drove through the streets in an open carriage, with military bands playing and guards of honour as he entered and got out of his carriage, at the entrance to the convent. On the 31st July, Captain J. E. Tewart joined the regiment, and took charge of No. 5 company at the King's Bastion. On the 15th of August, myself and several other sergeants of the garrison, with their wives, rode into Spain, some on horseback, more on side-cars, to witness a bull-fight at San-Roque. On arrival we put up our horses at an hotel, and paid a dollar each to go in.

Where the bull-fight was held is a large structure capable of containing ten thousand people. It is built of stone, with seats like a circus, and enclosed with a high wall of ancient architectural design, gaily ornamented, with flags waving all round on its summit.

One half of this enclosure is alloted and tastefully decorated, with an elaborately fitted box and a canopy surmounted with the Royal Arms of Spain, for the Royal family, and a splendid military band on a platform over the entrance. When drawing near the opening scene, the seats were all filled with a gaily dressed audience, the Spanish ladies in their gorgeous fineries, with their fans waving continually. In the ring were six mounted cavaliers, armed with lances and coats of mail, and six more on foot, with silk mantles lined with crimson across their arms, and swords drawn.

Then the gate flies open, and the bull rushes into the ring; the people cheer and shout; the bull roars and paws the ground, runs at a horseman, when the rider sticks him with his lance. Madly he rushes at a red cloak held out by a footman, and falls headlong on his face. In this way they tease him until he foams with rage. The footmen throw gaily dressed, loaded darts, and stick them in his neck, when the dart explodes with a loud report. This maddens him; he shakes his head, and rushes at a horse, tearing out his entrails and raising him on his horns; the footmen fool him with the red cloaks and loaded darts. When the bull corners a man, he slips into a side place made for that purpose. After he is well exhausted, and having over two dozen darts dangling from his neck, the professor undertakes to kill him. He plays with him a long time, fooling him with the red cloak and sword; at last, when he gets a good chance, he sinks his sword to the hilt just in the back of the head. When the bull gives the last roar and drops, throwing his life blood out of his mouth, the professor salutes the audience, who cheer him vociferously.

Three gay teams of smart ponies, with rich trappings, enter the ring and draw off the dead bull and horses; when the band plays while the ring is being cleared, for another fight. As we returned from the bull fight, we passed some Spaniards who were driving mules, the road being narrow, one of the sergeants shoved a mule out of the road, when the Spaniard threw a stone, striking one of the ladies, who were on the side car; then colour-sergeant Marshall jumped down to chastise the Spaniard; they closed on each other, the sergeant throwing him down in the scuffle; the Spaniard drew his stiletto and stabbed the sergeant, who cried out "I am stabbed," when the Spaniard ran away. Some British sailors who were passing at the time gave chase and caught him; one of the sailors took out his jack knife and cut the sign of the cross deep on the Spaniard's back, saying, "if I have to swear against you, I will have a mark so as I may know you again;" giving the Spaniards a good thrashing, they left them. The wound which the sergeant received did not seem much at first, but he was taken to the hospital where he lay for eight days, and died from the wound, deeply regretted by the battalion. The Spaniard was caught, tried, convicted, and transported for two years, on the sailor's evidence, who marked him on the back with the jack knife.

After putting in four months in camp at the Old North, and ball practice under our instructors, Captain Kerr, Lieutenant Nugent and Sergeant Parkinson, we were changed Front, where we went through a course of rifle instruction to the South Barracks. Here the colonel and officers encouraged all sorts of amusements amongst the men. Each captain purchased a boat for his company, and the sergeants got out a splendid outrigger 40 feet long, from Clasper, the famous boat-builder on the Tyne. In addition to the boating, Lieutenant Jackson, of the Royal Artillery, organized garrison reading rooms, where all the latest periodicals and newspapers, with excellent libraries, were at the service of the troops, and even schools where the men could learn English, French, and Spanish, and all sorts of amusing games, such as billiards, bagatelle, backgammon, dominoes, and chess. Lieutenant Jackson was a barrack-room word with the garrison. He made himself very popular among the troops by the unremitting exertions he used in order to improve the condition, habits, education, comfort, and amusement of the non-commissioned officers and privates of the garrison.

At those barracks the Roman Catholics and Protestants occupied the same church, the former at ten o'clock and the latter at eleven. The English Church chaplain, Rev. Mr. Gardiner, was a most eloquent preacher, and a very popular clergyman, so much so, that the sergeants of the 6th Regiment subscribed and sent to London for a beautiful bible, which we presented to him, with an address, couched in the warmest expressions of admiration and gratification for his ability as an eloquent preacher, as well as his sincerity, enthusiasm, passionate ardour, and unremitting attention to the spiritual and temporal welfare of the 2nd Battalion 6th Royal Regiment, who will long remember Mr. Gardiner as being a father to both Roman Catholics and Protestants of the battalion while stationed at Gibraltar.

The approaches both from the Neutral Ground and from the sea are guarded by a great number of very powerful batteries, so that the rock may be regarded as impregnable. Monkeys are very numerous and can be seen from the Alameda, looking down from the rock on the soldiers at drill, and running up and down the old Moorish Wall leading to the signal station ; some of them are very large. In visiting the company's barrack room, when orderly sergeant, one day, the men being all out at drill, I found a large baboon stealing the men's bread off the shelf in the barrack room. As soon as he saw me he sprung out of the window, on to a wall which divided the steep rock from the barracks, then stood and looked at me. They watch the barrack rooms from this wall, and when they see the men going out to drill they enter the rooms and steal the bread. The rock at its highest point attains an elevation of 1,440 feet above the sea. It is perforated by numerous caverns the largest of which is called Saint Michael's Cave, which has an entrance about 1000 feet above the sea. Thence there is a descent through a succession of caves, some ample chambers, others mere passages through which it is barely possible to creep, to a depth of 500 feet below the entrance; at this point the foul air has barred further ingress; but the roaring of the sea has been distinctly heard, which leads to the inference that these gloomy hollows have communication with the waves beneath. Large stalactites are found in most of the caverns and congealed stone of which many useful and ornamental articles are made by the soldiers and others, such as shirt-buttons, brooches, studs and rings, with several other useful articles. There are no springs of fresh water on the rock and the inhabitants are therefore compelled to depend on the heavy rainfall, and every precaution is adopted to preserve as much of the water as possible; large tanks are placed so as to catch the rain water off the roofs of the houses and conduits are made to guide the water from the rock surface into great public reservoirs. Among the latter, the Navy Tank, for the supply of ships coming to the port, is conspicuous, its capacity being 11,000 tons of water.

At present England guards this formidable rock with jealous care; every available point of defence bristles with guns; the steep rock is honeycombed with galleries and bombproof barracks; deep ditches with drawbridges, steep escarps, bar all approach, and batteries are hewn in the solid rock, frowning alike on friend or foe. The drawbridges are closed when the evening gun fires at sun-down and are opened at sunrise, by a sergeant detailed for that duty, who is called " the key sergeant," his post when not opening or closing the gates, is at the Convent guard, where he keeps the keys of the fortress. There are several pleasant walks about the rock, but perhaps the best is in the Alameda, and the gardens situated at the south end. They are prettily laid out, a bronze bust on a column has been erected in these gardens to the memory of *General Eliott, its heroic defender.* Plants and different sorts of tropical flowers, dwarf-palm, spanish-broom, the yellow blossoms of which are mixed with the varied colours of fuchsia, orange and oleanders interspersed along the beautiful walks and round the shaded rustic seats, with the profusion and aroma of the flowers, rendered it a most charming promenade, and during the fine evenings military band performances take place, when it is usually thronged with visitors.

During the summer of 1860, a war raged between the Queen of Spain and the Dey of Algiers, when about five hundred women and children of the Moorish Jews from Algiers fled to Gibraltar for protection; they were sent to the North Front where they were supplied by our authorities with tents and rations during the war, which lasted for six months, their husbands were kept behind to fight, and only a few old men accompanied the women to Gibraltar. After putting in a little over four years on the rock of Gibraltar, we embarked on the afternoon of the 25th June, 1862, on board H. M. S. " Himalaya," which lay at the New Mole, for the island of Corfu. As we lay at the wharf expecting to go to sea early in the morning, Rev. Mr. Gardiner came on board about eight o'clock, to bid the battalion a last farewell, the moon was clear and shone down with a silver brightness on the mass of red-coats who assembled on deck to hear Mr. Gardiner address the battalion. He stood on the quarter deck and delivered a most eloquent and sympathetic address, which touched the men's hearts, and drew tears from most of those strong soldiers who were present.

At five o'clock next morning we steamed out from the New Mole and proceeded round Europa point, passing the pillars of Hercules, and as we steamed out we gradually lost sight of the coast, which was beautifully illuminated by the rising sun, affording us a last glimpse at the old rock of Gibraltar. This magnificent transport, one of the best in Her Majesty's service, is kept up to man-of-war fashion in discipline and cleanliness. After a splendid voyage of five days we reached Corfu at two o'clock in the afternoon of the 1st July, 1862. No. 5 company, consisting of Captain Tewart, Lieutenant Hall, and Ensign Græme, myself and four sergeants, and one hundred and sixty rank and file, were ordered to proceed on detachment to Santa Maura, and No. 3 company to Ithica. During the afternoon the head quarters and the companies for Corfu disembarked, the companies for detachment stopped on board, and at four o'clock next morning the steamer proceeded with these detachments to their respective stations, arriving at Santa Maura about three o'clock on the afternoon of the following day, when we disembarked, the "Himalaya" proceeding on to Ithica with No. 3 company. The garrison of Santa Maura consisted of Captain Tewart (commandant), one garrison sergeant-major, four sergeants, and two hundred rank and file, including the artillery; that day I was appointed garrison sergeant-major and orderly room clerk besides. We were stationed at Santa Maura about twelve months. One of the Austrian steamers came in every Sunday morning with the mails from Corfu. I had to answer by seven p.m. the same day, when the steamer returned. This was the only mail during the week. The island of Santa Maura is separated from Greece by a broad lagoon which abounds with wild ducks; they came in immense flocks in the evening to feed during the night, and flew away at daylight. Many a night the officers of the garrison put in after those ducks.

We had a lance corporal named John Smith (a Yankee), who was in charge of a fatigue party outside the barrack gate, where he induced the six men to desert, the alarm being given by the sentry on the battery, that the fatigue party were escaping across the lagoon, I seized a rifle, ran out the back gate, loading as I went along, sighting it for six hundred yards. I fired at Smith as he was crossing the water, striking him in the heel, knocking the boot off his left foot, leaving it behind in the water where we found it with the bullet hole through it. After they got into Greece they were free, and we could not touch them; they carried the wounded man off with them.

A man named John Nobles, who was servant to Lieutenant Hall, robbed his master of thirty-six sovereigns and deserted into Greece. The sentry on the battery saw him with his dog early in the morning walking on the spit towards Greece, but did not suspect that he was going to desert as he told the sentry that he was going to give his master's dog a run on the spit, when he let him pass, as he was an officer's servant. About ten o'clock in the morning the officer missed his servant; his suspicions being aroused he opened his cash box, and found the money gone; he reported it to Captain Tewart, who ordered myself and a corporal to start after Nobles, the chief of police sending a policeman as an interpreter. We scoured the country, as far as Missolonghi, where we arrived about six o'clock in the evening, and were shown great attention, and treated well by the Tetrach, who sent an escort of cavalry with us next morning, besides furnishing us with horses. We divided into three parties, each taking a different road; towards evening, we halted at a village. I put up at a respectable private house, there being no public houses in the place; my escort were billeted on the people of the village. It being their dinner-hour, the hostess spread a clean white cloth on the carpet in the middle of the floor, on this were placed a pepper-box, salt cellar, and a roll of bread for each person, little mats were placed round on which the dishes were placed in succession; all sat down cross-legged round the cloth; a long narrow strip of white linen was spread round on our knees; there were eight persons sitting round this spread. A large soup-tureen containing a kind of thick soup and meat stood in the centre; when we were all politely invited to commence. They all dipped their spoons in the tureen, and asked me to join them, but I declined by saying that "I did not like soup just then." After soup other dishes, consisting of stewed mutton, fish, rice, milk, vegetables and fruit were handed round; they all helped themselves. The left hand is used to convey the food to the mouth, the thumb and two first fingers doing the duty of forks. There is a neatness in the Grecian way of manipulating the food that can only be acquired by care and long practice; the thumb and two fingers alone must touch the meat, the rest of the hand remaining perfectly clean and free from contact with it. An amusing incident occurred, tending to increase our merriment. Mustard, an unusual condiment on a Greek's table, was handed round, perhaps in honour of my presence. An old lady, not knowing what it was, took a spoonful, and before any one had time to interfere, had swallowed it. Her face became crimson, tears ran down her cheeks, she sneezed and appeared choking; but at last, with a supreme effort, she regained her composure, and tried to look as pleasant as circumstances would allow. It is considered a mark of great attention on the part of the hostess to pick the daintiest bit of food, and place it in the mouth of any of her guests. Native wine was handed round, in small tumblers. I managed to make an excellent dinner, being used to squatting down to my meals in camp before Sebastopol; therefore I was not at all awkward on this occasion. Dinner being over, the cloth was removed, when coffee and cigarettes were handed round. Next morning we had a cup of coffee and started off scouring the country, at last we passed through a wood where we saw Noble's dog, and close to him was the body of Noble covered up with a little earth. We immediately acquainted the authorities, who held a post mortem examination on the body. We then searched and found the guide that accompanied him, and had him searched, when the money was found on him, except two dollars which Noble had paid for horse-hire, for himself and his guide. When travelling along through the wood, this Greek guide, whom he hired to show him the way, murdered him for the money, and buried him in the woods. Only for the faithful dog we might never have found either the murdered man or the murderer. The money was retained by the Greek authorities until after the trial.

We then retired to Missolinghi when I returned the Tetrarch many thanks for the assistance he rendered us in securing the murderer and the money. He then gave me a letter of congratulation to the Commandant, when we returned to Santa Maura.

The guide was tried by the Greek authorities, when, by a force of circumstantial evidence, he was found guilty and sentenced to penal servitude,

CHAPTER XXVII.

SIR HENRY STORKS—ALBANIA—VISIT NICROPOLIS—THE BRIGAND CHIEF—TURKISH BATHS—COFFEE HOUSES—TURKISH LADIES' COSTUME—SERGEANTS' BALL—THE ROUTE—CORFU—ROUTE—WEST INDIES—THE VOYAGE—THE BURNING MOUNTAIN—GIBRALTAR—MADEIRA—TENERIFFE—SANTA CRUZ—CAPE DE VERDE ISLANDS—TRINIDAD—JAMAICA.

IN the month of October, Sir Henry Storks, Lord High Commissioner of the Ionian Islands, with his aide-de-camp, visited Santa Maura, when he inspected the troops, barrack and fortifications, and expressed himself highly pleased at the appearance and discipline of the troops, the cleanliness of the barrack and the good order and thorough repair in which the guns, shot, shell and fortifications were kept. Several of the naval officers of H. M. S. "Icarus," in which he came from Corfu, accompanied him on shore and invited the commandant to lunch with them on board. In November, myself, two other sergeants and three Greeks, went on an excursion to Previsa, a town in Albania, seven miles across the bay. We rowed across in a large four-oared boat. The entrance to the harbour was indeed a pretty sight, nothing could be more romantic than the little bay stretched out before us, the variety and beauty of the numerous groves of olive and fruit trees along the banks, the number of little boats gliding about on the smooth clear blue waters, and small vessels cruising from one island to another, with the tall minarets towering high above the numerous white houses, making up as charming a picture as could be imagined. On landing we were surprised to see the appearance of the town. A few of the houses are good substantial buildings and comparatively clean and comfortable; but the rest of the town had a dirty and slovenly appearance. The streets are narrow and crooked, the shops are little recesses from six to eight feet deep, without windows; they close with folding doors, which are thrown open during business hours. Here the occupant sits, sells, works and carries on almost every conceivable kind of business. In one of these places you can see a dry-goods merchant, with his stock stored in a little space not more than eight feet square. The floor is elevated two steps above the street and the tradesman sits behind a little counter. The customers stand at the open front and all the business is done in the street; every one sits down, the merchant sits at his shop, the mechanic at his work.

It is amusing to see what ingenuity they exercise in getting everything within their reach, that they may not change their position. After we had walked through several streets and visited the barrack, where the guard turned out, and the sentries presented arms as we passed their posts; we supposed that they did not know our rank or else they never would have presented arms, but we were neatly dressed in our uniform and swords and we supposed they took us for commissioned officers. One of the Turkish officers accompanied us round the barracks and showed us through the hospital. Oh! what a contrast between British soldiers' barracks and hospitals, and the Turkish, the latter are dirty and the men dirty, squatting round the rooms and lounging on their little dirty-looking beds, and the hospital was even worse; the smell was intolerable, the boards black and greasy, in fact everything was filthy and smelled strongly of oil and garlic.

We thanked the officer and left the barracks.

One of the Greeks who accompanied us took us to a friend's house where we had luncheon, which consisted of rolls of brown bread, cheese, salad, cakes and coffee. After which we hired six Turkish ponies and started off to visit the mines of the ancient city of Nicropolis. A ride of fifteen miles, in an easterly direction from Privisa, was soon passed in pleasant and cheerful company, the beauty of the groves, the luxurious vegetation, the mild and balmy air, all conspired to add to the pleasure of the ride; and now we are approaching the ancient city. What do we see? Before us immense ruins for miles around, old walls towering high in the air, wide enough to drive a coach and four on their top, with high arched doorways. A large amphitheatre with massive stone seats, encircled by a colossal wall, surmounted with ancient looking figures in marble, half man, half beast.

After visiting a great many of these wonderful old ruins and learning all we could of their ancient history from our guide, who was well informed and could make himself understood in English; at his suggestion, we took a detour to visit some robbers' caves, which he said were worth seeing.

One of the wild deep passes through which he led us is celebrated as the scene of the exploits of a robber chieftain, named Abdallah Niebhr. No one could go through this narrow pass without his sanction. The solitary pedestrian as well as the grand carriage were alike the object of his plunder. The whole country stood in fear of him; travellers trembled at his name ; a pasha on one occasion, attempting to pass here with his retinue, was shot dead by this daring bandit. For over forty years he contrived to elude capture and prosecuted his career of bloodshed, plunder and crime. At last he and his accomplices fell into the hands of the Turkish authorities and were sent to Constantinople. The passage is now safe and has been for many years, but the remembrance of these bloody atrocities often sends a thrill of terror through the heart of the timid traveller. Continuing our journey through olive groves, we arrived at our friend's house at seven o'clock, and had just time for a bath before dinner. This refreshed us after our journey in the hot sun and also increased our appetites to relish the the dish of lamb, roast whole, and stuffed with rice and pestacheos, besides other trimmings, consisting of rolls of brown bread, eggs fried in butter, cheese, garlic and oil, fruit and vegetables. Dinner being over, coffee was handed round, and at ten o'clock we retired to rest. After a good night's rest we were up early and had a Turkish bath. This is by far the best fitted and most useful part of the whole establishment. It comprises a suite of three rooms, the first is a square apartment chiefly constructed of marble, and terminating in a cupola studded with little panes of glass, through which the light enters; a deep reservoir attached to the outer wall, with an opening which is heated by a furnace built under it, a number of pipes attached to the furnace circulate through the walls of the bath and throw great heat into it. A graceful fountain conducts the water from the reservoir, and on each side of the fountain is a low wooden platform which serves as a seat for bathers, who sit cross-legged, and undergo a long and complicated process of washing and scrubbing. The second room is called the Touklouk, is constructed very much in the same style, but is smaller and has no furniture but a marble platform upon which mattresses and cushions are placed for the use of those who wish to repose between intervals of bathing, or do not wish to face the cooler temperature of the Hammam (the first room). This room is furnished with sofas, on which the bathers rest and dress after quitting the bath. Turkish women are very fond of this bath, and capable of remaining for hours together in that hot and depressing atmosphere. They smoke cigarettes, eat fruit and sweets and drink sherbet; and finally, after all the blood has rushed to their heads and their faces are crimson, they wrap themselves in soft garments and pass into a third or outer chamber, where they repose on a luxurious couch until their system shakes off part of the heat and languor that these baths produce. A bath being an indispensable appendage to every house, one is to be found in every Turkish dwelling.

The outer bathroom is a large stone building, lighted by a cupola, with wooden platforms running all round, upon which small mattresses and couches are spread for the men. A fountain of cold water stands in the outer hall of the public baths. Coffee houses are to be met with everywhere, and are very numerous in the towns. The Albanians resort to them when they leave their home early in the morning to take a cup of coffee and smoke a nargile before going to business. In the evening they step in to have a chat with their neighbours and hear the news of the day. Turkish newspapers are becoming common of late in these coffee-houses, and are to be found in all of them. Few of these establishments possess an inviting exterior or can boast any arrangements with regard to comfort or accommodation; a few mats are placed round on a raised seat, and some low stools for strangers; small gardens are attached to some, where the Turk may be seen sitting cross-legged and smoking his tchibouk, while others atone for the deficiencies of their interior by the lovely situation they occupy in this picturesque and luxurious land. What a Turk heartily enjoys is his tchibouk and coffee, sitting by the side of a running stream, or in some spot commanding a fine view. This quiescent pleasure he calls "taking kaif" (comfort), on the whole his capacity for enjoyment is rather of a passive than an active kind. The costume worn by ladies consists of a gown of cloth or damask silk, with a border of similar workmanship; opening upon the breast, it displays a handsome white silk gauze frill round the neck; the sleeves hang loosely at the wrists, covered by a velvet jacket, richly worked with gold thread; indoors they wear a red cap covered with pearls and precious stones; the slippers are equally adorned with embroidery and jewels according to the rank of the lady. The yashmak (veil), and feridji (cloak), are universally worn by Turkish women of all classes out of doors. The former varies according to the rank and place of residence of the wearers, from ordinary calico, to the finest tarlatan, while the latter may be of almost any colour or material, but green is the prevailing colour; the trowsers of red silk hanging loosely over a high-heeled and neat fitting yellow morocco boot, which rinkles over the ancle. As we were standing in the consul's office getting our passports vized, Sergeant Parkinson's rifle was accidentally discharged, the bullet passing through the ceiling over the office. The consul's lady had a narrow escape, for the bullet passed through her dress. After paying the consul fifty cents each for having our passports vized, and thanking our friend for the attention shown us while at his house, we departed, rowing back to Santa Maura where we arrived at nine o'clock in the evening, after enjoying three days' pleasure which will be long remembered by us.

At Christmas the sergeants gave a ball, and issued invitations to several friends and a few civilians.

On the 9th May, 1863, we were relieved at Santa Maura by a detachment of the 9th Regiment, the "Holy

Boys," who arrived from Corfu in the morning, by steamer, and we embarked on the same steamer in the afternoon for Corfu, arriving there by five o'clock next morning, when we were ordered on detachment at Vedo, a small island close to Corfu, but a strong fortification, commanded by Colonel Sankey, of the 9th Regiment, where garrison duty and field days were frequent.

On the 6th November, the British government agreed to give up the Ionian islands to the Greeks. On the 1st of January, 1864, Colonel Hobbs took command of the 2nd Battalion 6th Royal Regiment, vice Colonel Fraser, and on the same day we commenced to blow up the forts, before giving up the islands to the Greeks. In Vedo, the lunette and keep were blown up by the end of January, and Fortneuf and the citadel were all demolished by the 1st of March, 1864.

On the 4th of March, 1864, the 2nd Battalion 6th Royal Regiment, embarked on board of H.M.S. "Orontes," for Jamaica, in the West Indies.

On the evening of the third day we sighted Mount Etna, raising its fiery summit towards the sky, and sending up volumes of fire and smoke as it were among the stars, illuminating the country for miles round. Many of us stopped on deck till a late hour watching this grand phenomenon.

On the morning of the 10th of March, we arrived at Gibraltar, and moored alongside the New Mole. Here the regiment disembarked and encamped on the New Mole for a week, with a view to the health of the troops, during which time the ship coaled, cleaned and was fumigated. At the same time the troops got their linen washed, and everything clean and ready for the long voyage to the West Indies.

On the 17th of March we again embarked, and in the afternoon moved out from our moorings and proceeded round the New Mole, and passed Bona-vista Barrack, when we bid a last farewell to the old rock of Gibraltar, and as the day was well advanced, hastened on so as to pass through the straits before dark. Early next morning we passed the southerly point of Europe, and as we steamed on we gradually lost sight of the land, which was beautifully illuminated by the rising sun, affording us a faint view of the sun-scorched peaks of the African coast. The weather was delightful, with scarce a ripple on the water.

On the morning of the 21st of March, we passed close to the beautiful island of Madeira. The first impressions of this island are delightful and striking, with its luxuriant gardens smiling with gorgeous flowers, and its mountain sides cultivated almost to their summit with beautiful plants.

The product which has made the name of Madeira famous and familiar is its wine, now produced in no great quantities; this and the cultivation of sugar-cane form its principal trade. At twelve o'clock we passed the Desertas, a group of barren rocks.

March 23rd. At daylight the brilliant light on Cape Teneriffe was descried ahead. We ran in for the land, and the high precipitous rocks, all bleak and bare, here and there broken by deep and rugged clefts, rose in bold outline before us. Somewhat later, as the clouds cleared away, the celebrated Peak was in sight, a grand and solitary object towering to the clouds in seeming desolation; for although there is a certain amount of fertility on its sides, it was not apparent as we approached it. By eight o'clock we ran into the wharf at Santa Cruz, and, after a visit from the health officer, all was free for a run on shore while the ship was coaling. There is little at Santa Cruz itself to interest the stranger. The houses are poor structures, the streets narrow, but they are kept very clean; there are no public buildings with any pretensions to taste or elegance.

There is a sort of wondrous grandeur in this volcanic scenery—in the scorched craters of these enormous rocks, ribbed at the sides, no traces of life, no appearance of vegetation—all is arid, dry and parched, while away to the southward can just be discerned a fine picture of woodland scenery, arresting the eye at once by its great contrast, and, as it were, compelling one to admire the extreme beauty afforded by the charming landscape. Here and there were noticed inclosures of cactus, used in rearing the cochineal, which, with the castor-oil plant, appears to be largely cultivated for exportation. I and two sergeants, with our wives, entered a saloon to take refreshments, as well as to learn the customs and habits of the people. During the time we were enjoying the lunch, we heard the landlady say to her husband in Spanish, "charge them English well, they have plenty of money," fortunately one of the sergeant's wives, being a Spaniard, understood what was said, when they had a most amusing row in the Spanish language, the landlady coming off second best; she did not get as much out of us as she had anticipated. It was here that Nelson (1797) undertook an expedition against Teneriffe, which, although unsuccessful and disastrous, displayed great heroism and bravery. The two flags captured on this occasion are retained in this old cathedral, and the inhabitants still bear in mind the attack and repulse. Here the immortal Nelson lost his arm, and it was the only affair in which he was unsuccessful.

Toward evening we left the harbour of Santa Cruz. The bright moon-light affording us a capital view of the Peak, which frowned upon us in all its grandeur, its head hoary with many a winter's snow. A fine favouring breeze was with us all night; at dawn of the following morning the island of Teneriffe was looming far behind us on the distant horizon. From the present may be said to commence our dreary monotonous long voyage, from the pillars of Hercules in the east across the broad Atlantic to the West Indies. Life on board ship and the varied incidents at sea, all tend to rouse feelings and sensations which are reserved alone for those whose business is on the great waters. To the officers and soldiers—as well as the ladies, the routine on board ship, especially of this splendid transport, was entirely different from that they had hitherto enjoyed on shore. Fortunately the varied scenes were under most favourable circumstances as regards the weather.

On the morning of March 31st we sighted Cape de Verd Islands, and by two in the afternoon we took in coal at Port Grand, St. Vincent; here we had a good view of African negroes, who coaled our ship with baskets which they carried on their heads. They were very tall and powerfully built men, with no clothing except a little round their loins. What a contrast in the scenery between this place and Madeira! Here are barren rocks, and not the faintest indication of vegetation to be seen in any direction, although its formation is somewhat similar.

The town, if it can be so named, consists of a few straggling houses and the stores of the coal contractors, situated along the shore, while stretching away behind are several high, rough and jagged peaks and mountains, affording a fine background for the barren and uninteresting coast scenery.

Next day, at eight o'clock, we reached Santiago, another island of the same group; here we stayed for two or three hours. The houses, with a few exceptions, were poor specimens of habitations, nearly all built of stone, and one story high. The interiors present only a few articles of absolute necessity; of home comfort or cleanliness, in our sense of the word, they seem to have no idea.

The population appear to be made up of an intermixture of Portuguese settlers and negroes, who cultivate little patches of land in the valleys where are produced a few tropical fruits.

During the voyage our drum-major and a private fell

down the hatch-way, the soldier was killed, and the drum-major severely injured, so much so that it laid him up for ever afterwards.

After parade next morning the bell tolled, and the regiment were present to pay their last tribute to their comrade. The ship's captain read the beautiful and appropriate service for a burial at sea, and on reaching that portion, "we commit his body to the deep," it was slid out of the port, wrapped in a hammock, with a round shot at its feet, into the bright, blue, deep sea, to be seen no more until that day when the sea shall give up its dead.

On the 12th we cast anchor in the harbour of Trinidad, where two companies were landed on detachment. This is a very important port of the West Indies, particularly for the mail service, some eight or ten different lines reaching here monthly.

At four o'clock in the evening we left the anchorage under sail and steam, with a fresh evening breeze, running along at twelve knots an hour. On the 18th April, 1864, at 7 o'clock, a.m., the island of Jamaica was in sight. At nine o'clock we took a pilot on board to navigate the vessel through the intricate and dangerous narrows between the reefs. As the ship approached and rounded Port Royal, we cast anchor in Kingston harbour at eleven a.m. As we lay at anchor, the sight was indeed beautiful, the city with its white houses peeping out from amongst the dark green foliage; with Newcastle looming up in the distance with its white wooden barracks, on the side of St. Catharine's peak with its lofty summit towering towards the heavens, the mountain covered with forests of mahogany, cedar, yellow sauder and coffee plantations, and the valley covered with large green plantations of sugar-cane. Nature was indeed looking charming, the view in every direction was exquisite. look where we would, there were nature's beauties before us.

At four o'clock in the afternoon we disembarked and formed on the quay where we were surrounded by a conglomeration of the inhabitants of all shades of colour. After detailing two companies for detachment, one at Port Royal and the other at Uppark Camp, we marched off to Newcastle a distance of 18 miles, seven of which was up a steep mountain zigzag foot-path. The weather being so hot we did not attempt to march during the heat of the day. The word being given, we marched off with the band playing, followed through the streets by a motley croud of negroes, mulattoes, and creoles, raising a cloud of sand and dust as we advanced. After a very fatiguing march of ten miles we halted at a place called the gardens, where we piled arms and rested for two hours, resuming our journey at one o'clock in the morning, up a mountain road which tried many of our best marchers, arriving at Newcastle barrack at sun-rise, very much fatigued after the march during the close warm night.

CHAPTER XXVIII.

JAMAICA—THE EXHIBITION—MARKET—REBELLION—THE COMMISSION COL. HOBBS—THE VOYAGE—ROUTE—VOYAGE—QUEEN'S BIRTH-DAY —EDINBURGH—CALTON HILL—TOLBOOTH—QUEEN MARY'S ROOM—DUNOON—DISCHARGED—DALKEITH—GLASGOW—EMBARK FOR CANADA—THE VOYAGE—ARRIVAL—MONTREAL—KINGSTON—PICTON—THE DUNKIN BILL—THE MARQUIS OF LORNE.

THE barracks or camp were situated on a high ridge of St. Catharine's mountain, called Newcastle, famous for its exhilarating pure air, with immensely deep gullies on each side, each wooden hut, built on terraces, one above the other, consists of one room. The officers' quarters were neat little isolated cottages, surrounded with lovely flowers, trees, and shrubs. The parade ground was a large terrace, which had been excavated and levelled, with a nice mound round its lower edge, forming a promenade as well as a drill ground. We had one large wooden building where divine service was held by all denominations in their turn; it also served as a school house and lecture hall. The married sergeants' quarters were distributed on each side of the ridge, in separate little cottages, with flower gardens to each. The means by which the troops were supplied with water was a novel and most clever proof of our engineer's skill. From the upper end or source of the gully stream, which was many feet above the barracks, the water was conducted along the brow of the ridge by means of a large trough of bamboos resting on trestles, passing into a large reservoir situated a little above the barracks, from which pipes conducted the water to the respective quarters and rooms. Before this improvement, the water had to be carried from the bottom of the gully in large leather bags by donkeys, and was doled out to the troops daily. Above the barracks on a flat side of the mountain, Colonel Hobbs apportioned a garden for each company, which we reclaimed and cultivated, raising almost all sorts of vegetables, viz: yams, cocoas, sweet potatoes, cauliflowers, cabbages, potatoes, celery, lettuces, &c., besides pine apples and strawberries, with a variety of lovely flowers.

In the beginning of 1865, Colonel Elkington was appointed Deputy Adjutant-General at Kingston. During the summer we had an exhibition in the hall, of fancy, useful, and ornamental articles, manufactured by the soldiers of the battalion; and the number of articles, as well as the skill manifested in their manufacture, was very much admired by the visitors from the City of Kingston and the surrounding country. Among some of the distinguished visitors present, whose names the author entered in his note book, were, Governor Eyre and lady, General O'Connor and lady, Deputy Adjutant-General Lieutenant-Colonel Elkington and lady, and others. Some of the articles on exhibition were wonderfully good, and sold at a high price. A Lancashire weaver made a miniature loom out of the bones which he saved from time to time, and wove a miniature webb of fine texture on it to the amusement of those present. This was bought for fifteen pounds. William Lugden, a carpenter, made a model of the cantonment of Newcastle, which was sold to Rev. Mr. Fife for fifteen pounds. Henry Foreman, made a model battery from bone, sold for ten pounds; Corporal Gilchrist, a bed quilt, sold for nine pounds. Other articles, such as fancy work-boxes, shirt-buttons, and several articles of furniture and wearing apparel, too numerous to mention, were exhibited and sold.

We had a market every Wednesday and Saturday round the canteen, when the negroes from the country brought in all sorts of produce, some on donkeys, but most on their heads. A line of black women might be seen on those days, very early in the morning, coming to market along the narrow mountain path, with baskets of yams, cocoas, plantains, bananas, pine-apples, mangoes, oranges, lemons, bread-fruit and pomegranates, besides provisions in abundance. These people come miles with their loads, and barefooted, their clothes tucked up to their knees by a handkerchief tied round a little below the hips, securing them in graceful folds, with a light gay handkerchief on their heads.

We were enjoying every comfort in this delightful station, when we were aroused by a report that the negroes had broken out in open rebellion at Morant Bay. It appeared, from what we could learn afterwards, that a local preacher named George W. Gordon, had been for some time urging the black population of Saint-Thomas-in-the-east to rise in rebellion against the Government, telling them there was back lands which they could get, and urging them to pay him money for the purpose of agitation. This, it is said, was the doctrine he preached in his chapel. And a few compatriots of his named Paul Bogle, William Bogle, William Burie, James Burie, and others, were engaged in swearing in, drilling and organizing forces in order to attack the white population, when at dinner on Christmas night, kill them, and take their wives. But an accident occurred which fortunately, nay, providentially, brought this base conspiracy to light.

On the 7th October, 1865, which was Saturday, and market day at Morant Bay, a Court of Petty Sessions was held in that town. A man who had beeu convicted by the court for some crime, afterwards interrupted the proceedings of the court, and when the police endeavoured to arrest him he was rescued from their hands by the mob. For this act warrants were issued against two ringleaders named Bogle and several others.

On Tuesday, the 10th, six or eight policemen and some constables proceeded to Stony Gut to execute the warrants; they found Paul Bogle, who, after the warrant for his apprehension had been read to him, told them that he would not go with them. When they proceeded to arrest him, he cried "Help here!" and immediately a body of men, from four to six hundred in number, rushed out from Bogle's chapel and attacked the police; these men were armed with muskets, pistols, cutlasses, pikes, sticks and stones. The police were overpowered and severely wounded by the mob. In the meantime information of this rising was at once sent to the custos, Baron Von Ketelhodt, who applied to the governor for military aid.

On the 11th a meeting was held at Morant Bay, at twelve o'clock, and proceeded with its business till about four, when it was disturbed by the noise of a large crowd approaching, a few volunteers were drawn up outside the Court House; the crowd advanced; the Riot Act was read by a magistrate, when stones were thrown at the volunteers, who fired at the mob and retired into the Court House, when the infuriated rebels surrounded the Court House and set fire to it. The inmates were then compelled to leave the building, and endeavoured to conceal themselves; some fled with their families into the woods, but others were dragged from their houses and hiding places and beaten to death; some left for dead on the ground. On the 21st October, the Maroons marched out to meet them, when a sharp skirmish ensued, eventually the Maroons got the best of it, when the rebels fled. The letter of Baron Von Ketelhodt, written on the 10th October, requesting military aid was taken by the authorities into immediate consideration, and within twenty-four hours' of its receipt the 2nd Battalion 6th Regiment was on the march to Morant Bay, where troops were also landed from Spanish Town, and martial law was proclaimed in the affected district. After the troops had arrived, they took many of the rebels and had them tried and executed or flogged, according to the nature and degree of the offence. George Wm. Gordon was arrested on the 17th and placed on board H.M.S. "Wolverine," and conveyed to Morant Bay, where he was tried by a court martial on the 20th, and on the 21st found guilty and executed on the charge of high treason against Her Majesty Queen Victoria. Paul Bogle was apprehended on the 23rd, and on the 24th was conveyed a prisoner to Morant Bay, where he was tried and executed with other leaders. Had it not been for the prompt and stringent measures resorted to by Governor Eyre in crushing this rebellion, before it had assumed its intended magnitude, no one can tell how much more innocent blood of Her Majesty's subjects would have been spilled by the semi-savage rebels, urged on by the preacher.

Those who wish to know more about the question can find it by a search, with moderate diligence, in the blue books, or the pigeon-holes of the war office. What I assert here is from my own knowledge and experience, being present during the affair.

At the end of January, Colonel Hobbs took ill, and got deranged in his mind, when he was placed in the sanitarium under surveillance. In February, he was sent to England, accompanied by his wife and family, with two hospital orderlies, to guard and tend him. During the voyage, watching an opportunity when walking the deck, he jumped head first down the ash shoot. The ship hove to at once, boats were lowered to try and rescue him, but he could not be found; he sank to rise no more till that day when the sea shall give up its dead.

On the 24th March Her Majesty's Ship "Tamar" arrived at Kingston Harbour with the 84th Regiment, to relieve the 2nd Battalion 6th Regiment. On the 25th we marched from Newcastle to Uppark Camp, and there remained until the 1st April, 1867, when we embarked on board the "Tamar" for Cork.

In the afternoons the band played on the quarter-deck, and every facility was given to the men to enjoy themselves by the gentlemanly commander, Captain Sullivan.

The evening of the 6th May, a bright light at Queenstown harbour was seen, and the next morning we entered the port and cast anchor off Queenstown, where we hoped to land. But we were too sanguine; for after the mails were brought on board, a large official document was received, directing the regiment to proceed to Edinburgh, there to be stationed. After a short stay, we weighed anchor and steamed out of the harbour, but not before we got a supply of good fresh bread and beautiful Irish butter, which appeared to us most delicious after the hard tack and salt pork we were so tired of during the voyage. Next morning, amidst haze and fog we had our first sight of the English coast, as we passed up channel amidst a very maze of shipping, outward and homeward bound.

On the 9th of May, 1867, we cast anchor in the Firth of Forth.

At ten o'clock, a.m., we disembarked at Leith Pier and marched to Edinburgh Castle, "Modern Athens," amid a crowd of citizens, the band playing "Blue Bonnets o'er the Border," and other popular Scottish airs, during the march through the city to the castle, where we were to be quartered; then the usual bustle of taking over barracks, bed-filling, &c., was gone through. Edinburgh is a very small garrison, there being only guards to furnish, viz: The Castle, Hollyrood Palace, and Jock's Lodge. The forces consisted of the 2nd Battalion 6th Regiment and the 14th Light Dragoons. On arrival, the men had a good sum of ship's clearance to draw, and being flush with money, made it lively for the police about the Canongate and Lawnmarket, so much so, that the police undertook to take some of them to the station-house. This the soldiers strongly objected to, when a fight ensued; the police got the worst of it, and the soldiers were rescued. Afterwards they never attempted to take any of our men prisoners, instead of which they reported them at the orderly room, when the offenders were punished by the commanding officer. During the twelve months which the 2nd Battalion 6th Royal Regiment was stationed in Edinburgh, the officers were delighted with the society, which is regarded as unusually polished, from the predominance of the professional and literary elements in its composition. This arises partly from its being a university town, and partly from the presence of the Supreme Law Courts of Scotland, all the important legal business being attracted thither on that account; the lawyers have charge of most estates throughout the country, so that there are an unusual number of lawyers and accountants; its medical practitioners, surgeons and physicians have a high reputation. It is much resorted to for the sake of education, for its universities and medical schools, its high school and its numerous private schools.

There are four theatres, and abundance of amusements, including an open-air gymnasium, open to the public daily, admission six-pence. In the southern environs are fine, open fields, where the game "Golf" has been played from time immemorial. Excellent street-cabs are to be found, and street cars run on all the principal streets, and to the suburbs. From the castle, which crowns the highest point in the city, a splendid view of Edinburgh and the surrounding country, can be obtained. The old town, clustering along the heights extends gradually along the top and sides of the ridge which slopes downwards to the east.

The 2nd Battalion 6th Royal Regiment was stationed in Edinburgh Castle, over twelve months, when they got the route for Aldershot camp on the 30th May, 1868. Previous to the regiment leaving, I got my discharge, on the 26th May, 1868, after twenty-one years service of Her Majesty. I parted with the 6th Regiment and my coat with the deepest sorrow, and lost my regimental home and friends. I afterwards went to Dalkeith, a pensioner and civilian, and was employed as mess-man to the Duke of Buccleuch's regiment of militia, the Duke's Canaries, during their training. This town is about seven miles from Edinburgh, stands near the junction of the North and South Esk, and is a station of the North British Railway. It chiefly consists of one main street. It is one of the largest grain markets in Scotland, with a large and commodious market hall. Dalkeith Palace, the chief seat of the Duke of Buccleuch, is a large square structure overhanging the North Esk, amid fine grounds, in which the Esks flow and unite. The Duke's chapel stands within the palace grounds. While in Dalkeith I received two encouraging letters from Canada, one from my sister, and the other from my nephew, advising me to come to Canada.

After the training was over, I sold out my furniture by auction, and proceeded by the North British Railway to Glasgow, where I took an intermediate passage for Canada for my wife, daughter and myself, on board the steam ship "St. Andrew," Captain Scott, one of the Allan line, which was to sail on Tuesday, 14th July, 1868, for Quebec. This left us five days to wait in Glasgow, during which time I took the opportunity of visiting many interesting places in this industrial metropolis of Scotland, and one of its largest and most important cities. It is situated on the Clyde, in Lanarkshire. This river divides the north from the south side of the city, and is crossed by five bridges, much admired for their light and graceful architecture, and suspension bridges besides. Below the bridges ferry-boats ply at all hours. The city has somewhat a smoky aspect: while many of the streets are continually thronged with passengers, and noisy carts, cabs, and omnibuses. In other respects it has many attractions.

After paying the landlord at the George Hotel, we drove to the Broomielaw, where the ship lay alongside the wharf, when we went on board, and at 6.15 p.m., we sailed with the tide. The night was lovely, the clear bright moon threw a silvery light athwart the face of the deep glistening waters, as our ship dashed onwards, reaching Kingstown at 10 a.m. next day.

At eleven a.m. we weighed anchor again and proceeded on our way, and after a pleasant voyage of 15 days, arrived at Quebec, on the 30th of July.

On comparing chronometers, we found a difference in the time between Quebec and Greenwich of 5h. 44m. 49s.

From here we took the express train to Montreal, and put up at the Albion Hotel. The scenery along the line of the railway seemed to me so strange; the country was covered with wood; wherever I looked there was wood—everything seemed wooden.

At 8 o'clock next morning we took the train for that ancient limestone-fortified City of Kingston—the city of the Thousand Isles—where we arrived at 2 p.m., and drove in a cab to the Anglo-American Hotel, where we stayed till next day at 3 p.m., when we took the steamer "Bay of Quinté," for Picton. The scenery along the beautiful Bay of Quinté, from Kingston to Picton, was delightful. I stayed on deck during the evening, enchanted with the wild landscape and picturesque scenery, arriving at Picton at 8 p.m., when we rode in Mrs. Blanchard's 'bus up to my sister's.

I visited my friends for a month, when I went steward of Ontario College, where I stayed for twelve months, when I bought a property on Main Street. Here I went into the grocery business, during which time I messed the

16th Battalion, County Prince Edward, Volunteers, and the summer following I messed the officers at Picton, and again at Kingston, in 1871.

The same year I applied to the Council at Picton for a license, which was granted, for my house, which I named the "Victoria Hotel," where I carried on business as a hotel-keeper, until the year 1878, when I sold the hotel, through the effects of the Dunkin Act, after laying out a large sum of money in enlarging and building an addition to the house, also stables and sheds, For two or three years previous to voting on the Dunkin Bill, a few fanatics, in order to get their names before the public as great temperance advocates, not knowing of anything better to preach about, like the Turkish Dervishes, tried to make people believe that they were all saints, and everybody else sinners, although the temperance saints generally had a bottle in the garret or the cellar, which they used when not observed.

They held meetings all over the county, and any person who did not join them had no chance of being elected to any public office. Men who were ambitious were obliged to attend their meetings, in order to gain popularity, and dare not go into an hotel. An honest, straightforward, truthful man, unless he agreed with them, had a poor chance of being elected to any office. At any rate the Dunkin side got strong enough to carry the election. Most of those who were against it would not vote through fear of their neighbours; they said it made little difference to them whether there was license or not. Through this sort of intimidation the vote was carried by the Dunkinites and became law in the county. At the end of twelve months another vote was taken to repeal it, when the Dunkinites again carried the election; owing to several local orators who stood up where the Dunkinites held meetings throughout the county and preached against its repeal. These men, of course, gained popularity with the temperance party for the time being. But like the house that was built on the sand "the rain came and the wind blew and beat on that house and great was the fall thereof, because it was built on the sand." And now those who voted for the Dunkin Bill want to repeal it, seeing that it not only increases the number of places that sell liquor privately in the town, but that it deprives the county of a very large revenue. Notwithstanding that the Dunkin Act was superseded by the Crooks Act, and knowing that it was *ultra vires*, they tried to enforce it. Several cases of selling liquor contrary to the Dunkin Act were brought before the magistrates and fines inflicted; at last, seeing that it was not constitutional, they gave up trying any more. But when a man is to be hanged there is always a hangman to be found; so it was with the Dunkin Act, there was one found to try the cases, when almost invariably fines or imprisonment were inflicted, of the latter several hotel-keepers had a foretaste.

Knowing that these convictions were bad, they were appealed to a higher tribunal. There is one thing that we have good cause to be thankful to the government for, and that is for selecting and appointing just, learned and impartial judges, who know neither friend nor partisan when they sit on the tribunal to mete out justice and judgment, according to the law of the land. When these appeal cases came before the learned and just Judge of the County of Prince Edward they were all quashed.

LINES ON PICTON, BAY OF QUINTÉ.

Fair Picton ! what a blissful spot,
Where peace and happiness had been my lot,
But the Dunkin fanatics disturbed my home,
And sent me from you, far to roam.

Where golden corn waves in the breeze,
And sugar flows from maple trees,
And here in winter, on the plains of snow,
Gay dressed parties out a-sleighing go.

With noble churches of much renown,
Thy shady cemetery outside the town,
Where friends do go, when from labour free,
To dress the graves beneath the shady tree.

Where marble monuments lift up from grass,
Which mark the spot to strangers as they pass,
Where noble souls and friends so dear,
Having left this life, are sleeping quietly here.

T. FAUGHNAN.

After I sold out I thought I would not go into hotel business again, but I found it so dull, I leased the Anglo-American Hotel in Kingston, which however I again relinquished in February last, and am now living in Kingston.

At about 4 p.m. on the 29th of May, 1879, His Excellency the Right Honourable the Marquis of Lorne and his Royal Consort, Princess Louise, arrived at Kingston, for the purpose of laying the corner-stone of the Queen's College, having been invited for that purpose by Dr. Grant, the Principal of the Queen's University.

On arrival, the Royal guests were received by the corporation and other city dignitaries, professors, and officers of the Royal Military College. A Royal salute was fired from Fort Henry. After the singing of "God save the Queen," by over one thousand little school children, the Mayor read the address of welcome to the Royal guests, which was graciously responded to by His Excellency in a loud, clear, and distinct voice. After the address another song was sung by the children, led by Mr. Rackett, Bandmaster Dominion Artillery, on the cornet; after which a procession was formed, and the Vice-Regal party entered their carriage, which was drawn by four horses, with postilions. They moved off amid loud cheering from the people, escorted by a troop of cavalry commanded by Colonel Duff, with the corporation and members of the different societies in carriages. Crowds of people lined the streets, who cheered most heartily, as the Royal visitors proceeded along the route. The streets were beautifully decorated with splendid arches, appropriate mottoes, and evergreens. The Princess looked very much pleased, and bowed most graciously to the delighted crowd. The line of procession was kept by the 14th P. W. O. Rifles, commanded by Major E. H. Smythe. As His Excellency and the Princess alighted from their carriage at Mr. Geo. A. Kirkpatrick's house, where they were guests, the people again cheered and shouted, when the Princess and Marquis most graciously acknowledged the salutations. Major and Mrs. De Winton were staying at Mr. Stafford Kirkpatrick's. The Royal reception passed off to the entire satisfaction of all concerned, there being nothing to mar the proceedings.

In the evening His Excellency and the Princess held a drawing room in the City Hall, which was beautifully illuminated and filled up with swords and bayonets forming most exquisite designs and mottoes tastefully arranged by the gunners of "A" Battery Dominion Artillery.

The Cadets from the Royal Military College, commanded by Major Ridout, and headed by "A" Battery band, formed the guard of honour. About 9.30 His Excellency and Her Royal Highness Princess Louise arrived and were greeted by a Royal Salute. Next day at 11.30 a.m., His Excellency and H.R.H. Princess Louise laid the corner stones on each side of the front entrance of the Queen's College, and planted two trees, one of maple and the other of birch, in front of the entrance to the college. After which the degree of LL.D. was conferred on His Excellency by the Chancellor, who delivered to him the diploma, which was a beautiful work of art, being engrossed on parchment, in India ink and gold, with Royal Arms, and the crest of the noble House of Argyle within a chaste and elaborate border of the scenery, views, and buildings of the city.

At 3 p.m. His Excellency, the Princess and suite, accompanied by Mr. George A. Kirkpatrick, visited the Penitentiary. On arrival there, His Excellency and Her Royal Highness were received by Mr. Creighton, the Warden, who conducted the distinguished party through the institution, which was tastefully decorated with a handsome arch, on the top of which was a large and tastefully made crown of evergreens, with the Royal Arms beneath, and a large Union Jack floating from the tower. In the evening His Excellency and Her Royal Highness attended a concert at the Opera House. Mr. George A. Kirkpatrick, M.P., and Mrs. James were honoured with seats in the Vice-Regal boxes.

On Saturday, His Excellency and Her Royal Highness visited the different schools and hospitals. In the afternoon they visited the Royal Military College, where the troops, consisting of the Cadets, "A" Battery, Dominion Artillery, and the 14th Prince of Wales Own Rifles, commanded by Colonel Kerr, were formed in line, facing the city, and commanded by Colonel Hewett, R. E., the commandant. At 3 p.m., His Excellency, the Princess and suite, accompanied by Sir E. S. Smyth and staff, arrived on the ground, escorted by a troop of cavalry. They were received with a Royal salute, after which His Excellency, attended by General E. S. Smyth, Colonel Van Straubenzie, Colonel Hewett, Colonel Irwin, Colonel Wolsley and others of the staff, inspected the troops. The brigade then marched past, and afterwards were put through a sham fight, changing front to the left, Captain

W. C. Sand's company of the Rifles covering the advance in skirmishing order, which Her Royal Highness seemed to enjoy very much. The review being over, His Excellency, the Princess and suite, accompanied by Colonel Hewett and other officers, made a tour of inspection through the College, and afterwards Her Royal Highness the Princess Louise distributed prizes to the Cadets.

On Sunday, the Vice-Regal party attended Divine Service at St. George's Cathedral. The Service was read by the Very Rev. the Dean of Ontario, and the Lessons by the Rev. H. Wilson. His Excellency, accompanied by Mr. George A. Kirkpatrick, M.P., and Captain Harbord, A.D.C., attended Evening Service at St. Andrew's Church. The sermon was preached by the Rev. G. M. Grant, D.D.

On Monday His Excellency, the Princess, and suite took a trip down the river, accompanied by Sir Richard Cartwright, Principal and Mrs. Grant, Colonel and Mrs. Hewett, Mr. and Mrs. Gun, Colonel Irwin, Colonel Cotton, Colonel and Mrs. Van Straubenzie, the Misses Montalbert, Mrs. James, Mr. G. A. Kirkpatrick, M.P., Major Gildersleeve and others. On arrival at Gananoque, the Field Battery, under the command of Major Mackenzie, fired a Royal Salute. The return trip was made by the American channel, reaching the city about 6 p.m., when they drove to the residence of Mr. George A. Kirkpatrick, M.P.

The following morning about 5 o'clock the vice-regal party left Kingston by the steamer "Spartan," en route for Quebec. On their departure a Royal Salute was fired from Fort Henry. "A" Battery, Dominion Artillery, under the command of Lieutenant-Colonel Cotton, furnished a guard of honour. As the steamer moved from the wharf, the crowd cheered and shouted, to which His Excellency and H. R. H. the Princess Louise, most graciously bowed their acknowledgements.

Long live His Excellency the Governor-General, and H. R. Highness the Princess Louise!

LINES ON THE OCCASION OF THE MARQUIS OF LORNE AND THE PRINCESS LOUISE VISITING KINGSTON.

Of a Royal Princess we now can boast,
And drink a health and a loyal toast,
To Queen Victoria, whom God may spare,
Who honoured Canada with her daughter fair.

From deceitful enemies or their foes,
May God the Royal couple keep in sweet repose ;
And let nations see that this fair land,
Can uphold Royalty with heart and hand.

Kingston, fair city ! of the thousand isles,
Where the noble St. Lawrence so gently smiles ;
With its Royal Military College of much renown,
And the grand old buildings of this ancient town.

Though this city much of limestone smells,
There are British hearts that ever swell,
To respond to Royalty and one so fair,
As the Princess Louise who visited there.

Was e'er such honour paid to Kingston before ?
As a Princess and Marquis inside their door,
The honour paid her, was much deserved,
For she stood true and loyal when others swerved.

With the noble Marquis and the fair Louise,
The loyal Kingstonians were much pleased ;
At their reception Mayor Gildersleeve did preside,
With the city aldermen on either side.

To give a loyal welcome to those we love so dear,
And show our loyalty in old Kingston here,
For that we Kingstonians all are sworn,
To stand together,—aye, for Lorne !

T. FAUGHNAN.

So now here at the old limestone City of Kingston, I must give my gentle reader the parting hand of fellowship. We have had a long, and I hope interesting journey, from my enlistment to my discharge. I trust not an unprofitable one. We have travelled over the ground of battle-scenes, of blood, carnage and slaughter; stood on the hoary ruins of palaces and temples; we have seen Egypt, and that great and terrible desert.

Our time together has passed pleasantly; we part, I trust, mutual friends, and so ends the story of an old soldier, who only asks your pardon for the many defects and weaknesses in his simple narrative, and who also hopes it may amuse the young and old, and show them that a steady, sober and well-conducted man will ever get on well and be happy in the service of Her Most Gracious Majesty: whom may God long preserve, is the prayer of her humble and dutiful pensioner,

THOMAS FAUGHNAN.

KINGSTON, ONT., July 1, 1879.

www.ingramcontent.com/pod-product-compliance
Lightning Source LLC
Chambersburg PA
CBHW020948030726
47496CB00005B/1410